"A good addition to th
shelves which tells of
life of a Jewish famil
1900 when Uncle Hersch
to make a new life for himself
The story is told by Yankel, ten-year-old son of the family, who soon greatly admires his uncle and often acts as his interpreter. Uncle Herschel had been a felsher (paramedic) in Russia and intends to open a medicinal shop in America because he does not qualify either as a doctor or pharmacist. He has run-ins with a gangster, a local doctor, and the law but in the end comes out the winner. The characters of Uncle Hershel, Dr. Padilsky, and Yankel are well drawn and the story is amusing and nostalgic. . . . particularly suitable for school and young adult collections. . . . --Booklist

"Mr. Young reconstitutes the ambience of old Manhattan Avenue with an atmospheric precision that enables you to smell the horseradish that hung heavy on the weekend air." --N.Y. Times Book Review

"A gentle, mellow tale of past-the-turn-of-the-century Brooklyn in which nobility triumphs and the bad get their comeuppance." --Kirkus

Published 3/73 264 pp.
ISBN: 0-15-192690-5 LC: 72-91842

Harcourt Brace Jovanovich, Inc.
757 Third Avenue, New York, N.Y. 10017

Uncle Herschel,
Dr. Padilsky, and the Evil Eye

Other books by I. S. Young

JADIE GREENWAY
A HIT AND A MISS
TWO MINUTE DRIBBLE
CARSON AT SECOND
QUARTERBACK CARSON
CARSON'S FAST BREAK

Uncle Herschel, Dr. Padilsky, and the Evil Eye

A NOVEL OF OLD BROOKLYN

I. S. Young

HARCOURT BRACE JOVANOVICH, INC.
NEW YORK

ISBN *0-15-192690-5*
Library of Congress Catalog Card Number: 72-91842
Printed in the United States of America
B C D E

For Gerry,

my wife, my friend

Uncle Herschel,
Dr. Padilsky, and the Evil Eye

One

That Friday afternoon when Uncle Herschel came to us from Russia, I did not busy myself with conversation or idle loitering on the street as I might have on ordinary afternoons. I knew what chores waited for me on Friday. Arriving home, I pushed our door open without a flourish and hustled toward the front room on the right.

We were not a demonstrative family, so I did not pause at the door to see if my mother was in the kitchen-living room. I knew I would find her there when I would come back into the room after I had stowed my books in the tiny roll-top desk an affluent aunt had donated for my use.

I was hungry, very hungry, because the bready roll and butter I had carried to school in an oversized paper sack and eaten during the noon recess hardly filled my need and only held out a promise of further enrichment at three o'clock. So I turned immediately back to the breadbox in the kitchen, where I would find at least a round loaf of rye or corn bread from which I could lop off a sizeable hunk.

Then I saw my mother seated between the window and the big square table on which we ate, on which I did my homework, on which my father and mother read the daily newspaper. She was watching me and smiling, but that didn't stop my forward thrust toward the breadbox.

On a chair where I couldn't see him as I opened the door and across the table from my mother sat a man who would affect my living, my thinking very profoundly. He wasn't very tall, that is he was not very tall in his chair, but I was almost instantly attracted to him. He was thin, very thin; everything about him was spare—his hands (these I would almost call delicate), his face, his feet. In themselves these characteristics would make him unique, because most of the adults I knew were not thin or spare. However, as I stared at him I saw that his face and his head were narrow, his feet were narrow, and the shoes he wore were long and narrow and different from any shoes I had ever seen in the family shoestore where my father led us twice a year for our holiday shoes. This man's shoes were not only narrow, they were buttoned up rather high and the polish on them was dazzling. Then I became aware of the cane which stood between his feet and, as I raised my eyes, I saw his hands folded upon the head of the cane.

My mother said, "This is your uncle."

I continued to stare, and the man moistened his lips. He did not smile at me as most men ordinarily would to encourage a friendly gesture from a ten-year-old boy. He only licked his lips, and I noticed for the first time the little patch of hair under his lower lip. It was a narrow patch that ran vertically from under his lip to his chin, and as my amazed eye got to his chin, I saw his black bow tie, standing out from a starched winged collar and a stiff shirt which billowed out enormously from his chest.

Beards, of course, were not an uncommon sight, and if my uncle had worn a beard I would not have stared, nor would I have noticed the black bow tie, the starched winged collar and the boiled shirt.

He licked his lips again, and I wondered if his lips were dry. I hoped he would say something to me because I could not think of anything intelligent to say to a relative who was at the same time a stranger. I waved the large knife; I had to do something; I was feeling uncomfortable because he continued to stare at me. Then he licked his lips again, and I told myself this would lead him into a spoken thought. It did.

My uncle said, "Do you have whiskey?" He actually didn't say "whiskey," he said "*branfen*," which could be more readily translated "alcohol"; but my mother knew what he wanted.

"We don't have branfen," she told him, "Schiya makes a drink from cherries and alcohol–"

"Mm!" he said, as though he anticipated my father's combination of cherries and alcohol less than a tolerable substitute for what he wanted. He remoistened his lips.

"Who lives without branfen?" he asked.

"If one has to, one can live without branfen," my mother said. "Schiya doesn't need it and I don't need it and Yankel . . ." She waved at me to let him know I was called Yankel, actually a Yiddish embellishment for Jacob.

He took one hand off the head of his stick and waved it to reinforce what he was going to say. "Branfen is bread."

I heard it then for the first time, but I would hear it often as my association with him became deeper and more meaningful. Right now, I was probably a little displeased that he had hardly acknowledged my presence in this room. My mother saw me standing there near the breadbox as though I was not too sure what courtesy demanded of me.

She said, "Uncle Herschel is going to live with us. He just came from home."

Of course I knew what "home" meant, as my mother used it here. Home was the town, the shtetl from which she and my father had emigrated about twelve years ago. Home was not a place to go back to. It was only a frame of reference, because they knew that everybody's precious future lay here in this country. I readjusted my stare as though I could now appraise him from a new angle.

I had many questions I wanted to ask, but I would hold them for my mother when she and I were alone. I had learned not to articulate too many questions that came to mind as I entered upon new and intriguing situations. For instance, I had to think where my uncle would sleep. I could readily visualize him at the huge square table which could accommodate eight people. Beyond the kitchen and on a line with it was the bedroom where my father and mother slept. Then of course, there was the front room where I slept on the leather covered lounge.

"Come here," my uncle said suddenly. I walked toward him, stopped about three or four feet in front of him and leaned upon the wall. Uncle Herschel lowered his chin upon his hands, fisted on the cane handle, and slowly appraised me.

Then, without turning to my mother he said, "Bashful."

I glanced swiftly towards my mother, but she only regarded me fondly.

"How old are you?"

I told him.

"And what are you learning in school that you'll be able to use when you're a man?"

Here was a question to cope with. Normally a relative would ask me how I was doing in school. For that question there was one sure answer: "Fine." This answer ordinarily satisfied the inquirer, who I knew was not interested in the first place.

My uncle's question was another matter, about which I had just not thought. How did I know what I would be able to use when I grew up? I stared at him in some dismay. If he was going to live with us would I be subjected to this kind of badgering continuously?

I finally replied, "I don't know what I'll have to know when I become a man."

He ran his fingers over his mustache before he turned and smiled to my mother. "Smart," he said.

This I would learn about him: his penchant for declaring himself succinctly in one word.

"And Hebrew school?"

"I go."

"And what do you learn in Hebrew school that you can use when you become a man?"

"I learn to pray."

"You learn to pray. And do you learn why you pray?"

"I pray to God."

"You pray to God. And what is God?"

"Nobody ever told me. My *rebbe* says we mustn't talk about it."

"So good. So maybe someday we'll talk about God."

Again I sneaked a quick look at my mother, but she seemed to regard quite complacently his promise to talk to me about a forbidden subject.

"Take a roll and butter," my mother said. "Do you want tea?"

I shook my head and turned back toward the breadbox for one of the big bready rolls which my small mouth could not compass. I had learned to lay the roll on a flat surface and press down hard so I could enlarge its circumference by two or three inches and lower its height by almost a half-inch. I cut the roll open before I went to the icebox for butter. Very recently my parents had enlarged our culinary horizon by trading in our old icebox for one we thought was magnificent, opulent. The old box had a lid top so we had to reach down for what my mother laid in next to the hunk of ice. The new box had two compartments, each approached by a door.

The top compartment held the ten-cent hunk of ice which was carried up two flights every day or every other day by our regular ice man, who also sold us coal and wood in the fall and winter. Next to the ice or on it lay the butter, in a covered glass dish; I whisked it out, swiftly closing the door so none of the good cold would escape. Very early in my career as a boy I had learned to slam the door of the icebox in immediate haste so I would not hear the instant chorus about closing the door and not spoiling the food.

I laid a thick spread of butter on the roll, covered the spread and moved toward the front room. I knew what I had planned for that afternoon. Down the hall in one of the four-room flats lived a family of grown-ups. They welcomed me, I think, because my instinctive reticence kept me from intruding upon them. I would knock on their door every afternoon after I had come home from Hebrew school. At that hour none of Mrs. Fried's working family, her husband and her two sons, had yet returned from work, and I could sit on the floor in her front room (where her boys slept) and read yesterday's evening paper, the *Journal*, which her sons brought home.

Regularly, after I had read the cartoons, Maggie and Abe Kabbible and others, I would devour every news item, every editorial, every special column, all the advertisements, until her men would come home and I knew my father, too, had already begun to wash for his supper.

Thursday was my big prize day. On that afternoon Lily, the daughter in the Fried home, always gave me *Collier's* weekly—two weeks old but fantastically precious. I would clutch it to my chest and run all the way down the long hall home lest some intruder take it from me.

I always read it on Friday night and sometimes on Friday afternoon when Hebrew school was not in session. I read it avidly, the stories, the special articles, the editorials. Sometimes I was startled by what I read because the vehemence seemed strange to me, brought up in a house of supreme contentment and infinite peace. I was a hero along with the strong, hard-faced men in the stories, short and long, and I suffered with them as the conflict grew almost unbearable.

I heard my mother call to me to hurry to the baker for her two pans of chalah. This had been my chore for almost two years. In fall and winter, when our coal stove in the kitchen was delightfully hot and beckoning for potatoes and apples and chestnuts and herring on a sheet of manila paper, the chalah was baked in the stove. But now it was early spring, and we used our icebox and the two-burner gas range which stood at one end of the stove.

So in spring and summer my mother would carry her well-formed dough in two pans to the baker around the corner. The cellar under the bakeshop housed a huge brick oven where the baker worked all night. Every housewife who baked her own

Sabbath chalah brought her pans to this baker or to others in the neighborhood.

During the morning (this I learned when I ran this same errand in the summer months) perhaps a hundred or more women brought their pans to our baker. This assembly was exciting, many kids and many women exhorting the baker with specific instructions for their own baking. Some liked a light patina, others insisted upon a darker, deeper tan.

The baker listened patiently to each admonition and he seemed able to please everybody and I marveled that he could remember so many different stories and satisfy each. I concluded that he probably learned to associate every chalah with a face, so each loaf came to him as an individual endowed with a unique personality.

One exciting Friday evening I came home to report that my mother's chalah had disappeared from the baker's cellar. My mother accompanied me back to the baker. This time he was in the cellar, and as my mother strode in he looked around swiftly to the long table where he set up the pans as he hauled them out with his long-handled shovel. He held up his hand even before my mother could protest.

"Mrs. Glodsky has your chalah."

"Mrs. Glodsky?" This was an even greater indignity than stealing her pans. "She bakes for dogs." She pointed contemptuously to the huge pan in which rested two long, low breads intricately braided.

"That's Mrs. Glodsky's chalah," the baker said. "I went upstairs for a minute, and my wife stayed here. A man is a human being; I had to go upstairs. My wife doesn't know Mrs. Glodsky's chalah. Me, she couldn't fool. That's why she took your chalah. So take it and if you need me for a witness, I'll come."

"I wouldn't need any witness. I'll throw it in her face."

She pointed imperiously to the pan, I hefted it, and together we stalked back to our house where the Glodsky family also lived, on the fourth floor. The trek up four flights was memorable because at each landing my mother said, "Oh, my heart," and I didn't understand that moving straight up was impeding her breathing.

When we landed on the top floor, she sat down on the top step and I paused a few steps below, holding the large pan gingerly so I would not upset it and break the two long sticks of bread. I watched her as she struggled to breathe more regularly.

"Should I bring her her chalah?" I asked.

That seemed to revive my mother. "*I'll* bring her her chalah," she said, and as she stressed "I'll," I knew she would be emphatic.

She stopped one second when we reached the Glodsky threshold and then rapped firmly on the glass-paneled door.

Someone called "come," and my mother turned the knob and marched into this four-room flat, in no way comparable to the Frieds'. It was not dirty, just not well kept, like a horse who wears only leather.

"Here's your stinked-up chalah," my mother said. She turned, took the pan from my hands and slapped it on the table. The woman who had called to us to come in walked from her black cast-iron sink to the table and stared into the pan. She was a big woman; she billowed out fore and aft, and her features were cut in the same dimension. Her hair was caught up on the nape of her neck in a sloppy knot.

"Oh yeah," she said.

"Oh yeah," my mother mimicked her. "You didn't know this is your chalah. You didn't know you couldn't bake a chalah like mine if the shamus came to help you!"

"Look," Mrs. Glodsky cackled defensively. "So I made a mistake, so kill me."

"I should kill you? Eat your own chalah and nobody will have to kill you. You're a gonef, and the next time you steal my chalah, I'll give your whole family such an evil eye you wouldn't do it again."

Mrs. Glodsky hesitated before she turned to her washtub, which was covered by a long board and oiled cloth.

"I cut already a piece of the chalah."

My mother glared at her. "So bring what you didn't cut."

Mrs. Glodsky took the towel off my mother's pan. Her two chalahs came to light—tall, broad shouldered, deliciously inviting. She carried the pan to us as though she were offering us some kind of atonement for the wrong she had done. My mother snatched the pan from Mrs. Glodsky's hands and gave it to me.

"Don't be mad," Mrs. Glodsky pleaded.

"Why shouldn't I be mad? A woman likes her Sabbath to be beautiful. That's why she bakes chalah. You want good chalah, come to my house and I'll give you chalah for your Sabbath. A good woman doesn't steal for Sabbath."

She turned, and together we paraded triumphantly out of the flat bearing our chalah.

Today the baker was in his cellar. He saw me as soon as I had tramped down the six stone steps. As I set foot on the threshold he greeted me.

"Hello, schmendrick."

I never knew just what I meant to him when he called me "*schmendrick*," and, somehow, I never asked my parents. If "*schmendrick*" was a pleasant name, I had no need to involve them. If it was unpleasant and they objected, the strife would be more distasteful than the name. I never answered his call; I just looked past him toward the long table for the baked chalah. I hoped he would give up calling me "*schmendrick*" or he would forget if I pretended not to hear. I was wrong. He was a cheerful dope who had a name for every kid who came into his cellar. This I heard from the other kids. Only they never told me what he called them, and I never divulged the name he had for me. Once, however, while I was hefting my pan, another kid came in, and when the baker hollored, "Hello, schmendrick," I looked up puzzled that he should be repeating his greeting to me. He was looking at the other kid. So, I thought, even Sam is a schmendrick. Then as I walked to the stairs Willie traipsed in, and as I crossed the threshold I heard the baker call, "Hello, schmendrick."

I felt better instantly, and today, even though I still did not acknowledge his greeting, I went confidently to the long table. He looked over the big metal tub in which he was punching a huge blob of dough to watch what I would select from the table. I couldn't miss. I knew my mother's pan immediately and went for it.

"That's it. You got the best chalah. Tell your mother, she wants a job by me, she can have it in the best bakery cellar in Williamsburg."

I walked toward his table where his fists were beating a tattoo on the dough in the big metal pot. I set the pan on the table to fish for the three cents we paid him for baking the chalah.

"My mother doesn't work," I said stiffly.

"*Ha! Ha! Ha!*" he roared, "you're the smartest schmendrick who comes in here."

Elevating my nose, I hefted the big chalah pan and tramped toward the short flight of stairs. His belly laugh was an obbligato to my sturdy indignant gait. "*Ho! Ha! Ha! Ho!*" I kept my eyes on the pan and felt my way up the stairs so I wouldn't fall on the chalah and ruin the Sabbath. This part of the errand always dismayed me, and I was always relieved when I could kick on our door for someone to open it. Then I could bear the pan into the kitchen as if approaching royalty with a fragile crown instead of two large chalahs which I had just carried up two flights of treacherous, precipitous stairs.

Shortly after I came home my father arrived. I was in the front room as the door opened and I stood up to see how he would greet Uncle Herschel. Then for the first time I saw my uncle at his full height. My father was not tall—he couldn't have stood six inches over five feet—and my uncle was just slightly shorter.

My father had never really lived with people other than the workers he met every day in the pants-making shop and his family. He paused at the door and stared at Uncle Herschel.

"Look," my father said, "Herschel."

Uncle Herschel took my father's hand in both of his while he made the stick lean against his leg.

"Good, good," he said, "Schiya, good."

"How do you feel, Herschel? So long, so long. How is Hannah? How are the children?"

"Good, good, all good, all good."

My father had already ended his conversation. He transferred his lunch bag from his left hand to his right and just stood there.

"Wash and we'll eat," my mother said. She could always fill in every uncomfortable gap or lag.

"Nu," my father said, "go to the table."

This was his standard phrase as he reached for the key which hung near the door so he could go out to the toilet. My mother got up and brought a small dish. Then she set out four huge soup bowls. By this time my father had returned to splash in the black cast-iron kitchen sink.

Uncle Herschel had resumed his chair near the door and replaced his thin, delicate hands upon the head of his cane. He watched my mother move from the covered washtubs where she had set out her gefilte fish to cool against the evening meal.

She brought the bowl to the table where she ladled out a huge portion for each dish. My father cut slices off one of the chalahs and laid them on a large platter.

"Bring glasses," he told me, and I hurried to the closet and brought out four glasses which last fall had held the memorial candles my father and mother had lighted for the dead in their families. I knew why my father asked for the glasses tonight, Friday night, and waited to see how Uncle Herschel would greet my father's eagerly anticipated cherry liqueur.

He brought out the big gallon glass jug and poured some for my uncle and for himself and for my mother. For me he always prodded out a half-dozen alcohol-soaked cherries which I ate eagerly as dessert. He pushed a glass toward my uncle and he raised his own.

"Nu, to your health."

"To your health."

Uncle Herschel raised his glass and allowed some of the dark liquid to drain in between his closed lips as though he was subjecting it to some kind of supreme test. He stared into the glass as he savored the drink over and around his tongue.

"Sweet," he said, "sweet. For women."

My father looked swiftly over to my mother. This drink he offered proudly to relatives who came to our home Friday night or over the weekend.

"Schiya is not from the drinkers," my mother said.

My uncle waved his hand in a gesture I learned later to mean he was writing that person off.

"Who lives without branfen? Would you live without bread? Bread is worse for you than branfen."

In my home this could be a shocking thought. My parents had never talked at me, had never preached to me about the evils of drinking. Actually they didn't have to. The eloquent contempt in their voices as they described an occasional drinker was almost lyrical for me.

"Take a drink," Uncle said. "It won't harm you. Your whole body warms up. Your intestines become alive. You eat better. You sleep better. You want to do big things. What work do you do?"

"I make pants."

"Pants?" If my father had said he carved statues, my uncle couldn't have been more astounded. "What do you mean you make pants? You are a tailor?"

"A tailor I'm not. I just make pants."

"But I don't understand. In your town you were a merchant. You bought dried fish and eggs and you sold them."

"Oh," my father sighed, "that was in our town. In America I couldn't go in business. I was green, I couldn't speak English, I had no money."

"His brother took him in his shop, and they learned him to make pants," my mother said. "Gold he doesn't make, but we don't beg. Bread we have, thank God. Yankel doesn't go naked or barefoot, and we can pay the rent every month. So we thank God, and maybe someday he'll have his own shop."

My father turned a moment to shake a dozen or so deliciously soaked cherries into my glass. Everybody watched him because the cherries got choked in the neck of the jug and when they came out in a rush a flood of dark liquid followed. The liquid my father returned to the jug.

My mother said, "Let's begin to eat. The soup will get cold."

My father brought out a jar of white horseradish which he had scraped from the whole root the night before. Because the odor and the strength of the scraped root were normally strong enough to affect every person in the room, my father took root and scraper to the fire escape, where the air quickly dissipated the strength.

As we hurried through the first course, I noticed how my uncle devoured his portion and how swiftly my mother laid another fish cake on his dish. He bit off enormous hunks of chalah and dunked his fish in gobs of that very potent horseradish.

Once he paused long enough to say, "A delight," and immediately resumed his eating. We didn't have to wait for him to finish, because he ate so swiftly and so ravenously, he was able to look around at us and smooth out the two sides of his mustache. He reminded me of the tomcat who visited our home every night after supper. He never came while we were eating, but as my mother began to scrape the dishes we would hear him scratch at the door or begin a muted yowling if we did not respond quickly enough. My mother always spread yesterday's newspaper on the floor and dumped on it whatever was left on the plates and in the pots.

After he had dined sumptuously he always made the rounds under the sink and pieces of furniture where there were holes in the floor or where the floor met the wall. These tiny crevices my father boarded up regularly, but just as regularly they were eroded by mice teeth. Since the advent of our tom we were not bothered by mice, who probably caught his smell at their holes. Then Tom would sit down decorously very close to the hot oven and manicure his whiskers.

That's what my uncle was doing now as he told my mother that his Hannah was a very good woman but not a very good cook. My mother carried an oversized soup dish to each place at the table, carried it cautiously, although the long eggy noodles in the soup tended to stabilize the liquid.

Uncle Herschel soaked hunks of chalah in the soup and ladled them up to his mouth, and I marveled that such a small mouth could open so wide and take in so much liquid and so much solid.

My mother was preparing to lay a quarter of chicken onto each plate, the chicken which had made the soup so deliciously tasty, but Uncle Herschel waved her off telling her not to serve it to him.

"Why? This is a pullet, sweet as sugar."

"I don't eat meat."

"You don't eat meat? So how can you live? How can you be strong?"

"I eat eggs, all kinds of beans, nuts."

She continued to stare from him into the pot she was holding.

"This is some kind of insanity. Why don't you eat meat?"

"Animals eat meat. Animals eat other animals."

"So why do you eat fish?"

"Fish is not an animal. I don't eat fish all the time."

My mother teetered uncertainly from side to side, not knowing how to accept his determination not to eat meat. I didn't know then, but I know now, how well-fed we were with the best cuts of meat at fourteen cents a pound, liver and lung tossed in if we agreed to take them.

"Maybe just a little piece, just the thigh."

"Feh! When you talk about a chicken's thigh, I see his thigh. Would I eat his thigh?"

I stared and held my mouth open because "his" meant mine,

and I had just crunched off a succulent hunk from the thigh I was holding.

We continued to eat the chicken and the boiled carrots and onions and, of course, chalah. My mother ate her meat with her eyes glued to Uncle Herschel, as though reproaching herself for not having known he was not a meat eater.

The talk around the table was minimal even though there was a stranger in our midst. No one really tried to make conversation, possibly because everyone except Uncle Herschel was too intent upon the good, juicy chicken.

When my mother had cleared away the dishes, she brought saucers and tumblers and into each poured about an inch of essence of tea, which had been brewing on the gas range ever since we had begun to eat. Then she filled each tumbler with hot water from our enormous tea kettle.

"Get the sugar," she told me and I went for the glass bowl which contained the sugar cubes. I was a little boy when I learned to hold the cube of sugar between my teeth or in a corner of my mouth while sipping hot tea. It was a precarious procedure, and I wasted or ruined many cubes of sugar until I learned not to take big swallows that would instantly inundate the cubes and soon dissolve them.

Then my mother carried a huge platter to the table. On it lay the oversized apple cake she baked so well and which we adored. With a sharp knife she cut squares out of this cake, always a Thursday chore, which the baker proudly baked.

This evening's tea drinking would be a revelation for me. Uncle Herschel nibbled on the huge square of cake my mother cut for him, but he approached the tea drinking as though it were a ritual. As I tried to take my first sip and stopped because the tea scalded my tongue, he took a big swallow and another and another. Before I had ventured my first sip, Uncle Herschel returned his tumbler to the saucer and my mother instantly refilled it.

Normally, my father drank two tumblers every night; to me

his two-tumbler drinking was not extraordinary. But as one tumbler followed another to Uncle Herschel's saucer I gawked, and I wondered how such a slight man could hold so much liquid. He did not eat all of the cake my mother set before him, but he drank four full tumblers of tea. When he finished the fourth tumbler I gasped, but my parents did not seem to notice.

At last he pushed his saucer toward the middle of the table, leaned back in his chair and took from his pocket something that looked like a silver box. It was almost square, and it was thin. With one finger he pressed some mechanism that caused it to spring open, and he pulled out a cigarette.

I was fascinated by that cigarette because although my father smoked, tonight was Friday; and my father did not strike fire on Friday night. Uncle Herschel held a light to the cigarette, and he seemed to draw in not only all the smoke but all the air in the room. The smoke sank deep into his head or his chest, and then slowly some of it drifted out his nose and throat. He looked at my father, who was interested in his second tumbler of tea.

"You don't smoke on the Sabbath?"

"No."

"Foolish."

"I am a Jew."

"So you'll have a golden tombstone."

"No, it's not that. It's not allowed on the Sabbath. It's forbidden."

"Who forbids it?"

"Who forbids it? God forbids it."

"It's in the ten commandments?"

"No, it's not in the ten commandments, but God said six days a week you work and on the seventh day you rest."

"So if you strike a match on the Sabbath you're not resting?"

"You mustn't light fire on the Sabbath."

"So you light fire the way they did three thousand years ago?"

"What God said three thousand years ago is as important now as it was three thousand years ago."

I later developed a tremendous affection for my Uncle Herschel, but he distressed me when he took advantage of my father's naïve approach to a good deal that was secular and even more to matters that had religious overtones.

I was happy when my uncle suddenly stopped talking about cigarette smoking on Friday night; but he continued to smoke cigarette after cigarette, and I began to count the butts that piled up on his dish.

"How soon will you send for Hannah and the children?" my father asked.

"Ah, that is a good question. My children, I don't have to bring over. They are all old enough to bring themselves and I will bring Hannah . . . soon."

"So, what will you do?"

"You mean what work will I do?"

"Yes."

"That is another good question. What work can a felsher do? I won't work in a shop making pants. I can work in a hospital, but I can't be a doctor because I wasn't a doctor in Russia and they won't let me be a doctor here. I can't speak English so I can only help people who speak Yiddish or Russian."

"Pa, what's a felsher?" I asked.

My father looked at Uncle Herschel, who accepted his invitation.

"Russia is a very large country, much larger than this country. It doesn't have a lot of things you have in this country, like toilets and those cars that run on tracks. It also doesn't have many doctors. There are so few doctors that the government is worried about it. The whole country is divided into guberniehs like the states in the United States. Every gubernieh has a few doctors, but they never get into the small towns, the villages. In these places the sick are taken care of by a felsher. He does everything for the sick. I am a felsher. In America I'm a nothing because I can't write a prescription, I can't do anything a doctor can do. But I'll find what to do."

I was very proud. My mother had told me she had a brother who was a doctor in Russia and now an almost-doctor would be living with us. I couldn't wait to tell Muttel and Bootsie, whose real name was Sam. That night long after my father had turned off the gas light in our kitchen mantle, I thought excitedly about what had happened to me this afternoon and evening. I turned in my cot to look towards the front room where Uncle Herschel had retired on the lounge, which my mother had covered with a soft blanket and a sheet, and I saw a frightening glow. Then I remembered he was probably smoking his last cigarette of the night.

I had no way of knowing when I fell asleep, but when I awoke, my mother was already padding around the kitchen, preparing for the day. In my household there was no lingering in bed. Even on the Sabbath when chilly weather demanded heat, I provided it. This morning was dark and gloomy and wet, and my mother said, "The house is very cold."

I threw off my quilt, dressed quickly, folded the cot and left it to roll into the front room later. Then I crumpled up old newspapers, laid them on the grate in the oven, and firmed in among them a half-dozen thin, wood splinters that would quickly catch the fire from the burning paper. Our wood was always housed behind the stove, where in a few days the kindling had time to dry. This wood I laid in on the thin pieces, making sure there were enough spaces for drafts to spur the flames. Then I placed small pieces of coal on the kindling so they would catch the rising flames quickly. I got the covers ready as I struck first one match and then another and applied them to both ends of the oven. The fire caught and spread swiftly, hungrily to all the paper, to all the slender pieces of wood and finally to the kindling. I knew then the fire was set and soon I would be shoveling heaps of hard coal into the flames where they would take hold securely. Soon the welcome heat would spread over all the rooms, and we would be comfortable. My mother put the coffee pot on the oven for the water to boil so she could drop in the coffee she had ground, together with a spoonful of chicory.

On Saturday and Sunday mornings, when there was no hurry to leave for school my mother laid in potatoes to bake and cuts of herring on pieces of manila paper cut from store bags. This she did this morning as my father came into the kitchen to wash at the sink.

By now Uncle Herschel had emerged from the front room, dressed as he had been when I left him last night, his hair carefully combed down flat, and he appeared to have shaved.

"When did you get up this morning?" my mother asked my uncle.

"Early."

"But today is not a working day. You didn't have to get up early."

He waved his hand at her. "Nobody lives while he's sleeping."

Then he did something I had never seen before. He took out his cigarette box, extracted a cigarette and held a light to it. I had never seen my father light a cigarette before breakfast, only after he had eaten and, of course, never on the Sabbath. He went to the window and leaned against the side to stare out into the street where the horse-drawn wagons had already begun to clump on the cobbles.

"We'll eat potatoes and herring and sliced onion for breakfast," my mother told him. "I'll put in a potato and herring for you?"

He didn't turn. He just said, "Coffee."

My mother was dismayed. "No potato, no herring? A person has to eat."

"Coffee."

"But how can a person live without eating? A person has to eat to live."

"A pig eats to live."

"You're not a pig, but how can you exist on coffee?"

"Trust me, I've been existing for forty-eight years. If I eat potatoes and herring and onions will it add to my years? And if I drink coffee, it won't take away from my years."

Soon the coffee began to brew, and its aroma spread deliciously over the house. We peeled our baked potatoes, laid some butter on them and allowed it to melt. We never used salt on the potato because the herring was quite briney, but this combination overlaid with a slice of onion and of course eaten with chalah was exquisite.

Only Uncle Herschel was not stirred by the pungent smells on the table. Once he broke off a piece of chalah, dabbed some butter on it and munched it slowly until my mother filled his tumbler with coffee. He poured in some milk from the pitcher, a bluish colored milk, only slightly diluting the strong coffee. My mother always boiled the milk as a precautionary measure, I guess, and allowed it to cool. This made the cream rise to the surface, and she would spoon it off for me. Such a luxury was reserved for the weekend, however, because in my home the only milk was that which my mother budgeted for us at five cents a quart.

The color of the coffee did not upset or discourage Uncle Herschel; he drank enormous quantities, holding the sugar cube expertly between his teeth or somewhere in his mouth. He drank the coffee with vast, astonishing gulps, murmuring a little with each gulp.

When he had consumed three tumblers full, he pushed the tumbler from him as he had done last night, and again began a series of cigarette smoking.

"This herring is good," my father said.

I never knew whether he was consciously complimenting my mother when he talked about the good herring or the good chicken or the good soup. Perhaps that was his reticent way of thanking God for helping him provide for our daily needs.

"Good!" my mother said. "I paid two cents for it."

"I've got to think about making a living," Uncle Herschel said, "but what to do is another story."

When he paused, nobody spoke. We waited for him to continue because he appeared to be revolving a thought in his mind which he would presently manifest in words.

"You think I'm a failure?" he said.

We stared at him; this statement was so positive, so disconcerting, and I did not want to disturb my faith in him.

"Why does a man leave his whole family in one country and go to another country? Because he is a failure! This is strong, but how else can I say it? I know it's been on your minds ever since I suddenly appeared in your home. I'm a felsher in Russia, a somebody in a village, but I'm not happy. If I can't be a doctor, I don't want to be a felsher in Russia. How does one measure success? In two ways: how much money can I earn, and what is my standing in the community? Money? Nobody has money, so the peasants pay with produce. So if I need a pair of boots or if my children need clothing, I have to trade the produce or the livestock the peasants bring me. This is not a way of life. I was beginning to choke. I hated what I was tied down to, and I had to tell my Hannah, 'I must get away. I must go to America, where maybe I can change from a failure to a person with dignity, and where I'll be able to earn a good living for my family.' "

"Maybe you can work with a doctor," my mother suggested.

"Doctors! They know nothing, and they convince each other about how much they know."

"Maybe you can work in a hospital," my father said.

"What will they let me do? In America, you have examinations and you have licenses, and how can I take an examination if I can't read and understand English?"

"It's really a problem."

"Problems are meant to be solved and if I think long enough I'll solve it. I have in my mind prescriptions for all kinds of misfortunes—corns, pimples, sour stomach, toothache. As soon as I have enough money I'll start making these prescriptions, and I'll be able to sell them to drugstores, to people."

"You mean you'll make drugs?" I asked.

Uncle Herschel looked at me. "I won't make drugs. I'll buy

drugs, and then I'll put them together into something people can use when they have a pain some place or something bothers them."

"But if a person is sick, shouldn't he go to see a doctor?"

"He can go to see a doctor, and if the doctor knows what he's doing he'll give that person my prescription. In that way, the person will do without the doctor who will make mistakes. I'll open a store and people can come in and tell me what's wrong and I'll give them a medicine."

Nobody had an answer for what Uncle Herschel proposed to do, and nobody could tell him he would be practicing medicine even if he never touched the patient.

He said, "Would you let your son walk with me through the streets? I haven't had time to look around, to see the stores. . . ."

"Of course. Get your hat and coat, my son, and go with Uncle Herschel."

It was an experience even walking down the long, long hall on the street floor. The hall ran to the wooden staircase which led to all the flats upstairs. We met nobody there, but when we came into the street at least three of my friends were out preparing to play gutter soccer. They stared as I strolled out by my uncle's side. They must have glanced only swiftly at me, but Uncle was surveyed quite extensively: his suit, his stiff shirt and bow tie, his little under-the-lip beard, his dove-gray hat, which he wore rakishly, and above all his stick.

"We're choosing up a kick ball game," Googsie said.

When I shook my head, Sam asked, "Where you going?"

"For a walk with my uncle," I said, loud and proud.

"Is that your uncle?"

"Yeh."

"What's he carrying that thing for?"

"Because he's a doctor," I lied.

"No kiddin'?"

"He's a doctor?"

"But he's a doctor just came from Russia. He's stayin' with us until he can open up an office, and I'm taking him for a walk around the neighborhood."

"When you comin' back?"

"When we're finished walkin'."

"I got a sore on my toe. Will he look at it?"

"Nah, he's not that kind of doctor."

I looked back once as we retreated from the boys because I wanted to see how my story had affected my friends. It had indeed, because their mouths were still open and they stood there immobilized.

I said to Uncle Herschel, "This street we're on is Manhattan Avenue."

"How?"

"Manhattan Avenue."

He repeated that, but all the *a*'s came out as short *e*'s. I repeated the name of the street, and he nodded. He had already learned it.

We had turned to our right. "This is McKibbin Street. On this street all the doctors live, and there's a big house where I think they have bathrooms in their flats and electricity."

We paused. The houses I had indicated were all on the right. I knew about the doctors' houses, private houses, because the sons of two doctors were in my class. One was a very handsome boy, I could almost say a beautiful boy, and I knew why because several times I had seen his mother. Once she had swept into our classroom to talk to our teacher. She was so tall, I almost gasped, and she had the prettiest face I had ever seen. I remember I had stared and stared as she spoke to our teacher from under a wide-brimmed, flowered hat, and when she said good-by to the teacher she beckoned to her son. She adjusted his tie, said something to him, and bent over to kiss him. Nobody snickered because all the boys were breathless with her great beauty and because very few of our parents could have come into school to speak the teacher's language so intimately.

Nobody envied this kid his mother or his high place in our

neighborhood circle because he was a nice kid who never talked about his parents, about his father the doctor or about his mother the beautiful lady.

We walked into the middle of Cook Street. I stopped in front of the house that all the kids avoided because in it lived and worked the doctor known to all the natives as "Crazy Padilsky." Dr. Padilsky was probably not an old man. As I grew older and older I continued to hear stories about his short temper, about his violent rages, about his sharp tongue. He, too, wore a goatee, but it was much more extensive than my uncle's.

I told my uncle about an incident I had witnessed in the hall just outside our flat. We had known that the mother across the hall from the Frieds' was very sick. It had seemed to me that another doctor was in her home every day. One day as I walked out of my flat, I had heard a disturbance down the hall and I stopped to listen. The hall was very dark, but presently the disturbance moved towards me. A tall man emerged out of the gloom of the hall. He was carrying a bag and he was preparing to go down the stairs. Because I was standing on the landing facing him curiously, he had to pause. A young woman—the sick woman's eldest child—was pursuing him, and she caught him on the landing. She laid an imploring hand on his arm.

"Please, Doctor," she said, "tell me what's the matter with my mother."

From the way he swung around to her, I sensed he was very angry. Evidently that question had been asked and rebuffed once before.

"Did you go to college?" he thundered at her.

She lowered her head and shook it almost despondently.

"Then if I tell you, will you know? Go to college and then come and ask me."

I remembered thinking that the woman would be dead by the time her daughter got out of college.

He had turned abruptly, pushed me aside with his bag and strode angrily down the stairs. I had watched the girl sit on the stairs and cover her eyes while the neighbors tried to soothe her.

My uncle did not interrupt my story, and when I finished he said, "Very often when a man hollers loud he's trying to conceal something."

"What was he trying to conceal?"

"Maybe what he didn't know about that woman's sickness. Maybe he was angry with himself because he didn't know, because he was so helpless."

We walked on to Broadway, stopping at the corner to watch an elevated, wooden train thunder by. My uncle didn't say anything, although he had already sampled the marvel of this modern conveyance that had brought him and his bag to my home.

I showed him the many stores on Manhattan Avenue which sold men's suits and women's dresses and coats and shoes for the whole family. He stared into many store windows, but without comment so I did not know what he was thinking.

Then suddenly he said, "On this one street there are more stores and more to buy than in any of the large cities in Russia."

Just that and nothing more. He asked to go down a side street and he chose Cook Street. We had walked about fifty feet from Manhattan Avenue when he stopped and pointed to an empty store, elevated about ten feet from the sidewalk.

"Why is that store vacant?"

"I don't know."

"Do you think it's for rent?"

"I don't know."

"Come, we'll find out."

As we came closer, I saw a small card pasted on the inside of the glass door panel. Because the writing on the card was in script, I took a little time reducing the swings and the writing curlicues so I could read the legend. The last line indicated "ring the bell."

"I have to ring the bell," I said.

My uncle leaned forward to peer at the card and nodded. I rang the bell.

Almost instantly a big man appeared. He was so tall, he was almost terrifying, and his height was further enhanced for me by the fact that I was looking up at him from a lower step.

My uncle said, "Ask him if he speaks Yiddish."

The man beamed down at us. "I put on my teffilin every morning," he said.

Now I saw he wore a big pleasant grin revealing a mouthful of gold. As he spoke he shoved his rolled-up sleeves towards his shoulders. His arms were heroic like the bottom part of a fat whiskey bottle. The rest of him, his chest, his shoulders, was fashioned like his arms—outsized.

"Is the store for rent?" Uncle Herschel asked.

"The store is for rent."

"We can perhaps look at the store?"

The man unhitched a whole jangle of keys which hung from his belt and turned toward the store door. He unlocked it, pushed it open, and waved us in. I waited for my uncle to precede me.

The store was hot and dusty. It was small, about fifteen or twenty feet deep and fifteen feet across. When I turned to look behind me I noticed, really for the first time, that the whole storefront was one huge pane of glass. My uncle was standing in the middle of the store turning to all points of the compass, surveying, for what purpose I could not imagine, sucking now and then on his lower lip, while the renter waited quietly to one side leaning against the wall.

Directly in front of us was a door. My uncle pointed to it with his walking stick. "What is there?"

"Go in and see," the man said.

We went and as my uncle pushed the door open with his stick, we came into a room as wide as the store but only about six or seven feet deep. At one end was a sink. Uncle Herschel saw it at once. He said "aha," went to it, and turned the faucet. Water flowed swiftly and readily.

"How much rent do you ask?" he said.

"Twenty-five."

"Twenty-five dollars? A year?"

Even I knew this was a silly question. My father paid eight dollars a month for our flat. That was eighty-four dollars a year, and this is a store!

The man laughed, but there was no cruel overtone in his laughter.

"How long are you in this country, Uncle?"

"Two days."

"So, good. Someday you'll be a good businessman. In this country a man rents a store and pays rent every month. This store costs twenty-five dollars a month."

My uncle consulted his goatee. "I'll be able to rent this store next month?"

"Sure, if nobody rents it this month."

Uncle Herschel swung around like a soldier performing a maneuver.

"Come," he said to me.

"What did you want to rent the store for, Uncle?" the man asked.

"I want to make things."

"What things?"

"Like patent medicines."

"Are you a druggist?"

"No."

"Then maybe a doctor?"

"Maybe you know what a felsher is?"

"Felsher. Of course I know a felsher. My whole family was always treated by felshers. Wait. I have an Aunt Sarah. She lives in Bath Beach in Brooklyn. She's always saying if only a felsher could look at her she'd get better right away. Maybe you'll go to her?"

Uncle Herschel turned to me. "Do you know Bath Beach?"

I said, "No."

The man said, "Where do you live? I'll send my wife. She has my Aunt Sarah's address, and she'll tell you how to get to Bath Beach."

"We live on Manhattan Avenue. Seventy-nine," I told him.

He wrote it on the back of an envelope he pulled out of his back pocket. I told him my uncle's name, and he promised his wife would come to us.

We continued our walk to Broadway, where we turned left toward Batterman's department store. Here we stopped and he stared and stared, while I waited for him to have his fill of awe and wonder. At last we turned away and returned to Manhattan Avenue.

Back at our flat, we found that my father wasn't home. He had gone to the synagogue on Moore Street where he prayed in the Sephardic congregation. Every Saturday of the year was a privileged praying day for him, because he could go directly to the synagogue upstairs where he would pray with the cantor. On High Holy days we prayed in the basement synagogue, because the prices for seats upstairs were drastically out of his reach.

My mother had already washed the morning dishes and dusted the front-room furniture. When we came into the house, we found her at the kitchen table reading today's installment of the romance which was started fresh twice a year.

"Put more coal on the fire," she told me.

I took off one stove lid to see where the coals needed replenishing and began to shovel more in from the coal box.

"Where did you go?" she asked, after my uncle had hung up his hat and coat behind the front room door.

"We found a store for Uncle," I said.

"A store? What do you need a store for?"

Uncle Herschel came in to remind her he had spoken of it last night, and if he was going to make medicines he wanted to sell them.

"Who will come to you?" my mother asked.

My mother was not profound, but she could ask blunt, disconcerting questions. My uncle did not often smile or laugh, but in response to this question evidently he had to smile.

"As long as there are people who are not willing to admit

they're sick, I'll be able to sell a lot of medicines that will help them."

"So, may God help you in what you're doing."

"When Schiya comes home I must talk to him about a carpenter to make shelves for the store and about buying what I'll need."

My mother looked at him as though she was making up her mind about asking the next question.

"Do you have the money to open such a store, to fix up such a store?"

Uncle Herschel shrugged, and this shrug almost always characterized his attitude toward and his discussions about money.

"God will help."

"But God won't pay the rent."

"I will go to a loan group. We heard about them in Mogliev."

"They will want security."

"I'm a felsher."

"I hope that will be enough."

Two

I went out to play one morning a week after Uncle Herschel, the felsher, came to us from Russia. My Saturdays were normally divided between play on the street in the morning and the library in the afternoon, where I lingered for only a very short time in the children's room. The books and magazines in that room did not interest me. I would wait until the librarian turned her back or until she was called away so I could sneak into the adult room. I had a need to read the magazines I found there—*Life, Judge, Literary Digest, National Geographic*—and many books in the stacks. I discovered Verne and Chambers and Sienkiewicz and Dumas and McCutcheon.

The adult-room librarian was an adversary even tougher than the one in the children's room. She surveyed the readers from her desk, recessed at an angle into one corner, and woe to any young person who dared open his mouth. I knew she might heave me out because my feet hung off the chair, so I sat near her but at such an angle that she could not see my legs. In order to compensate for my lack of height, which would almost beckon her to me, I always sat on three or four magazines, stacking them stealthily before I sat down. As I finished each magazine, I leaned forward and substituted it for another I had been sitting on. During these two or three hours when I read voraciously and without selectivity or guidance, I grew enormously.

Today I came home early enough so my father and I could go to our little compartment in the cellar for the week's supply of coal and wood. We carried a candle to light our operation and two sacks, one for coal, the other for wood. We needed all hands: my father shoveled coal into his sack, I threw kindling into mine and propped up the lighted candle. In that tinderbox where the tenants stored sixteen or more tons of coal and many cords of wood, I had to keep my eyes fixed constantly on the candle.

After we had disposed of the coal in the coal box beside the stove and the wood under the mantelpiece behind the stove, we washed and got ready for a supper of fish and soup and chicken and, of course, my mother's delicious chalah and apple cake. We knew that in the normal course of rotation she would bake her almond bread next week.

We had just mustered all our forces for the gefilte fish when someone knocked on the door. We waited, because our neighbors knocked with one hand while turning the doorknob with the other. One of them even announced herself, fitting her words to her actions. "I knock and I enter," she would say, as she thrust the door open. She went into that routine one day as I was standing in the doorway of the front room in my underwear. She didn't retreat. She gave me only a casual glance, waved at me and told my mother I didn't have anything to startle her or excite her. I went back into the front room, puzzled by what she had said, and forgot it almost immediately.

When the person who knocked didn't come in, my father said, "Come."

A middle-aged woman came in. I looked swiftly from her to my mother. I had to guess they were about the same age. She stopped at the door and said, "I want to talk to the felsher."

When all eyes turned to Uncle Herschel, she, too, looked at him.

My mother said to me, "Bring a chair."

I went into the front room for one of the leather-upholstered, straight chairs we had there around our round claw-footed table. It was so tall and so heavy I had to drag it into the kitchen.

"My husband Sam told me you are a felsher," the woman said.

"Your husband told you the truth."

"I have a very sick aunt."

"What's the matter with your aunt?"

"She can't catch her breath."

Uncle Herschel nodded, and I thought he was waiting for her to invite him to visit her aunt.

"Would you go to visit my aunt?"

"I'll go."

"Oh good, oh good. My aunt believes in felshers. They took care of her in the old home, and she doesn't like American doctors. She thinks they know too much. They make her nervous with all their questions and their examinations. She knows she goes to a felsher, she tells him what's wrong, and he gives her a medicine."

Uncle Herschel toyed with his goatee but he didn't take up the theme this woman had presented.

"When can you go, Felsher?"

"Tomorrow."

"My aunt lives in Bath Beach. Do you know how to go there?"

"No "

"I'll tell you."

"Listen," Uncle Herschel pointed to me. "He will go with me."

She outlined the route: the ride to Manhattan on the Broadway line, the walk to Park Row, the Fifth Avenue line to Bay Forty-fourth Street in Bath Beach.

My mother said, "Write it. You won't remember."

"I'll remember."

"Write it. If you should forget, you'll both be in trouble."

I hurried to my schoolbooks, tore a page out of my notebook

and came back into the kitchen. The woman waited for me to lay the paper on the table before she dictated slowly enough for me to write.

"My aunt has a lot of friends who believe in felshers," she said.

"Good," Uncle Herschel said.

"I'll run to my aunt now to tell her you'll come tomorrow."

"Good."

"My aunt will bless you."

"Good."

"Good-by, everybody, and have a good, prosperous, healthy week."

After the woman left, we seemed to hang a moment saying nothing, perhaps because Uncle Herschel seemed so absorbed in some deep thought. Then he reached over for the paper on which I had written the directions, tore off what I had written and took from his pocket a beautifully scrolled pen.

"Ink," he said.

I hurried to the front room for our bottle of blue ink. Then for the next five minutes as we watched in silence and some awe, he wrote swiftly on the paper. When he finished, he replaced the cap on his pen, reread what he had written, and pushed the paper toward me.

"Take this to a druggist," Uncle Herschel said. He hauled out a pocketbook and took from it a dollar bill.

"Where did you get American money?" my mother asked.

"In Rotterdam."

I took the paper and the money, stuffed them into my pocket and hurried to the drugstore two blocks down. On the street I picked up my friend Muttel.

"Walk me," I said.

"Where you going?"

"To the drugstore."

He fell in by my side. "Somebody sick?"

"I'm going for my uncle, the doctor."

"He sick?"

"No." I looked at him almost pityingly. "My uncle has to fix up a medicine."

"Wow! Your uncle does that?"

"Sure, what do you think?"

"I don't know. I never seen a doctor fix up a medicine."

"Well, my uncle does it."

The druggist looked puzzled when I gave him the list of drugs. He said "*hmm*" and "*umm?*" and then nothing; but his head inclined at a sharp angle and his eyebrows went up.

"This isn't for you, is it?" he asked.

I thought he was incredibly dopey. "Nah," I said, "it's for my uncle."

"And who's your uncle?"

"Herschel."

"Herschel? Does he have a last name?"

"Kessler."

"So what does he need with all these drugs?"

"He's going to make a medicine."

"Oh? Is your uncle a doctor?"

I looked around at Muttel, whose eyes and head had rotated on a well-oiled swivel between me and the druggist during our dialogue. I knew that doctors did not ever make a medicine and that doctors wrote their prescriptions and messages on important-looking pads on which their names and other mystic signs were printed. I couldn't lie to the druggist because he would be suspicious if I told him Uncle Herschel was a doctor, so I had to tell him the truth. I leaned forward and whispered, "My uncle is a felsher."

The druggist stared at me, and I quickly realized he hadn't heard.

"What?"

I tried desperately to lower my voice and at the same time make it audible for this man who evidently did not hear too well.

"My uncle is a felsher," I said.

This, Muttel heard. "What's a felsher?" he demanded.

The druggist crackled the paper between his fingers, undecided how to define a felsher for a little American boy.

"It's a kind of doctor, isn't it?" I said.

"Um . . . yes," the druggist said generously, after he had looked from my eager, worried face to Muttel's inquisitive eyes.

"We'll wait outside for it," I said. "Come on, Mutt."

I hustled him out of the drugstore and into the street, where we watched a huge wagon drawn by two tremendous broad-backed horses pull up to the curb to unload beer barrels. This chore was very familiar to us because saloons grew on every corner, saloons to which I would sometimes go for a pitcher of beer on a warm Friday night. Of course I couldn't go in, but I would slide the pitcher under the swinging doors and give the bartender the ten cents for this huge pitcher which I had to almost cradle home.

Last year during the Chanukah week when I had got twenty-five cents from my mother to commemorate the holiday season, I spent my money in a dizzy orgy. I bought candy in many varieties, I bought cracker-barrel cookies, I bought a Wild West magazine and still had one nickel left at the end of the week. At this point I had lived well and excitingly. There was nothing else in my limited world to buy for a nickel, until I walked by a saloon. Then I turned to my parents and told them I was going in for a glass of beer. It was weeks before I could live that down.

In about ten minutes I went back to the druggist. He had a package for me for which he asked fifty-four cents. I counted the change and pocketed it carefully. I was happy that Muttel did not fog me with questions about my uncle, because normally I am not a very good liar. I did, however, tell him very proudly that my uncle and I would go to visit a patient tomorrow. He was impressed. He said, "Yeah?"

I nodded.

"Around here?"

"No. In Bath Beach."

"Bath Beach? Is that in the United States?"

"It's in Brooklyn, dopey."

"I didn't never hear of it."

"Well you're hearing now."

"I gotta tell the fellers. Bad Beach! It sounds like something else."

"Yeah, well it isn't."

On this note we parted.

Uncle Herschel took the package from me as soon as I entered the house. He went immediately to the sink where he washed his hands over and over. Then he opened the package and laid out first a medicine bottle, then three or four little packets which he unwound slowly.

"I need a mixing bowl and a small spoon," he said.

My mother came to look. "Is this kosher?"

He clucked between his teeth. "Don't be a cow. What can be kosher or not kosher about drugs? Besides, any rabbi will tell you you can use even pig if you save a life. A mixing bowl and a spoon."

My mother brought them, but she did not look at my father; he was certainly more religious than she. We watched as my uncle uncorked the bottle into which the druggist had poured a white liquid. This liquid, "alcohol" Uncle Herschel had explained, he emptied into the mixing bowl and slowly added the drugs one by one until he had a golden liquid. He continued to stir this brew for almost a minute.

When he stopped to study the logistics of transferring the liquid from the bowl to the narrow-necked bottle, my mother brought him a funnel so he could complete the operation.

I set out with Uncle Herschel on our expedition to Bath Beach the next morning at ten o'clock. Sorry that Muttel and my other friends were not on the street to see me off, I turned around several times before we reached the corner of McKibbin Street, but alas there was no one on the street to gape at us, to envy me.

Our trip into Manhattan was uneventful. Uncle Herschel insisted upon riding on the open platform, clinging to his hat as the train passed the Hewes Street station and Marcy Avenue station and on to the Williamsburg Bridge. He didn't talk because he must have been full of the marvel of this long wooden vehicle, speeding down elevated tracks at what must have been extraordinary speed for both of us.

The bridges particularly, spanning the East River with the older Brooklyn Bridge within quick sight, must have stirred him. When we were halfway across, I heard him take a deep breath and whisper, "God's work." This, of course, surprised me, because in these two days since he came to us he had not shown that he was very godly.

Then the train dipped into the subway, and we were at Delancy Street. We had one more stop to get to the Bowery, where the woman had instructed us to disembark and walk to Park Row and the Fifth Avenue train. This station I had never seen. The tracks were all elevated. They came in off the Brooklyn Bridge into a vast, high-ceilinged, domelike station. There were many platforms and many tracks, and it took some time before I found a sign that indicated on which platform we could find the Fifth Avenue train.

As we waited for the train to pull in, I counted three big wooden cars rolling slowly up to the huge stop mechanism at the end of the track. We moved back from the tracks not wanting to interfere with this monstrous conveyance as it came to a halt. A man in a blue uniform straddled the space between the two cars, seized two iron handles and heaved hard on them pulling them toward his body; and the gates swung open for each car. As a mass of passengers spilled out onto the platform, the man in uniform took off his gloves, slapped them together, and strolled slowly off the car platform to the station platform.

When he came closer to us, I stepped forward and asked, "Is this train for Bath Beach?"

"Bath Beach."

"Can we go in, now?"

"That's what it's there for."

I waited for my uncle to precede me into the car where we

found a seat for two facing the door. As soon as we sat down, my uncle took out his cigarette case and held a light to a cigarette. He had time for one long drag before the man in the uniform suddenly loomed in the doorway like some monstrous apparition. He was a very big man with a big red face that was exposed to the elevated wind for about twelve hours each day. He stared at us from the doorway, his hands on his hips, his elbows sticking out, invisible beyond the frame of the door. His eyes were fiercely alight.

"Now, you wouldn't like some beer with that cigarette?" he asked.

We looked at him because he seemed to be looking at us and talking to us.

"Whom is he talking to?" Uncle Herschel asked me in Yiddish.

I said, "I don't know," and I turned to look behind me. My uncle and I were the only ones in the car.

"Put out that damned cigarette," the man bellowed at us.

"What does he want?" Uncle Herschel asked.

"He wants you to put out the cigarette."

Uncle Herschel took the cigarette from his mouth and stared at it as though he couldn't understand how a cigarette could have offended this big man at the door.

"Ask him why I should put out the cigarette," my uncle said.

I said, "Why?"

The man in the uniform stamped toward us, grabbed the cigarette out of Uncle Herschel's fingers causing him to stand up tall and indignant, and ground it out on the floor. Then he swung around and pointed to a sign which read, "SMOKING on this train FORBIDDEN."

"Wynchu foreigners go back where you came from?"

Uncle Herschel said, "This is a wild animal."

"You're not allowed to smoke on this train, Uncle."

"Why?"

"I don't know. That sign says it's not allowed."

He read the sign, making out the words in upper case letters:

"smoking" and "forbidden." He pronounced it "*verboten*," and he knew what that meant.

Because I knew how often Uncle Herschel smoked, I suspected this long ride would be a hardship for him. On the way into Manhattan, however, he had no problem, because he had tossed away a butt as we had entered the station and apparently had no need to light up another cigarette until we came out to the street at the Bowery.

In about five minutes the man in the uniform hollered "all aboard," stepped out to the car platform, heaved on the handles and closed the gates. We were on our way. For about ten or fifteen minutes we watched every station as we pulled in, and I read the signs on each one to Uncle Herschel. I must confess, I knew as little about Bath Beach as he, but I relied upon my ability to speak English to ask for directions. I could sense a restless uncertainty in Uncle Herschel as he alternately got up to stare out the window and leaned forward to rest his chin on the head of his cane. I knew why he was behaving like a nervous cat and I promised myself I would soon get up and walk over to that immense keeper of the gates to discover how far we were from our destination.

As we pulled out of the station we had just hit, I decided that it was time to do this errand, but Uncle Herschel anticipated me. He got to his feet so resolutely, I was almost dragged to mine by some kind of molecular attraction. I was right on his heels as he strode out to the platform where the man in the uniform was comfortably implanted upon the long window at the rear of the car.

Uncle Herschel took a firm hold of the iron grating, because the train was lurching, and faced the man in uniform. He had been staring out into the space we were swiftly leaving behind us when he sensed my uncle's presence in front of him.

"Mister," Uncle Herschel said. "Son of a bitch."

The man in the uniform looked at him incredulously.

"What'd you say?"

I don't think Uncle Herschel could have translated the other man's question, but the tone and the amazed upward lilt of that question alerted him he should repeat his question.

"Son of a bitch," he said, this time even more firmly for emphasis. "Son of a bitch."

The man in the uniform took a menacing step toward my uncle and said, "You say that again and I'll kick your ass."

Then I saw a stranger move forward to my uncle. This man had a conciliatory look on his face as he touched my uncle's arm. My uncle swung around to face him, and his expression was very clear to me: why am I being beset on all sides? He didn't speak to the stranger; he waited for the man to declare himself.

"Mister," he said in Yiddish, "why do you throw yourself in his face?"

"What do you mean, 'throw myself in his face'?" my uncle demanded indignantly.

"Such a word you don't call a man. He'll hit you if you do." The man shook his head at my uncle's indiscretion.

"What word?"

"Son of a bitch."

"What are you talking about? I want to go to Son of a bitch. Why should I call him that? 'Son of a bitch' is a place. I want to go there. I asked him to tell me when we get to Son of a bitch. That's why he wants to hit me? Is everybody crazy?"

I thought I knew what had happened, and I reached over to tug on the man's sleeve. "He doesn't speak English," I tried to explain, "and he got mixed up between that word and Bath Beach. We want to go to Bath Beach, and he wanted to ask you how far we have to go to get there."

The man in the uniform looked from me to my uncle, who repeated "Bath Beach" as though he had just made an exciting discovery.

"Okay," the man conceded, "put a leash on him and keep him in his seat and tell him not to go callin' no names. When we get to Bath Beach I'll holler."

I said "Come back" to my uncle, and we went like sailors rolling in a tossing sea, almost falling into our seats as the train stopped suddenly in a station.

For a few minutes we rode on in silence. I was thinking that the story of our adventure on the Fifth Avenue train would make delightful retelling, but I would have to sacrifice it lest the story downgrade our illustrious guest.

"What did I say to him?" my uncle asked.

"You said a dirty word."

"What do you mean a dirty word? In your city you say a dirty word as a name for a place?"

"No, what you said was a dirty word."

"What did I say?"

I hesitated, but he asked for it. "Son of a bitch."

He mouthed the word. "And where are we going?"

"Bath Beach."

He repeated the two words once, twice, three times.

"Where did I hear son of a bitch?"

"Maybe in the street. Boys use it a lot."

"That, I will have to remember. If I say to an American 'Bath Beach,' even if I'm angry it'll be good; but if I am not angry and I smile and I say 'son of a bitch' to an American, he'll want to hit me."

I told him he was right, and for the next ten minutes as he leaned over the head of his cane, he said the two words over and over. When the man in the uniform leaned into the car to bellow, "Bath Beach," I could see a grin on his red face. I was happy he was no longer angry with us.

Once on the street, we followed the street signs, asked questions and very soon we came to the street we were looking for. We found the house and I rang the doorbell. As we waited I looked up and down the street. All the houses were small like the doctor's house on McKibbin Street, only these were all built of wood. I had never gone into a one-family house before, and I looked forward to this visit.

A man opened the door and looked from me to Uncle Herschel. He said, "Yes?"

Uncle Herschel said, "You speak Yiddish?"

When the man nodded, Uncle Herschel said, "I am the felsher."

The man opened the door wide and we followed him into a dark narrow hall. We stopped at a doorway, and the man pointed to a large room on the left. "You can wait in here," he said to me in Yiddish.

He led my uncle to a short flight of stairs, and I went into the large front room. Against one wall was a sofa like the one in my Tante Luba's house. And all around set at many crazy angles were tables and large and small chairs, some upholstered and stiff-backed like our dining room chairs and some overstuffed and deeply inviting. I had never sat in a deep, soft chair except when I visited Aunt Luba with my parents and the older people were drinking tea in the dining room.

I lowered myself into one of these soft chairs, and I felt myself sinking out of sight but did not resist. I put my hands on the arms, and I just revelled in this unusual luxury for a few minutes. Then I noticed a book on the table to my right and I heaved myself forward so I could reach it. The cover read "*The Count of Monte Cristo* by Alexandre Dumas." In my browsing in the library stacks I had never before seen this title. I turned to the first page and began to read, speeding hungrily through the book; I knew where I would go tomorrow afternoon right after I'd eaten my postschool roll and butter. Edmond Dantes became a fascinating character; his strange and unpredicted arrest as his ship docked roused me to a high pitch of anxiety and concern.

When Uncle Herschel stood in the doorway and said "come," I closed the book regretfully and went with him. On the way home he was quiet, almost pensive, permitting me to lead him from one train to another and down Manhattan Avenue to our home.

My mother was chopping some of the huge hunk of liver she had gotten free from Berger's Meat Market. She had fried it in chicken fat, and now, as she chopped away with a wide chopper in a wooden bowl, she added onion and moistened it with chicken fat. She looked up as we came in.

"Nu?"

"She'll die."

"We all have to die, but when?"

"Maybe in a month. Nothing will help her now, nobody will help her. Only God."

"I thought you don't believe in God."

"I don't believe in the God who has to be worshipped in a schule, but a man has to believe that somehow what is happening to us on earth has a design. You call it God. Good, I'll say it's God. But to me God is God, and he won't be any better to me if I go to schule every day and praise him. My God doesn't need that kind of fawning."

"So, you live with your God however you like to. Are you hungry?"

"No."

My mother looked at me, and I nodded. I was hungry, and I was disturbed by what he had said about God. What did he mean when he said people went to schule to praise God, and his God didn't need that kind of worship?

"How do you pray to God, Uncle?"

"I don't."

"Never?"

"Never."

"But isn't that what a good Jew is supposed to do?"

"Then I'm not a good Jew."

"But what is a good Jew?"

I saw my uncle look at my mother as though he wanted to consult her about the propriety of answering that question, but my mother's head was bowed over the wooden bowl.

"Better you should ask your father," he said.

Three

I met Muttel later Sunday afternoon and mentioned casually that I had just returned from visiting the patient in Bath Beach. He stared incredulously, still not convinced that Bath Beach was an area in the United States. He asked some of my other friends if they had ever heard of it, and when they supported his ignorance he turned to me, saying it was all a hoax, there was no such place, and I had told him a deliberate lie about some place I called Bath Beach that was really another place.

"I can't help it if you're a dope and you never heard of Bath Beach," I said.

"All right, I never heard of Bath Beach, but did Sam, did George, did Jugie?"

I agreed they had never heard of Bath Beach either, but that wasn't enough for Muttel. When I insisted, Muttel said suddenly, "All right, you're such a smart guy, let's ask the only guy around here who knows if there's a Bath Beach. Let's ask Callahan."

"*Ho! Ho!*" Everybody laughed. Callahan was the red-faced cop who walked up and down Manhattan Avenue. None of the kids ever really knew Callahan, because he was not the kind of uniformed man one of our sheeny kids could really approach.

If we ever paused across the street from my house to stare into the windows of the big restaurant where well-dressed men and women came to dine and Callahan sauntered up, he'd growl, "Get the hell away from them winders before I break your ass." I always wondered why he offered to break only one and whether that was meant to serve as a warning to all of us.

We would "get the hell away" a good distance and in chorus chant at him, "Brass buttons, blue coat, can't catch a nanny goat." We would repeat that rhyme three or four times while Callahan, his hands clasped behind him, would try to stare us down. He wasn't very good at that, and we would yowl over his discomfiture. Actually, the only one who was any good at staring people down was the principal of the all-boys school I attended. (Jimmy O'Donnell was the biggest man I knew, and I can recall thinking that only big men like him could become principals. My present teacher in the 5B was a man, but I was sure he could never become principal because he wasn't big enough.)

So when Muttel suggested we appeal to Callahan we hooted at him, because Callahan would no doubt clutch us by our collars and shake us silly.

"All right," Muttel said, "I ain't a fraidy cat. I'll ask him, and if there ain't no such place, you'll go through the mill."

I accepted the challenge. "Bath Beach is in Brooklyn, and if Callahan says so, you'll have to kiss a pig."

"I wouldn't kiss no pig."

"Yeah, you see, fellows. He's afraid I'm right. Okay, you won't have to kiss a pig. You'll have to go to Hymie's pushcart and swipe five mickeys."

For a moment Muttel hesitated as he weighed going through the mill against swiping five potatoes from Hymie's pushcart. Hymie was an easygoing peddler who always added his pilfered losses into the price of his potatoes and onions. However, he must have been a frustrated soccer player because every now and then when he grabbed a hand that was intruding upon his potatoes, he would send the intruder off with such a rousing kick in the behind that the victim couldn't sit for days. No kid ever disclosed to his parents why he couldn't sit because his parents would punish him severely for stealing.

I suppose Muttel thought about all this before he agreed he would suffer the pushcart penalty. Together, then, we set out to find Callahan. We knew we could walk as far as Johnson Avenue without worrying about the Italian boys who lived on Johnson Avenue and the streets beyond, leading to Greenpoint. Sam said Callahan had walked by about a half hour ago, but, then, we knew Sam was no mathematical genius and a half hour could have no real meaning for him. We walked to Boerum Street, the next corner, crossed over, and proceeded toward Johnson Avenue.

Officer Callahan met us halfway up the block. We stopped when we saw he had crossed Johnson Avenue, and I think he saw us at the same time. True to form, his hands were locked behind him as he walked. Even as he mounted the sidewalk off Johnson Avenue, I could see a glint in his eye and a wariness in his gait. Although he could have caught us many times when we were not aware of him, he never approached us in physical belligerence. It's just that his mien was sometimes fierce and his tongue, sharp.

Because we did not run as he came up to us, his thoughts probably mounted in succeeding layers of suspicion.

"What're you doing up this far?" he demanded. "Them wops catch you, they'll kick hell out of you."

"We were looking for you, Mr. Callahan," I said.

Now he surveyed our faces with even graver doubt. Not only had I called him Mr. Callahan, but I had advanced the most unlikely possibility that we were seeking him out. He spread his legs, gripping his hands even more firmly behind his back. The hostility or the make-believe hostility between the Jewish kids and the Italian kids on Johnson Avenue had only face merit, because we saw each other, talked to each other, played with each other on a first-name basis in school. Only on the street were the Italian kids adamant about our living below Johnson

Avenue. Actually, we never cared too much; but this invisible fence bothered Officer Callahan, and he was constantly alert to avert conflict.

"We wanna ask you a question," Muttel said.

He paused, to be assured by Mr. Callahan that he would be receptive.

"All right, ask your question."

"Is there a place called Bath Beach in Brooklyn?"

"Of course there's a Bath Beach in Brooklyn, and it's a place where the likes of you couldn't live."

"You see?" I said.

Muttel wasn't convinced. "How do you get there?"

"How? Fifth Avenue train and Fifth Avenue trolley."

"There, you see," I repeated.

I know we should have thanked Officer Callahan, but we were now so consumed with the errand Muttel would have to run that we turned and hurried to Seigel Street where Hymie's pushcart stood. Nobody shopped on the Sabbath, and only the big stores on Manhattan Avenue, Graham Avenue, and Broadway were open for business then; but Sunday was a big shopping day for the Jewish housewives. We knew where Hymie's pushcart would be and we knew that normally there were up to five potatoes loose under it.

We escorted Muttel to the corner, where we huddled out of sight to observe his maneuverings behind and under the pushcart. We knew he would wait until Hymie began weighing off two or three pounds of potatoes and onions so he could lower himself under the cart, grab the potatoes like a scavenger, stuff them into his shirt, and race for freedom.

We watched him almost breathlessly, because we were only clandestine thieves and sometimes all our poorly laid plans would explode in our faces. Everything went well for Muttel until he forgot he was under the pushcart after he had poked six potatoes into his shirt. He thought he had cleared the pushcart and he raised himself suddenly and vigorously. He crashed his back into the cart, causing the stick which supported it at one end to pull out. The pushcart tipped down, scattering potatoes and onions all over the street.

Hymie dropped the bag he was weighing, screaming, "You son of a bitch, you son of a bitch," and raced for the tilted pushcart where it had struck the ground. The potatoes and onions dribbled sickeningly off the cart. Muttel had disappeared, and our first urge was to flee this disaster area. Then I remembered my father had always said we must help people who were less fortunate. When I started to cross the street, my friends cried to me fearfully.

"I'm going to help him," I said.

They railed at me that I was out of my mind, that Hymie would hit me over the head with that support, but I continued toward the cart.

"Get outa here, you bastard," Hymie yelled at me.

I had picked up two handfuls of potatoes, which I carried to the cart.

"I want to help you pick up–," I started to say.

"I don't need your help. You and your friends. You should live so long, what friends you are to me. It's a good thing the street isn't wet or you'd hear from me. Wait, I'll go to your school yet and tell your teacher."

I continued to pick up the potatoes and onions disregarding his continuing tirade. In a minute my friends were at my side, shoveling up the potatoes and onions and laying them gently, almost penitently, on the cart.

Hymie returned to the bag in which he was weighing off five pounds of onions, and, as he tossed in onion after onion to achieve an accurate weight, he continued to rail against modern children. They were not like the children in the old home where respect for an older person was a prime consideration in a child's upbringing. We completed our task and stole quietly away. We didn't go to look for Muttel. This adventure had ended in a near disaster and all our taste for a feast of mickey charred in a tin can went suddenly flat.

I went home to read the Jewish paper *Forward*, if my mother had done with it, or the special articles in yesterday's paper. On Sunday and Saturday I never went scrounging for reading to the Frieds'. My mother had seen to that. "Let them be on Saturday and Sunday. The family is home; they don't need you."

Uncle Herschel was reading today's edition of *Forward* and my mother was preparing the dinner—rolled cabbage in a huge pot. In another pot a thick soup aromatic of dill and parsley and parsnips and lima beans, and split green peas, was simmering gently. I went to the wood area behind the stove to look for yesterday's *Forward* and retired with it to the front room.

Suddenly we heard a wild scream from the house next to ours. My mother dropped the meat she was rolling and ran to the window. Uncle Herschel took off his pince-nez glasses, laid them on the table and he, too, hurried to the window which my mother had opened wide.

The two houses were joined with an areaway between them, two windows almost meeting at an apex from which ran the common wall for both our kitchens and our front rooms. Between the two windows was a space about five or six feet wide. My mother was holding a long-handled spoon which she used to reach out and knock on the window.

"Jennie, Jennie, why are you screaming? Why are you screaming?"

Instantly Jennie flung the window up and bawled something incoherent at my mother.

"I don't understand you, I don't understand you," my mother said.

Jennie stopped, took a big swallow of air, and screamed more distinctly, "My mother, my mother. I can't wake her up."

"What do you mean you can't wake her up?"

"She said she was tired about twelve o'clock and she said she'll lie down for a while. I just tried to wake her up, but she just lies there. She just lies there."

Uncle Herschel said, "Let me, let me," and my mother moved aside for him to get closer to the window. "Is your mother breathing?"

"Yes! She's breathing and everything, just like she was asleep, but I can't wake her no matter what I do."

I had come closer to the window now. I knew Jennie very well because she called me her little brother and she had cakes for me that she and her mother baked.

Uncle Herschel leaned over to look down into the shaft, two floors below.

"How can I creep over to that house?"

"Don't go this way," my mother said. "Go down and into the next house and up two flights. Don't go this way."

Uncle Herschel shook his head impatiently at her. "I must look at her immediately. Do you have a board?"

From behind my mother I said, "Your ironing board, Ma."

Sometimes she spread a blanket and a sheet on the kitchen table to iron, because the table was the right height for her. At other times she laid a stout board that my father had covered with a cloth from the back of a kitchen chair to the washtub or the back of another chair.

I ran for the board, which my uncle laid across the two window sills, spanning the shaft and hugging the two buildings.

"Hold it," he told Jennie, and he repeated the admonition to my mother and me. And while my mother watched fearfully, Uncle Herschel crawled out on the board, took a firm hold of the window casement of Jennie's flat and lowered himself into the house.

Jennie watched him, and she must have wondered why he was responding to her call for help. My mother must have sensed some misgiving in Jennie's face as she moved aside for Uncle Herschel to clamber down from the window ledge.

"That's my brother," my mother said, "he's a felsher. Let him look at your mother."

"I'm going over there," I called to my mother and I ran for the door. I knew my request to follow Uncle Herschel across the shaft would be futile because I had asked to do this so often and had been denied just as regularly.

I fled down the two flights of stairs, ignored Muttel, who had been loitering near the house to try to explain how he had miscalculated the distance from the middle of the pushcart to the end, and galloped up the two flights of stairs to Jennie's flat. I didn't knock. I just opened the door and stepped into the kitchen.

I tried to peer into the bedroom, but Jennie was standing in the doorway. I walked softly up behind her and saw my uncle hunting for a pulse in her mother's left wrist. Then he took out his watch and he stared at the face for what seemed like an hour. He laid her arm on the bed and slowly raised first one eyelid then another. Jennie covered her mouth with her hands so she would not scream as Uncle Herschel backed away from the bed. For a long time he stood there, staring and fingering the little thatch of hair under his chin.

"How often did this happen?"

"Often? This is the first time. This never happened before."

Again he returned to his goatee, while I waited breathlessly for him to perform a miracle.

"Send for a doctor," he said.

Jennie was surprised, and I must confess I, too, was surprised and even disappointed.

"But you're a felsher," Jennie said. I could appreciate the distress in her voice; I felt it with her.

"In Russia I could do what a doctor could do. Here in America I'm nothing. You have to send for a doctor."

Jennie wrung her hands and looked about her helplessly. "My father won't be home until eight o'clock and I can't leave her—"

"I'll go," I said. "Which doctor should I call?"

She clutched at me and kissed me. "The best, the best. Get Doctor Padilsky."

I drew back a little inwardly at the thought of walking up to that monstrous character's door, but I said "all right" and hurried to the street.

I ran every step of the way to Cook Street and I paused at the door only long enough so I would have the breath for speaking. Somebody who wore a little white apron and a little white something on her head came to the door of Dr. Padilsky's house when I rang the bell. She was very decidedly not Jewish, and before admitting me she studied my shoes to see, I suppose, if they were too dirty and would clod up the hall. Then she inspected the rest of me.

"Yes?"

"I want to see Doctor Padilsky."

"Now what would you be wantin' to see him about?"

"There's a lady in Seventy-seven Manhattan Avenue. She's dying."

She continued her study of my face for another ten seconds while I fidgeted unhappily on the stoop. Then she closed the door, and I wondered whether I would have spunk enough to follow her in to the presence of her distinguished master. She reappeared with a pencil and a notebook.

"Tell me her name, and she better not live too high up. Doctor doesn't like to go above the second floor."

I gave her the information she needed and thought, What a ridiculous thing to tell me. Suppose a person who lives on the fourth floor gets sick? Will his family have to litter him down to the second floor?

"Doctor will be there as soon as he finishes his dinner."

"But this lady's dying."

"I told Doctor. He said patients never die while he's having his dinner."

I heard the period on that sentence as she closed the door. For a few seconds I stared at the door; then I hurried back to Jennie's house. She caught me as soon as I opened the door.

"Is he coming?"

"He'll come as soon as he finishes eating. He says nobody dies while he's eating."

"He should only drop dead. Last year he came here because my father was vomiting and sick, and after he examined my father he called him all kinds of names—a 'pig,' a 'fat slob'—because he said my father ate everything that a normal animal wouldn't eat."

I looked at Uncle Herschel because he had chanted the same lines to my father only two days ago, but my uncle was not thinking of the doctor. He sat in a chair near the bed, and he did not take his eyes from the woman's face. She didn't look sick to me, although I had been creative when I described her condition to that person at the door. Uncle Herschel held a light to a cigarette and for the half hour that followed he smoked constantly, moving toward the bed regularly, recurringly to touch the woman's face, to hold her wrist and measure against his watch the intensity and speed of her pulse.

Each time, Jennie brought her hands up to her mouth as Uncle Herschel retreated and she whispered, "How is she?"

Several times he gave her an indifferent answer, but this last time he shrugged. "She's still alive."

Then suddenly the door flew open as though it was motivated by some wild fury, and that man flung himself into the room. Because the door crashed against the wall, Jennie and I started and we moved away from this tide.

"So, where is she?" the doctor exclaimed.

"She's in there," Jennie pointed. She shrank from his searing presence. He strode into the room and saw my uncle sitting almost serenely in that chair near the bed, smoking his everlasting cigarette.

"Who is this?" Dr. Padilsky bellowed.

"Shah, don't holler," Uncle Herschel said.

"Who is this?"

Jennie stuck her head into the doorway. She suspected, and correctly, that she was going to be caught between these two men.

"He's a felsher," she said.

"I don't care if he's the King of Jerusalem. Get him out of here."

"I'm staying," Uncle Herschel said quietly.

"He's a felsher," Jennie repeated, and I thought she would begin to cry.

"I can't examine a patient with an audience."

"I'm not an audience. I know as much about what you're going to see as you do. In Russia I practiced medicine maybe before you did. I can't practice here yet. Just go ahead with your examination. I won't bother you."

"Out! Out! Young lady, either he goes or I go."

"*Shah! Shah!* You're a doctor. You won't run, and you wouldn't want this girl to report that you ran from a patient just because a felsher was in the room."

My uncle got up and stomped out of the room, not because he was angry, but because he was walking out of the room. As he cleared the threshold the door slammed shut with a blast.

Uncle Herschel found a chair and held a lighted match to a cigarette. "He's either crazy," he said, "or he's a good actor."

Jennie hovered over him unhappily. "I knew he would do that," she said, "but my mother is so sick."

"I told you to send for him," Uncle Herschel reminded her.

We endured the ten minutes that slithered by, each in his own medium. Jennie paced up and down wringing her hands and cracking her knuckles. Each crack reverberated in the room. I had fastened myself upon a wall opposite the door and I didn't stir from that posture. Only my uncle appeared undisturbed.

When the door opened, it did not tremble as when it was shut. Dr. Padilsky came out a little more subdued.

"Your mother has sleeping sickness," he said.

"That we already know," Uncle Herschel said.

The doctor swung on him, and all the fury he had borne into the sickroom rose to his face and his tongue. He was standing where the light shone on his face, and I saw that the skin was badly blotched and scarred. I wondered, did doctors get sick, too?

"What do you know? What do you know?" Dr. Padilsky demanded.

"That she has sleeping sickness."

"So you know she has sleeping sickness. Did you go to college?"

"I went to the body."

"So you went to the body. Did the body talk to you?"

"I have eyes and I have hands, and I could read what others found in bodies."

"So you saw, so you touched. Did that make you a doctor?"

"I lived with diseases and I read what others knew about these diseases and what they did for them, and a lot of people went on living because of me."

"You're a charlatan like the rest of your kind, who know nothing and who are like leeches on the stupid and ignorant."

"The difference between you and me is that you have a license to be a charlatan. Let's see if I'm a charlatan. You write a prescription, and I'll write what I used to prescribe in Russia."

"Pah! I don't recognize you as an equal." He held a piece of paper in his hand. "Take this to your druggist," he told Jennie. "He'll tell you what to do."

Uncle Herschel took a small notebook from his pocket, tore out a page and wrote swiftly on it. He gave me the paper before he turned to Jennie. "Take the prescription to the druggist, and then ask him if what I wrote is the same as what the doctor wrote."

I hurried to the drugstore. On the way I studied both papers, trying to distinguish any characters on one sheet that I could relate to the words on the other; but this was a hopeless undertaking.

I gave the prescription to the druggist and waited for him to *hmm* and *umm* over it before he said, "Come back in an hour. It'll cost seventy-five cents."

Then I laid my uncle's paper on the counter. The druggist stared down at it. "What's this?"

I told him, and as I spoke proudly and fearfully he read what Uncle Herschel had written. Then he clucked.

"That's the man who wanted those drugs I sold you yesterday?"

"Yes."

"He's all right. A felsher! He knows his business, and that Doctor Padilsky is crazy."

I hurried back to Uncle Herschel with joy and pride in my heart. He accepted my story quite calmly, but Jennie did not seem to hear. She had returned to her pacing, and it was disturbing to watch. I backed away from her, I tried to shut out the unpleasant spectacle.

"Go back home," Uncle Herschel told me. "I'll stay here until her father comes home from work."

I was happy to go, because that sleeping woman in there and her distraught daughter were beginning to distress me. When I got home I gave my mother Uncle Herschel's message and had to tell her the whole sequence of events. She knew Jennie's mother very well, because in the spring and summer they sat at their windows talking about their children and about their husbands and about their families.

Uncle Herschel came back about two hours later. My mother had fed me so I could retire to the front room to do my homework on the round dining-room table. Normally I worked at the kitchen table while my parents read the newspaper so we would have the expense of only one light.

I came into the kitchen, wanting to hear what Uncle Herschel would tell my parents about the sleeping woman in the next house.

"What kind of curse is this?" my mother asked.

"She's a sick woman. She has sleeping sickness. What is sleeping sickness? Some people say it is a curse from God, but God wouldn't bother sending such a curse on one unimportant woman. If the Czar had sleeping sickness, I might agree that this could be God's curse, but this woman!"

"Will she get better?"

"Will it rain next month?"

"Will it rain next month?" That was the kind of enigmatic answer I would get to many of the questions I asked him, for which there were no answers or for which he did not know the answers. However, I didn't mind, because even in those answers I found, after reviewing my question, that I had learned something.

Four

Many weeks went by, and during those endless days Uncle Herschel would disappear early in the morning and come back in time for supper. All of us assumed he was hunting for work, for some kind of professional attachment to some hospital, to some clinic where they could use his skilled hands. He never told us where he had been, whom he had seen, what success he had had or what failure. My mother would sometimes talk around his preoccupation, but she never asked him directly.

"What can a felsher do in a hospital in the year 1912?"

"They don't need a felsher in a hospital."

"But suppose a felsher should get a job in a hospital. What could he do?"

"I know too much. As soon as a doctor asks me questions and I give him answers, I become too old. I age in front of their eyes. They won't say I can be a doctor, and I know too much to be an orderly, and I'm too old to wash floors."

"That's what they tell you?"

"That is not what they tell me, but a fool I'm not."

"So what will be?"

"God and I will get together and think up something."

"And about the store you wanted to open on Cook Street?"

"Ah! Now you're coming closer to what I think I'm going

to do. If I can get started there, then I can make a fortune with my medicines."

"So?"

"I'm thinking about it. This I have to do. I won't let those doctors push me into the ground. As I told you once before, in Russia I was a failure in my own eyes because I felt I was wasting myself in that village and everything I had learned, but at least the peasants respected me, looked up to me. I must do something that will permit me to have a respect for what I am doing. Once and for all I must wipe out of my mind the thought of failure."

I could sense how pridefully he said that, and I could visualize also the perplexed attitude of the doctors who interviewed the goateed little man, erect and alert, holding his cane as a scepter. I recall standing on the corner of McKibbin Street and watching him approach from Broadway. McKibbin Street was a busy thoroughfare with a trolley running one way as well as many single- and double-spanned horse-drawn trucks.

As he came to the corner this day, three trucks were moving east and two others had begun to cross Manhattan Avenue, rolling west. Uncle Herschel didn't hesitate for one minute. Ignoring those huge Percherons he stepped off the sidewalk to cross the street. He raised his cane as a flag or a baton, and I was amazed to see the truckers pull up their horses to watch him walk leisurely to the other side of the street.

Of course they told him raucously and profanely what they thought of him, his mother, his father, his ancestors all the way back, but he continued on serenely, never once disturbed by the uproar around him.

When he saw me gaping at him, at his cold-blooded insouciance, he said, "What are they hollering about?"

I waited for him to step up on the sidewalk before I said, "They're hollering because they were afraid their horses would run you down."

He waved his cane. "Horses have more sense than they. Horses won't run you down. They run around you."

"But they're in harness."

"They would turn unless the driver held them straight. Let's go back to that store."

I led him to Cook Street, where Sam welcomed us enthusiastically. "Ah," he exclaimed, "the felsher. My wife told me you came to her aunt's house. She's already better. You hear, already better."

Uncle Herschel stared at him because he had not yet convinced himself about that lady in Bath Beach, but he did not offer a rebuttal. Instead, he held out his cane as though he were cutting a path for himself into the store. Sam moved back, impressed by the majesty of the cane and by his respect for this learned man.

"I will need a carpenter," Uncle Herschel said.

"I'm a carpenter."

"On this wall I will need shelves."

"On the whole wall?"

"On the whole wall."

Sam nodded, said "wait a minute," and ran from the store. In a few minutes he reappeared with a long sheet of paper, a carpenter's folded rule, and an odd flat pencil. I watched as Sam ran the rule from floor to ceiling, from back wall to front window; wrote figures on his sheet; and asked questions about the height of the shelves, their depth and their width. He drew a picture as he made his measurements, and Uncle Herschel stood by, apparently admiring what Sam was creating on paper.

"Pretty," Uncle Herschel said.

"I'll let you know how much it will cost after you pay rent for the first month."

"Tomorrow."

"Tomorrow."

We headed home, but as we approached the house Uncle Herschel said, "Come, show me how to get to that woman's house."

I led him to the flat and in the dark hall knocked on the door. Jennie shuffled to answer it; I could hear her weary step on the oilcloth that covered their floor. She peered out at us but she could not make out our faces because there was no light at her back.

As we came in a voice in the gloom near the window said, "Make a light, Jennie."

We stopped near the door and waited for Jennie to strike a match. I could hear her fumbling in the metal matchbox and the sharp scratch against its abrasive front. She carried the lighted match to the gas jet that hung from a pipe extended down from the ceiling. The gas streaming up from the jet into a gossamer-thin mantle caught the light and came up a big, bright glow.

"Papa," Jennie said, "this is the felsher. You know him." She touched my head.

Papa sat in a corner between the table and the window, his sloping shoulders hunched over the table, his stunned eyes looking out at us over dark half-moons.

"Come in," Papa said bleakly.

"How is the mother?" Uncle Herschel asked.

Papa only turned up his palms where they were resting on the table, and Jennie said, "She's sleeping."

"Can I see her?"

Jennie came around to lead us into the bedroom. Uncle Herschel stopped at the bed and said to me, "Bring a candle."

I wondered why he asked for a candle when there was a gas jet jutting from the wall, but I realized later that they had only kerosene lamps and candles in the Russia from which he had come. But Jennie understood what he wanted. She came with a match, and when she caught the gas the flame was small. Uncle stared at it.

"Make it lighter. She won't know about the light."

He held the patient's hand, touched her head, and took out his watch to count the beats in her pulse. Then he leaned against the wall and stared on and on at her while I shifted restlessly from one leg to another. Jennie was too tired to question him, so I was sure she didn't hear Uncle say, "She may get up tonight."

But suddenly Jennie jumped and ran to clutch at him. "What did you say?"

"Your mother may get up tonight or tomorrow morning."

"Oh! Oh! Papa did you hear? The felsher says mama may get up tonight."

"Or tomorrow."

"Oh, what do I care! You said she'd get up."

"Yes."

"Oh! What should I do—what should I do when she gets up?"

"Nothing."

"Nothing? How can you stand there and say nothing?"

"She will ask for nothing, so you'll do nothing."

"But how will she look? Will I be able to talk to her?"

"You'll be able to talk to her, and she'll answer you."

"I'm going crazy. Here my mother lies like she's dead, and now you say she'll wake up and I'll be able to talk to her and she'll talk to me!"

"You just told the whole story."

"Just like that? How can I believe you? Look at her. She doesn't move. She doesn't even cough. She just lies there."

"You'll see when she gets up."

"What should I tell her if she asks me what happened to her?"

"She won't ask you."

"How, she won't ask me, when she wakes up after she's been like dead?"

"She won't ask you."

"But why?"

"She doesn't know what happened to her."

"How can that be? You tell me something I can't believe, I shouldn't believe."

"Believe it or not, she won't ask you, and you shouldn't tell her."

"So I should just let her lie there?"

"No. She can get up if she wants to, and she can walk around."

"And eat?"

"Light—an egg, soup, maybe white meat from a chicken, a lot of liquid—tea, water."

"And medicine?"

"The urotropin—what the doctor prescribed for you."

"That's all?"

"What else can I tell you? Even the doctor won't do any more for her."

"Maybe God will."

"Maybe God will."

The door was suddenly propelled open as if motivated by a monstrous wind. Without ceremony, a brassy voice that I knew belonged to Dr. Padilsky announced itself to the man who was still sitting apathetically in the chair by the window. The doctor shrugged himself out of his coat dropping it on a chair near the table.

He stamped into the bedroom without looking at anyone, flung his bag open, raised the sleeping woman's wrist, took out his watch and studied it briefly.

"She didn't wake up?" He threw out this question assuming that the right person would field it.

"No," Jennie said.

"Your mother will wake up sometime tonight or tomorrow morning," he said.

"Oh!" Jennie exclaimed.

"What's the matter? Did I give you bad news?"

"No, oh no, I'm just so happy. The felsher just told me the same thing."

"Felsher!" he snorted.

Uncle Herschel turned and walked slowly out of the bedroom. He took out a cigarette, held a light to it, and dragged and dragged on it.

"When she wakes up, she won't know what happened to her," the doctor said. "You don't have to tell her."

"Oh!" Jennie said.

Because he suspected the reason for Jennie's second exclamation, he only looked at her to emphasize his annoyance.

"If she's hungry, give her light food, egg, soup, chicken–the white meat–and a lot of liquid–tea, water."

"The felsher told me everything." Jennie hardly breathed the words.

"So the felsher told you, so the felsher told you!" the doctor bellowed.

He hefted his bag and strode into the kitchen, stopping to glare at Uncle Herschel. "Who asked you to come?" the doctor demanded.

Uncle Herschel took another long drag and expelled a vast, irritating span of smoke. "Why do I have to explain to you why I go where I go?"

"Because I'm a doctor and you're a felsher."

"And it bothered you that I know what you know."

"You know nothing."

"I just said that."

"You have no right coming into this house to practice medicine."

"I don't have to practice; I've already learned how. I didn't give her a prescription, although I know what you know about that. I've seen and treated more cases of encephalitis than you can count until next Friday."

"Just you let me catch you practicing medicine, you charlatan!"

"You're a little boy."

"I'll show you what a little boy who's a doctor can do."

"You're a foolish little boy. Anybody can give advice to a sick person. Even you know that. I wouldn't tell them I'm a doctor, because then they'd have a picture of you in their minds for me. That, I don't need."

Dr. Padilsky sucked his lower lip. I stared into his face and I could see that the sores on it seemed even redder. His fury must have been uncontainable because his reputation as the wildman of the medical profession was widely proclaimed throughout the neighborhood. For years he had browbeaten and intimidated everybody, and only Uncle Herschel had stood up to him. He clapped his badly crushed hat on his head and burst out of the house.

Uncle Herschel calmly continued to smoke while we watched him pace the kitchen floor, shaking his head and setting and re-setting his lips over and over as though he wanted to rid himself of an obnoxious taste. Then suddenly he grabbed up his coat, said to Jennie, "Call me if she does anything strange," and motioned me out of the house.

Five

Down in the street Uncle Herschel said to me, "Come with me. I want to buy brandy," and we headed in the direction of Boerum Street. Knowing the store to which he was leading me, I was apprehensive, because it was on the other side of the invisible line the Italian boys had drawn for us at Johnson Avenue.

"Isn't there a store this way?" I asked pointing toward Broadway.

"No, this is a good store. I like the bottles in their window."

"No, we mustn't go there."

"Why?"

"Because Italian boys live there, and they hit Jewish boys who go there."

"Italian boys? Do their fathers come out to hit Jewish boys?"

"No, only Italian boys."

"So come. This is America. In America a Jew is not afraid. In Russia the pogroms are started and helped by the police. In America the police are on the side of the Jew. Come. You're going with me."

This would be my first lesson in the behavior of boys who were accompanied by their parents. I walked fearfully by his side, wondering what I would do if, when we crossed Johnson Avenue on our way to Montrose Avenue, we were suddenly jumped by a throng of Italian boys. I kept swiveling my head from side to side, and my uncle knew what was plaguing me.

"Dogs become very angry when another dog whom they don't know suddenly walks by their yard. They bark, but when their master comes out with a stick, they slink away."

I said, "I know, but these boys don't bark."

I stopped, completely immobilized. On the same sidewalk, coming toward us was Jimmy, one of the biggest of the Italian boys. He was probably only a little older than I, but he was so much bigger and stronger. When he was in my class last year, he had always greeted me by making a bitter disarray of what I had wrought so carefully with comb and water.

Uncle Herschel didn't notice I had stopped; I was literally scared stiff. Jimmy was walking by himself, carrying a short stick which he slapped against his thigh to keep time with his gait. Jimmy always carried a short stick, and even a playful pat with it made quite an impression on the buttocks.

He didn't stop. As he strolled by me, he raised the short stick in greeting, and in reply I could only gawk at him, here on Manhattan Avenue one-half block beyond the boundary line. Then I saw a man and a woman behind him, and I heard the woman call, "We'll turn down Johnson Avenue, Jimmy."

I hurried to catch up to Uncle Herschel. He had missed me but had not altered his pace, and when I fell into step by his side he turned to look at me.

"It's the same all over the world," he said. "I saw it in our village in Russia. The peasant wanted to live in peace and he rarely bothered the Jew and he did not let his sons bother the Jew unless the police stirred them up."

He carried his brandy home, and as my mother talked to him he poured himself three glassfuls. Neither my mother nor I made any comment about his drinking, but I gaped, never having seen liquor consumed with such sureness.

He told my mother about his adventure with the doctor in the house next door, and he laughed. He didn't laugh very often; actually this was the first time I had seen him lay his head back and cackle. Something in his throat seemed to interfere with the fullness of his laughter, but he was delighted with his story and with the doctor's discomfiture.

"You better watch out for him," my mother warned.

"Why? Because I gave them advice? I didn't tell them I'm a doctor; I didn't take money from them. Anybody can go in there and advise them. Nobody can say that the advice can't be given or that they have to take it."

"I don't know, but with such a man, you shouldn't fool around."

He waved his hand at my mother. "I upset him because I know what he knows, and that mustn't happen to a doctor. He surrounds himself with all kinds of mumbo jumbo and rejects completely what was handed down from grandmother to grandmother. Wait, someday he and other doctors will suddenly discover that the grandmother remedies are not so stupid."

"We went back to look at the store," I said.

I wanted most urgently to talk about the store. I had always envied the boys who fussed importantly behind counters of retail stores, and I looked forward to the possibility that I might yet achieve that eminence in Uncle Herschel's store.

My mother looked at him. He was battening down the cork in the brandy bottle. "Really?" she asked.

"I brought with me five hundred rubles. With the five hundred rubles I'll be able to open the store with shelves and buy drugs to start making my medicines."

"Medicines? Don't you need a license for that, like a druggist?"

"Those medicines, I won't worry about. There is nothing in the drugs to hurt anyone, and only a few are for drinking."

"I'm afraid."

"So you're afraid. Tomorrow I will go to the druggist and ask him where he buys his drugs. . . ."

"Why don't you go tonight, Uncle," I asked. "I'll go with you and tell him who you are. He already knows you from what you sent me to buy. . . ."

My uncle looked at me and then across at my mother.

"Go with him," my mother said.

He laid his hand on my head. "Good boy," he said.

I glowed; these were the only words of praise he had ever spoken to me.

"When you come back, Schiya will be home," my mother said.

I went with him, proudly leading the way. As we came into the street, Muttel was standing near the door. He took my arm, and I knew he wanted to explain how he had permitted a disaster to ruin our plans for a weenie roast, but I shook him off.

"Wait," he said. "Wynchu lemme tell you what happened?"

"Can't you see I'm doing something important with my uncle?"

"But I gotta talk to you."

"You don't gotta do nothin'. I'm busy. Tomorrow I'll talk to you."

Uncle Herschel had not paused to listen to my dialogue with Muttel. He was proceeding confidently down the street. I wondered how he knew how to get to the drugstore, but he did not falter, and I ran to catch him at the corner of Boerum Street.

The druggist was a gray, tallish man whose hips were infinitely wider than his shoulders, which drooped over his chest. His face reminded me of a rooster with drooping eyes, because his cheeks were distended downward and he appeared to be carrying something in these pouches that made them sag so.

He was standing behind the counter as we opened his door and seemed to be staring off into space, space that was not just limited to the store. As we crossed his line of vision he failed to acknowledge us. We were almost upon the counter when suddenly he became alert. He knew me, of course, but did not associate me with the elegant cane-carrying gentleman who had come in behind me. He waved to me, said, "Hello there, young feller," and, impressed by my uncle's appearance, turned to look inquiringly at him.

I said, "This is my uncle, the felsher. You remember, you sold him some drugs."

The druggist reversed his eyeballs, "Yes, yes indeed."

Uncle raised his walking stick like a conductor signaling to a choir in his orchestra. "You speak Yiddish?"

The druggist grinned. "How could I survive in this neighborhood if I didn't?"

"Good, then we can talk. I came to ask you a favor."

"Ask."

"I need drugs, a lot of drugs, and I want you to tell me where you buy yours so I can go there and buy from them."

The druggist needed time to digest this request.

"You know, mister, I get all kinds of crazy requests in this drugstore, but in twenty-five years nobody ever asked me a question like that."

"This is the first time?"

"Yes!"

"So you have to get used to things that happen to you only once and never again. For instance, you were born only once and you're going to die only once and if you think hard you'll find you've had a lot of things happen to you only once."

The druggist licked his lips, and his eyes seemed to take on another light. "All right, just tell me what you need so much drugs for, and I'll give you a name and an address."

"I want to make some medicines."

"To sell?"

"To sell."

"But you're not a druggist. You're not even a doctor, and in this country a felsher is a nothing. They won't let you sell anything."

"The drugs will be harmless."

"That's what you say, but suppose they're not?"

"Then I'll go to prison."

"*Ho! Ho!* Look how he talks about prison. You're not a spring chicken."

"To whom do I have to prove that my drugs will not hurt anyone?"

"I don't know, but if you do hurt somebody, look out."

"Are you going to give me the name and address?"

"How long are you in this country?"

"Four weeks."

"Four weeks! You talk as if you've lived here four years."

"Put a silly chicken in a strange coop, and she'll learn her way around the coop very fast."

"*Ho!* You'll make a million dollars yet."

Six

Uncle Herschel had gone back to the store on Cook Street the next morning. He recited the story that evening as we ate a supper of my mother's garlic borscht, made from a number of shredded beets, two or three hunks of garlic, about two pounds of meat, and two or three marrow bones. Eaten steaming hot and when I had to angle around the chunks of meat to ladle up all the shreds of beets, it was just another world. I always saved the meat for last, retaining a little of the succulent soup so I could combine the meat with the liquid.

Uncle Herschel had gone into the store, he told us, and Sam had given him the completed drawing of the wall shelves.

"It will cost you thirty dollars," he had said.

"Twenty," Uncle Herschel had said.

Sam had been dismayed. He had held out the drawing and he seemed to implore my uncle's understanding and sympathy. "Look, look at the plans."

"I looked."

"And you think it isn't worth thirty dollars?"

"To you it can be worth fifty dollars. To me it's worth twenty."

"But do you know how much I'll have to pay for lumber?"

"I never bought lumber."

"So if you never bought lumber, how can you know this job isn't worth thirty dollars?"

"Because I never bought lumber."

"I wouldn't want to do business with you every day. You'd eat my heart out."

"In Russia a good carpenter would take ten rubles for this job and thank God."

"We're not in Russia, and for that I thank God."

"Then you'll make the shelves."

"I should live so long how hard it is for me to make those shelves for twenty dollars."

"Make, make."

"You'll have to give me some of your medicine. I'll need it for my heart."

Before he had left Uncle Herschel had paid rent for one month, to begin as soon as Sam painted the store and set up the shelves. Then he had gone to Manhattan by himself to buy the drugs he would need. When my father asked him how he had found his way to Third Avenue, he said he had looked around until he had seen what he judged to be a Jewish face.

Only once had he misjudged, but happily. The man he had accosted peered at him and said, "I speak Russian." When Uncle Herschel had told him in glittering Russian that he had just arrived fresh from Russia, that he was a felsher and that he was looking for a wholesale druggist to buy supplies, the Russian had embraced him, taken his arm, led him to the establishment and waited for him.

When they came out the Russian had again taken command and steered him to a store—an "inn," my uncle called it—where they had been served gallons of tea and a strong kind of liquor. The Russian had written Uncle's name on a small piece of paper together with our address. He had promised to tell the Russian colony a real felsher had come to town. Alas, either the promise and the horizon disappeared somewhere into an oblivion or the drunken Russian lost the paper. Nobody from the Russian colony ever called on Uncle Herschel.

In about a week, the drugs were delivered to our house. I was on the street in a choose-up game of soccer, which we played with a stocking ball. The stocking ball is a monument of resourcefulness and ingenuity. We would take a stocking, black of course, and cut off the foot. Then we would scrounge around for rags. When we had sewed up one end of the sock (I learned later we were actually using the art of stuffing derma), we would stuff in the rags, pounding the stocking so it would be tight and hard, until the ball was about six inches in diameter. Then we would sew up the other end, a procedure that required a refined piece of tailoring. We now had a stocking ball that we could use as a soccer football and that would last for at least one full week of enthusiastic kicking.

In this game, each player had a turn at kicking the ball. The object was to kick it across the corner to score a goal. We couldn't run the ball back when we caught it, but if we missed a catch the other team took possession for another kick. We enjoyed the game, particularly when only three or four played on each team and there was a lot of open, unprotected space on all sides. I had just caught a kick and was looking around for Simon, whose turn to kick had just come up, when I saw a truck coming up Manhattan Avenue from Broadway. It was a small truck drawn by one horse, and it swayed as the iron-rimmed wheels ground over the cobbles.

I waited almost breathlessly for that truck to cross McKibbin Street, not noticing that Simon had produced a vigorous kick almost in the path of the oncoming horse. One of the boys, roaring across the street to make a catch, was nearly propelled into the path of the truck, and the dismayed driver stood up, flinging himself back as he jerked frantically on the reins.

"You dopey bastard!" he screamed at the kid.

"I'll be right back," I called to my friends as I raced toward the truck and waited for the driver to decide to make a big sweep in the street so he could stop in front of my house. He pulled up his horse and stood up to look around at the numbers on the houses.

"Over here," I called to him. I was dancing, unrestrained, on the curb. He dragged on his reins, pulling the horse's head to the left so he could execute a full turn. Then, having tied up the reins, he jumped to the street from his lofty perch.

"You delivering drugs?" I asked as he walked to the rear of his truck. He ignored me, so I asked the same question twice in the same breath.

"Wynchu wipe your nose and get the hell out of my way."

I rammed my hand at my nose and realized he was only making a phrase. "I want to help you."

"Git."

"I know where you're taking those drugs. They're for my uncle."

That stopped him. He picked on his nose speculatively.

"Is your uncle home?"

"No, but my mother's home, and I'll show you where to take it if you let me help you."

He hefted a small parcel out of the truck, giving it to me before he brought out four oversized packages.

"Let's go," he said.

My friends had paused in their play because the horse and wagon had encroached on their field and they wanted to see what part would be given me in this saga of huff and puff. Holding the small package against my chest with both hands, I turned swiftly to see how they would react to my involvement in this business.

I hustled busily, proudly toward the door and the long hall that led to the stair well at the rear of the house. None of my friends called to me, and I wondered what this silence portended.

The truck driver and I moved the drugs into the house in about three or four trips, and each time we returned to the street, I looked at my friends to learn by word or gesture how they were taking my defection.

They weren't all there. I saw Muttel and Tubie and Willie sitting on the curb, their backs to me, but I didn't call to them because we had to run one more trip before all the packages were safely stored in my home. I watched my mother sign her name on the receipt where the truck driver had marked an *x* and proceeded to the front room near the windows where we had stacked the packages.

Standing before the parcels, I thought how wonderful it was that my uncle could convert these drugs into something magically valuable for all people, sick and well. My mother came in behind me to stare at the packages also, and I turned to look into her eyes to see whether she, too, felt the near wonder of it.

"Uncle Herschel is a very smart man," she said.

"Oh boy, I wish I could be smart like him."

"You'll be, you'll be. Your father's father was a rabbi and my father was a rabbi, so why shouldn't my children be smart like Uncle Herschel?"

I should have told her this several weeks ago, but we were so excited with the coming of Uncle Herschel that I had forgotten and just couldn't suddenly and without a lead-in say, "Ma, my teacher made me poet laureate of the class."

I told her now to reassure her that her children would be smart or at least as smart as Uncle Herschel. She stared at me because she had never heard of a poet laureate.

"I know what a poet is. The *Forward* prints poems by Bialick, but what is the other thing?"

"A poet laureate—that means he thinks I'm the best poet in the class and my poem will be published in the school magazine and I'll get a prize at the end of the year."

"Show me the poems you wrote."

"I can't. They're in school, but I'll write a copy and I'll bring it home."

"Good. Papa will like to hear your poems."

Nothing more. Perhaps Freudians could have a field day over

the fact that my parents were never effusive with me, but I didn't mind, because I was never embarrassed by public displays of affection, which can be obnoxious to kids.

I went back to the street, where my three friends were still mooning on the curb near my house. They accepted my presence without comment.

"Game break up?" I asked.

"Crap," Willie said, "you oughta know. You broke it up."

"I did not. I just went to help that guy."

"Help that guy! You think he couldn't carry those packages upstairs without you?"

"No, but I wanted to help him."

"Sure, and helping that guy was more important than playing our game."

"Ho! If you had an uncle like mine, you'd help him too."

"What's so great about your uncle?" Willie asked.

We knew about Willie. He was an orphan both ways who lived with a childless uncle and aunt. His aunt was a wizened little woman, very religious, who I learned later wore a very bad wig, always awry and always oddly off the beam. He never went near her on the street although she would often pause to watch him play in our games. It was not a pleasant thought, but I sometimes wondered if he was ashamed of her. I don't think he minded so much her calling to him and talking to him in Yiddish, because all of us spoke that language to our parents. What must have bothered him, I think, was the way the end of every sentence soared up and away as though she were asking a question.

His uncle was our ice and coal man, and although he was a little taller than my father, my father seemed ten feet tall in comparison. This man, Ike, was bowed over into almost a semicircle, because the burdens he carried on his back weighted him down dreadfully. When he walked to and from schule on Friday night and Saturday morning beside his wife and Willie, he became a reincarnation of the Hunchback of Notre Dame, whose picture I had seen in a magazine the month before.

So now I was not surprised when Willie spoke so disparagingly about my uncle, but I had to bristle.

"What's so great? What's so great? Is your uncle a felsher?"

"What's a felsher?"

"A felsher's an almost-doctor, that's what a felsher is, smarty eyes."

"I thought you said your uncle's a doctor, Yankel?," Muttel said.

"Well, a felsher's like a doctor in Russia, and that's what they call him—a felsher."

"Pish! You told me he's a doctor."

"Listen, when Mrs. Teitelbaum got sleeping sickness my uncle went in her house and he told Jennie what's the matter with her mother and when Crazy Padilsky came he didn't have anything to do because my uncle told her what prescription to take and when her mother would wake up and crazy Doctor Padilsky didn't tell her anything different."

"Yeah, but he ain't a doctor."

I had made a terrible mistake trying to explain the differences and similarities between Uncle Herschel and a doctor. I jumped to my feet. "Let's play," I said.

"Nah."

"Who wants to play now?"

"All right, then I'll go upstairs and help my uncle unpack his drugs."

They stared at me.

"You thought I was just running up and down for nothin'. Well, I wasn't. I was carrying up drugs—lots and lots of drugs, and from it my uncle's gonna make medicines and all other kinds of great things like hair tonic."

"No kiddin', Yank," Muttel gasped.

Sometimes when he was excited, he cut my name short.

"No kiddin'."

"In your house?"

"Nah, not in my house, you dummy. Who ever heard of a felsher making important medicines in a house."

"Where, then?"

"In a store on Cook Street."

"No–kiddin'!"

"And my uncle's gonna have a sign on the window that's gonna say, 'Russian Felsher,' and I–am–gonna–be–his assistant."

"No kiddin'," Muttel said. "Can I come watch you?"

"Nah, my uncle's a felsher. He wouldn't want dopey kids around him. Does Crazy Padilsky let you come in his office when he's examining a patient?"

They were shuttered silent by my logic, and I reveled in my importance.

"I'll ask my uncle if he'll let you come in on Sunday, because he won't be making medicine on Sunday."

"Would you?"

"Sure. Now I gotta go help unpack the stuff."

"Can I come with you, huh?" Muttel pleaded.

"Nah, first I gotta go to the Frieds' to read the paper and last week's *Collier's*. Then I'll go home to unpack."

I could see in their eyes a new jealousy, a new disbelief that I would be going anywhere but home. I ran joyously up the stairs to the Frieds' because I had achieved a victory out of an almost certain censure and possible banishment from street play for at least two days.

Mrs. Fried opened the door when I knocked and laid her hand fondly on my head. She returned to her stove and I went on to the front room on the left where they always kept the newspaper and *Collier's* for me.

"Here's a piece of mandelbread," Mrs. Fried said.

I took it and thanked her. In my mother's presence I would have looked her way first, and she would have nodded or said, "Take, take."

Seven

That afternoon I hurried home because I thought Uncle Herschel might be preparing to do something with that huge assortment of drugs which I was eager to participate in.

He was home but sitting quietly at the kitchen table. Near him was the bottle of liquor he had bought a few days before. I greeted him and my mother and hustled into the front room to hang up my coat and lay my books away on the floor of the closet.

When I came back into the kitchen I went for a roll in the breadbox and the butter in the icebox. I took the buttered roll to the table, where my uncle had just poured out some brown liquid.

As he held a light to a cigarette I heard him say, "For a few months after I open the store, I won't make any money and I'll have to pay rent. The question is, How can I earn some money to have, to use during those bad months?"

"I know," I said. "You can sell something on Seigel Street or on Moore Street. Everybody sells things on Seigel Street or Moore Street."

My mother laughed, and Uncle Herschel stared at me.

"What does he mean?" he asked my mother.

"On Seigel Street and on Moore Street men come with pushcarts to sell everything except meat and dairy. They even sell fish. They sell everything."

"What would I be able to sell?"

She shrugged, and I said nothing because I hadn't really thought about it and couldn't imagine what he could sell there which would not lower the dignity of a felsher.

Someone knocked on our door and my mother said "come."

When Callahan pushed the door open and appeared on our threshold, my mouth dropped, my mother said "oh!" and my uncle just stared. My mother suddenly became frantic, because a policeman in one's home was as terrifying as an arriving telegram. She got up and clutched her face.

"Ask him what he wants," she called to me.

I obeyed her literally. Callahan hitched up his pants with his elbows and said, "I been hearin' stories about drugs you're keeping in this here place."

I looked toward my uncle, who had just held a light to a fresh cigarette. I translated for him what the policeman had said. My uncle seemed to deliberate over that question.

"Ask him who sent him here."

I asked him. He said, "Nobody sent me. I came by myself because I like to know what's goin' on on my beat, and when I hear a story like this, I'm gonna find out."

I translated for my uncle, and he blew out some more smoke before he said, "Tell him he has no right to come into this house to look for anything without a warrant."

I began to protest to him that I couldn't say that to Callahan, but the policeman held up his hand. He had heard the last word and he understood.

"Is that your father?" he asked me.

"No, he's my uncle."

"Well, if he can't talk English how'd he know about a warrant?"

I translated, and my uncle leaned over casually to break a stick of ash off his cigarette. I saw a tiny wisp of a smile maneuvering around his mouth.

"Tell him that for three years before I came here, I read everything I could find in Odessa about this country, and that I memorized the first ten amendments to the American Constitution."

I listened in amazement as he spoke, and when I repeated his message to the policeman his eyes became fixed in the same astonished stare.

"I'll be damned," he said.

"Tell him," my uncle said, "I have nothing to hide from him, but I want him to know I'm showing him the drugs because I want to. Ask him who told him we have drugs in this house?"

Callahan sniffed as he tried to make up his mind about revealing his source of information, and I think Uncle Herschel's invitation to inspect what he had no right to see helped his thinking.

"One of your friends," he said to me.

"Who?" I bristled.

"The kid you call 'Snotnose.' "

I blew out my cheeks. "That guy! He's not my friend. He stinks."

"Well, he told me you got something dangerous in this house, and knowing that you people, you Jewish people, mind your business and never get into trouble with the law, I just had to see for myself."

When I had translated this for Uncle Herschel, he got up and said, "Come in here."

Everybody followed him into the front room. He opened two cartons, rummaged around in them and came up with two boxes. As he read the long Latin names, Callahan tried to keep up with him. Next Uncle Herschel placed the two boxes on the table, pointed first to one and then the other, held up two fingers, and rammed the fingers into his hair rubbing vigorously.

Callahan stared at Uncle Herschel's charade, then he looked at me and said, "Shampoo?"

I said yes and told my uncle, and everybody began to laugh delightedly that they could reach such a quick rapprochement with two fingers.

"Is your uncle trying to tell me he's going to make shampoo out of those powders?"

"Yes, and he's going to make other things, too, and he's gonna open a store on Cook Street to sell them."

"Cook Street? Ain't that interestin'."

"The man is painting the store now and putting up shelves."

"A big man with red hair?"

"Yes."

"Name's Wolf."

"I don't know his name."

"Well, tell your uncle I'm sorry I barged in like this. Tell him I'll see him in his new store, and tell him I'll expect some of that brown stuff he's got sittin' on his table now and some of that lekach."

He pronounced it "*lekack*," thus providing a good family story for many years. When I told Uncle Herschel what Callahan had said, "*lekack*" and all, he said, "Bring another glass," and when we returned to the kitchen he held up the bottle. The policeman showed the palm of his hand to indicate he would have to decline the invitation, but my uncle had already poured into the fresh glass. He brought it to Callahan and held it close to the officer's nose. Callahan sniffed and raised his eyebrows. "You got good taste in liquor," he said.

Uncle Herschel paid no attention to what Callahan had said because he did not understand it, but he moved the glass toward the policeman's face. Then Callahan did something that convulsed us. He took off his big round hat with his left hand, took the glass from Uncle Herschel, held the hat in front of his face, and with a quick flip of his hand gulped the two or three fingers of liquor my uncle had poured for him.

He said, "I'm savin' you the need to lie about my drinkin'." Then he straightened his face, winked, clapped the hat on his head and left.

My uncle said, "In the darkest days in Russia when Jews were being killed right and left, I never ran into a peasant to whom I couldn't talk and whom I couldn't convince."

Eight

We were excitingly occupied for the next few days. Jennie called to us to tell us that her mother seemed to wake up at intervals of thirty-six hours. I went with Uncle Herschel to see Mrs. Teitelbaum as she sat in the kitchen, poised like some kind of coldly unveiled creation. She ate what Jennie placed before her with a vague disinterest in what was going on in the house; I had never seen such a curiously stupid expression in any face before. She permitted Uncle to hold her wrist while he consulted his watch.

Just before we left Uncle told Jennie to be sure to induce her mother to pass her water regularly or complications would set in. Jennie then asked if she should send for Dr. Padilsky so he could examine her. Uncle Herschel shrugged. "Send for him. He won't tell you anything I haven't told you, but whatever he tells you will be legal."

Jennie didn't know what he meant, but she said she would send for the doctor as soon as her father came home and she could leave her mother.

"I'm going to the store," Uncle said. "Do you want to come with me?"

I knew I had homework to do, but my father would not be home before seven and we had almost three hours until seven.

As we approached the store we noticed that Sam had smeared some kind of white paint or wet powder over the store window. When we came into the store he explained he did not like working for an audience. Often watchers would plague him by knocking on the window and pointing to something he was doing that did not sit well with their notions. If he ignored them, they would continue to knock until, possessed by a fury, he would fly to the door to drive the tormentors from the storefront. They would flee only to return momentarily to their places in front of the window.

Sam was working on the shelves, which he had laid out on two wooden horses. We watched him set the shelves in this section, and while we were there, he braced them on the wall with angle irons. Then he joined us where we stood, about ten feet from the wall, and said, "I'll need two weeks to finish, maybe three weeks, because tomorrow my shop is opening again and I'll be going back to work."

I looked at my uncle. He was caressing his little beard, and I knew he was thinking something very deep. Once he murmured, "Three weeks."

Sam said, "Three weeks can be like an hour or like a year."

Uncle Herschel looked at him, but I couldn't say for sure that he had heard what Sam was saying. He said, "We'll be back in a few days," and we left. On the way home he did not speak, and I walked proudly by his side keeping an exact rhythm with his walking stick.

On our way upstairs I said, "I'm going over to the Frieds'," and I disappeared. For the hour and a half that followed, I forgot my uncle, his medicines, the store on Cook Street, even my position as poet laureate, as I read hungrily the *Journal* and *Collier's* weekly. I left the Frieds' when their younger son came home, knowing they would be preparing for supper and remembering how my mother had instructed me.

My father had not yet come home, but Uncle Herschel was sitting with his bottle and a glass and a cigarette between his fingers. My mother was frying hamburgers murmuring unhappily that Uncle Herschel would have nothing to eat.

"Cheese," he said. "Give me cheese and bread and vegetables."

She rummaged in the icebox and presently brought out a big cake of farmer cheese on a dish. "Better eat now. Schiya won't like cheese on the table with meat."

He smiled but did not object. I stared in a kind of bemused wonder as he ate the cheese with cucumber and tomato and a boiled potato; our family had never before encountered this kind of impasse. Whatever my mother served us we ate, and we never ever thought to mix milk products with our meat. Uncle Herschel finished eating before my father came home, and my mother cleared away the dishes so eagerly, I was sure she was relieved.

My uncle said, "All food comes from the ground in one way or another, and in one way or another it returns to the ground, so why can't we mix it in our stomachs?"

"We are not allowed," my mother said uneasily. She did not have easy or ready answers for his teasing, mortifying questions.

"You are not allowed?" he repeated. "I haven't met anyone who can tell me who does not allow it."

"I don't know. It is not permitted."

My uncle shook his head but did not continue his irritating inquiries into her beliefs. He took up the *Forward* and turned toward the gas light.

When my father came home, Mother served the hamburgers, a heaping mound of potatoes, and sliced onions and cucumbers in vinegar.

"Schiya," Uncle Herschel said, "if you wanted to peddle something in a pushcart on the street, what would you sell?"

My father looked at my mother, surprised at the question because no one had spoken of peddling on the street.

"I don't know. What do they sell on the street? Fruit, fish, herring."

"I don't want to sell what everybody else sells."

"If you don't want to sell what everybody sells, so what can you sell?"

This question seemed to complete the circle; my father had tossed the question back to Uncle Herschel.

"The store won't be ready for three weeks, and I can't just sit still for three weeks without earning a penny. I've got to pay you for the food I eat here. I know Schiya works hard and he can't feed me. I must earn some money.

"I know you've been wondering about what I've been saying to you. Here, now, for a few weeks I've been telling you I felt I've been a failure in Russia and I wanted a new fresh start in America. I've tried with doctors and hospitals and they listen to me and they can't think how they can use me: I can't be a nurse because I know too much, and they won't let me be a doctor because I don't have a license. So again I'm a failure. But . . . I have a plan to use the knowledge I've acquired, and it's a good plan. However, the plan will take time, so until then I must earn some money without thinking of myself as a felsher. I must sell something–and not myself."

A kind of uneasy silence followed that statement, and then my mother recited what had happened this afternoon when Callahan came calling. My father's eyes were large and startled as he listened; I knew how he regarded involvement with the law.

When I awoke the next morning I found that Uncle Herschel was not home. My mother fretted over his disappearance because she had not prepared breakfast for him. We never saw my father. He always left so quietly at six o'clock that we did not hear the water boil for his tea or his maneuvering around the icebox and the breadbox, where he cut himself the few slices of bread he buttered for breakfast and the two or three he cut to take for his lunch with a hunk of cheese or black olives or a tomato.

I had my breakfast of tea and buttered rye bread and left for school. Nothing unlikely or unseemly happened in school that day. I was startled only once when Muttel broadcast aloud what

I had confided to only him, that I was converting Dickens' *A Christmas Carol* into a play and that I was writing out all the parts.

My face flamed brilliantly as Mr. Samuelson turned to look at me and ask, "Is that so?"

I said, "Yes."

"And will you let us hear it when you're all ready?"

I had not thought about it, at least not boldly enough to consider a public presentation of what I was doing, but in response to this sudden prodding, I said, "I have to finish the parts first and then pick kids for the parts."

"We'll look forward to it," he said, "and you let us know when you're ready."

My mother fretted over Uncle Herschel's early departure and she wondered where he might have gone. When she asked me if he had mentioned going anywhere so early this morning, I told her he had said nothing to me.

I didn't see him again until about four o'clock, when I recognized his walking stick almost two blocks down. We weren't playing a game; we were only idling with the stocking ball, so when I saw him trying to maintain a jaunty walk unbalanced by a huge flat carton he was carrying in his right hand, I yelled to Muttel to come with me and sped down Manhattan Avenue toward him. I waved my hand as I ran, and when he saw me he lowered the carton slowly and leaned rather wearily on his cane.

"Take one side," I instructed Muttel, and we lifted the big carton between us. It was not heavy, only wide and cumbersome, so between us the weight was negligible. Uncle Herschel walked behind us, and Muttel and I soon devised a game out of our errand: miss the cracks. Sidewalks in those days were paved with flagstones, so cracks were many and widely diversified. He who stepped on a crack lost a point, and soon we tried to develop a technique which would force the opponent to step on a crack.

By the time we got to my house we had become so expert that Muttel had only five cracks and I had five. Because of the size of the carton we carried it fore and aft, one behind the other. My mother watched the procession but didn't have time to ask what we were carting before Uncle Herschel followed us in.

Muttel was eager to stay and see what my uncle had brought home. He confided to me later that he had been sure, because Uncle was a felsher, that the carton contained at least one human arm and one leg for home study and review.

When we were alone, Uncle Herschel opened the carton and revealed to us what my mother declared was the most beautiful collection of ladies' collars she had ever seen. She stared into the big box.

"Where did you get this?"

Uncle laughed his very small cackle. "You have a sister? Well, she's my sister, too. I know she has a son who manufactures these, so I decided to go to his factory. Don't ask me how I found him. I had a name, I had an address, and like when I looked for a Jewish face I had no problem. I told him what I wanted, and he gave me two hundred collars. He wouldn't take money. He said, 'When you sell them come back for more, and I'll charge you for these and for the next two hundred.' "

"Let's see what you have there," my mother said.

We laid out the ten different styles on the table and we counted twenty in each style. My mother touched them gently, almost caressed them, I thought; even in my eyes they were dainty and pretty. Then Mother stood off to admire them.

"Ach," she said, "how much will you ask for them?"

"He told me fifty cents."

She made a clucking noise with her tongue. "You'll sell," she said, "you'll sell." Then she said, "You'll need bags."

"Bags?"

"Of course. When a woman buys a collar, you have to put it in a bag. If you buy a herring they wrap it in a newspaper, so a collar you'll have to put in a bag. On Graham Avenue near McKibbin Street there's a stationery store. You can buy a package of two hundred bags. Go."

"How much will it cost?" Uncle asked.

My mother didn't know. "Give him a dollar," she advised.

As I came into the street, Muttel jumped up from the curb where he had been sitting, waiting impatiently to discover whether his guess had been correct.

"Walk me," I said.

"Where you goin'?"

"Over to Graham Avenue."

I think every kid likes to build his own climaxes, and I knew that Muttel was ready to respect my need.

"What for?"

"Gotta get something."

"What?"

"You'll see."

There could evidently be no advance from here, so he told me what he thought was in the carton he and I had brought home.

"You're nuts," I said.

Nine

I talked to my uncle as hard as I could to convince him not to venture into Seigel Street without me, because there would be rock-hard characters behind and in front of the pushcarts, who would not know he was a felsher and would not respect him for it even if they knew.

When my mother joined in my plea, he agreed to let me go with him as soon as I came home from school. My mother promised to prepare a buttered roll for me to eat on the way or when we had chosen a base of operations.

At three o'clock the next day I was like a restive horse waiting at the gate for a gong to ring. When Mr. Samuelson said we could go, I exploded out of the room almost running over Muttel. He yelled to me, demanding to know why I was in such a hurry. I turned my head only long enough to call to him that I would reveal the cause of my urgency to him tomorrow.

I raced up the stairs and burst into our flat. Uncle Herschel was hovering over a tumbler of tea, and he turned leisurely as I pulled up at the door.

My mother said, "Sit down and eat your roll. Uncle Herschel wants to drink a glass of tea before he goes."

I stared at my uncle and I marveled that he could be so cold, so untouched, so calm about this new adventure. I could feel my blood churning in my chest, in my veins. As I ate my roll, I got up and walked around the room and sat.

"It will get dark soon, and there won't be anybody on the street," I said.

My mother looked out. "No," she said, "many women like to shop later in the afternoon. They cook in the morning."

I had to yield, but I was impatient to storm out to Seigel Street and set up a display, a glittering array of splendidly designed collars which the women would quickly seize upon and almost tear from our hands. I had never really watched my mother or my father drink tea as I watched Uncle Herschel this afternoon. I wondered about each long sip, as though he were inhaling the liquid, and I wondered what was happening to the tea during the interval between imbibing and swallowing until I saw his Adam's apple flutter.

When he finally set the glass down in the saucer I sprang to my feet, raced into the front room, grabbed the cords around the carton and dragged it into the kitchen.

As I opened the door and maneuvered around holding my end of the carton, my mother said, "Pooh, pooh, let it be with lots of luck." I was happy. My friends had not yet come into the street, so I would not have to explain to them later what had inspired my sudden haste and now this errand with the carton Muttel helped me carry.

When we came to Seigel Street, we walked the length of the block between McKibbin and Boerum without glimpsing even a tiny area where we could set up our wares. Only one spot appeared to be even slightly promising. It was about two feet wide, hardly enough for the carton and Uncle and me. On one side of this opening was Hymie's pushcart and on the other, Schmuel's.

Hymie I knew very well, because my mother often bought onions and potatoes from him and he would often pat my head and ask me what I was going to be. "A doctor? A lawyer?" I never had an answer for him because I detested head patters and always wished I could slap his obnoxious hand away. Such an action, however, was unthinkable, so when I was about nine years old I told him I wanted to be a horse thief. That, of course, set off a wild explosion of laughter and an even wilder coughing spasm, but he never forgot. As soon as he would see, me he'd exclaim, "Aha! How's the horse thief?"

He didn't disappoint me as Uncle Herschel and I crossed the street and came up on his blind side.

"Hey," he hollered, "how's the horse thief?" And when he saw the carton my uncle and I carried, he really bellowed, "Bet you got a horse in there—a horse you stole."

He fell over the pushcart, *haw*ing and *hooh*ing until he couldn't catch his breath and began to cough. We stood there, holding our carton and waiting for him to get over his spasm. Then as Hymie dried his eyes, heaving his chest, Uncle Herschel said, "You speak Jewish?"

"Of course."

"I don't like your cough."

Hymie held his handkerchief away from his eyes so he could see who had suddenly infiltrated upon his personal concern.

"*You* don't like it. You think I like it?"

"You should do something about it."

"Oh, I do. I cough, and every day my cough gets stronger and stronger."

"Don't laugh. If you'll come to my house, I'll give you something for it."

Now Hymie really stared. This time he made a thorough survey of this character, strange for Seigel Street with his narrow goatee, starched shirt and walking stick.

"You'll give me something for my cough! And who are you?"

"He's my uncle, and he's a felsher. You know what a felsher is?"

"Why shouldn't I know what a felsher is?"

"That's my uncle."

Hymie looked suspiciously from Uncle Herschel to me and

to the carton. He pointed to it. "What does he carry in that—his medicines?"

Again he exploded, heaving with the exertion and the strain on his lungs. Uncle Herschel leaned on his stick and waited for the paroxysm to end.

"Listen," he said, "I'll tell you why we're here. I just came to this country from Russia. I'm very green. In about three weeks I'm opening a store on Cook Street, where I'll make my own medicines to sell them. Until then I've got to make a living. That's what we have in the carton—lace and linen collars for women. We want to sell them to make a living. If you come to me in three weeks, I'll give you something for your cough."

Hymie's mouth had opened wide, and when Uncle Herschel had finished he said, "Why didn't you say so? Here, move in here, I'll push back a little."

He walked around to the other end of his pushcart to pull it back a foot or two, but instantly we heard a bull voice bellow, "Where the hell you going?"

Hymie turned to stare at Schmuel. They had been perched on each other's tails for years. They never agreed about anything, but they would never permit another peddler to separate them.

"What are you hollering?" Hymie asked blandly.

"What am I hollering? You're climbing on my pushcart. That's what I'm hollering."

"Hold your balls. For the shit you got piled on your pushcart, you don't need no more room."

"Who says? You gotta leave me two feet between my pushcart and yours."

"Who says?"

"I says. Everybody says."

"If you say, then I say shit on you. If everybody says, I say shit on them."

"A gentleman."

"I gotta be a gentleman to sell onions and potatoes? I need the room for my friends. Good? They're gonna sell something beautiful. Maybe yet you'll take one home for your wife. Don't be a schmuckhead and give them room."

"I don't wanna buy anything for my wife. She'll throw it at me, and you stop pushing."

"I stopped, I stopped. Now, mister," he turned to us, "you got room on the sidewalk. Just turn the box the other way, the policeman shouldn't say you're blocking the sidewalk. He'll come over anyway to see what you're selling. When he comes, you don't say nothin'. Leave him to me."

Uncle Herschel said, "You are a good human being. I'll remember you."

We maneuvered the carton around so the narrow side was parallel to the curb, and when we had pried off the cover Hymie came around to stare into the contents.

"Hmm," he said, "What are you asking for those?"

"Fifty cents."

"How will the customers know? You gotta make a sign. Here, you got a bag?" When I gave him one, he knelt on the sidewalk and with a black crayon printed a huge 50¢ on it. Then Hymie rummaged under his pushcart and came up with a piece of wood. He fitted the bag over the wood like a hood and asked for the carton cover. Dropping the carton into its cover, he rammed the piece of wood between the two with the bag facing the sidewalk. He went around, hands shoved into his pockets and lips set, as he contemplated how his handiwork would affect the prospective customer and said, "That ain't enough. You gotta holler. They gotta know you're here. I'll show you. Women! You wanna buy a *beeooteeful* collar for your dress? A *beeooteeful* collar. It's one dollar in the store. Come on over and look. It's only fifty cents. Only fifty cents! Cost price, cost price."

All the peddlers hawking their wares suddenly stopped, not because his voice was unfamiliar but because the tune was different. Three or four women who were buying herring and groceries from the stands close to the houses turned and looked toward him. He pointed to our carton. I was fascinated by his delivery, by his unorthodox diction, and I tried to remember not only what he said, but also the order of his dissertation.

"Here," he said, "I'm a lucky guy." I looked at his pushcart and wondered what he meant. "I'll start you off. You see. I'll buy the first off you, and the rest'll go like hot cakes."

He hauled fifty cents out of his pocket and held it out to Uncle Herschel.

"What is that?" Uncle asked.

"Fifty cents! I want to be your first customer."

"No, not that way. I don't need your money. I don't need charity."

"Charity, my ass. I'm paying you for a collar. I want a collar for my wife."

Now Uncle Herschel understood. He stroked his little beard and said, "Take what you want."

" 'Take,' he says to me. What do I know about women's collars. If you asked me to pick a sack of potatoes or onions, I could take one look and I would know, but collars!"

"Then close your eyes and take one."

"Close my eyes? Just my luck, I'll pick one she'll like, and she'll say a woman picked it out for me. Kid, you pick one for me. Then I'll be able to say a boy picked it out, and she'll say, 'Sure, you picked it out–a man with a boy's mind.' Or she'll say, 'Why are you bringing me a fancy collar when I ain't got a dress to put it on.' Kid, if you have to get married, don't get married to a woman."

"What did he say?" Uncle Herschel asked for the first time, as though some overtone in Hymie's voice had stimulated his curiosity. I told him. He smiled his slow, dry smile.

"What would you do if you were not married?" he asked.

"I'd find myself a woman."

"But always a woman."

"What do you think I am–a freak?"

"So pick out a collar."

Hymie motioned to me, and I dug my fist into the top layer of collars and came up with two. I dropped one back into the carton and held up the other. Hymie laid his head to one side and said, "Good?"

"Good," I said.

"So put it in a bag, and I'll take it home."

I started to drop it into a bag, but then I remembered how meticulously the man in the dry-goods store would fold the shirts my mother bought for me. I laid the collar in the carton, knelt, folded it clumsily finding I had too many fingers, and shoved it into a bag.

"*Ho!* You should get a job in Batterman's," Hymie chortled.

I gave him the bag; he gave me a monumental wallop on the back and said, "Awright, go ahead and holler."

"What does he want?" Uncle asked me.

I told him and immediately launched into the long line I had heard from Hymie, trying hard to remember everything he had included in his tirade.

"Women!" I yelled in my high subteen voice. "Women! Come on over and see the *beeooteeful* collars for your *beeooteeful* dresses. A bargain! In a big store you'll pay one dollar. We charge you only fifty cents, a half-dollar."

I had cupped my hands around my mouth for greater resonance and had attracted some attention. One or two women edged over to squint into our cartons. I knew they wouldn't buy our collars, because I had watched them paw two herrings the herring man had laid out for them on a sheet of newspaper, to test the width of their backs.

Uncle Herschel laid his hand on my head and said, "Where did you learn to holler this way?"

"I didn't learn. I just heard Hymie holler, so I hollered the way he hollered."

"No, I'm not talking about your holler. I'm talking about your being here and doing this from your heart. Someday you'll be a good person."

"You're my uncle. I'm only helping you."

He smiled. "I don't know about God, but I'm hoping your God will be good to you someday."

One of the women, who was very nearsighted but didn't wear glasses, sidled over to get closer to the collars.

"Fifty cents apiece," I said to her.

"I know, I know," she said. Then she went through a ritual of wiping her right hand on her skirt, which I did not understand until Hymie suddenly bellowed, "Take your goddamn herring hands off them collars, you yenteh."

She straightened up like something off a chute, and because she had been startled she exclaimed, "Break your head, bastard!"

"You just had your hands on Jake's herrings, didn't you?"

"Why is it your pig's business?"

"These people are my friends. If you stink up their collars with your goddamn herring stink, what are they gonna do with their collars–hang them around your herrings?"

"You are a big shit."

"I'm a big shit! *Hah!* You'll get to know this yenteh. She feels every potato and every onion she buys by me. That's the way she takes their temperature."

"You should drop dead how long you'll wait before I buy from you."

"*Hah!* I need to make a living from you like I need smallpox."

I looked at Uncle Herschel and I realized he was enjoying this dialogue in Yiddish between Hymie and our near customer. A tiny smile puckered his lips at the corners, and he reached into his pocket for his cigarette case.

After he had lit the cigarette and the rage of battle between Hymie and the woman had eased off, he reached down, selected three collars, and held them close to her face. At first, she backed off, annoyed no doubt by this sudden unlooked-for onslaught. Then she moved in to peer into my uncle's face and at his pressed suit and starched shirt.

"Who is this?" she demanded.

"What do you care who I am? Look at these collars. I'll hold them up for you to see. These collars can make you look beautiful."

She sniffed and stepped back. "Who sent for you? For whom do I need to be beautiful? I'm lonely like a stone. For fifty cents I can buy herring and potatoes for a whole week to eat."

She started to turn away, but Uncle called to her.

"You're a widow?"

"Fifteen years."

"Then how do you live?"

"How does a Jew live? Jews don't let their own starve. I live, I get from Malbush Aroomim, I get from other places. A Rockefeller I'm not, but I live."

"Take a collar."

"No." She said this so fiercely I had to look at her pinched poverty once more and this time in some wonder. Uncle smiled at her.

"You think maybe this is charity. Don't be silly. I'm just asking you to share with what I haven't got. Take a collar."

"I don't need your charity."

"But I'm not giving you charity. I need charity. Can I afford to give you charity? Why would I be selling these collars on the street?"

"I don't know. I don't need your collar. It wouldn't fit me anyway. It wouldn't fit my dress."

"Don't you have a sister whom you visit?"

"I have a sister."

"Good, then take a collar. Let's say if you take a collar, you'll bring me luck."

She looked down into the carton but did not reach down for a collar. Instead she raised belligerent eyes to Hymie, who instantly put his palms on his chest. "Don't look at me. They're not my collars."

"You were hollering a couple of minutes ago."

"I just didn't want you to put your herring hands on these new beeooteeful collars."

"Drop dead."

"Pick out a collar for her," Uncle said to me. I couldn't be persuaded by merit or beauty; I reached into the carton for any collar, folded it neatly and stuffed it into a bag.

As I held it out for her she said, "My sister will think I have a lot of money to spend on collars."

"Then send your sister to me. I'll explain to her how you got the collar."

I touched her hand with the bag, and she seemed to sense the magic in it. She took it quickly and stuffed it into the bottom of her cloth shopping bag, hardly raising her eyes to uncle as she murmured, "I give you a pretty thanks."

As she hurried away, Hymie made a clicking noise in his throat.

"A millionaire you won't be, if you give away all your profit."

Uncle Herschel moistened his lips. "How can a person live by herring and potatoes alone? This one collar can sustain her for a year. Did you see the way she looked at those collars? I got more satisfaction out of her thanks than I will if I sell the whole box of collars today. So I gave her let's say thirty-five cents. It's only money. What is money? It's only something you use to get something you need or something you want. I've never worried about money even when my family was large and feeding it was a problem. Somebody always provided."

This startling lack of concern I saw and heard later when he was entrenched in the store on Cook Street. Women would ask for a reduction in his price on a bottle of some medicine or some preparation for the hair or the skin.

"Why?" he would ask.

"Because I don't have any more," they would answer, and he would say, "Take it for nothing. You'll pay me if you need another bottle."

Soon two women had engaged Hymie's attention, and immediately I began to recite the virtues of what lay in the carton at our feet. Some women turned. One approached and bent over to rummage through our neatly assorted piles, and I watched her wanton progress through the order we had so carefully arranged. I said nothing, while Uncle stood by in some kind of reverie, but Hymie's eyes moved constantly back to our carton from his potatoes and onions.

When at last this woman paid for two collars, he gave us a triumphant look, and I went down to restore order to the ravaged carton.

"Holler good, kiddo," Hymie encouraged me, and I did.

Then I saw a pair of huge shoes in front of the carton and, above the shoes, a pair of blue uniform pants. I raised my eyes to meet the pair which belonged to the blue uniform pants. They stared, unblinking, down into the carton.

"What have we here?" asked the blue uniform.

I got to my feet and I would have tried to explain "what we have here," but Hymie called from his scale, where he was weighing off a huge number of potatoes, that he would be right over.

"What is them things?" The policeman pointed into the carton.

I reached down for one, thinking a demonstration might be helpful to my inadequate explanation. "Ladies' collars," I said.

Hymie bustled over. "I want you should meet my friends, Officer Lucas. This gentleman is like a doctor in the old country—not a real doctor, but I betcha he knows moren some of our doctors. So until he gets settled, he wants to make a quick living. That's why he's selling these ladies' collars. This here's his nephew. Good boy." He stopped and looked around conspiratorially while Officer Lucas continued to stare into the carton.

"What size dress does your wife wear?"

"Now how the hell would I know that?"

"So, is she a big woman?"

"Like me."

"So pick out a good collar, nice and big," Hymie instructed me.

I had not thought of sizes in the collars. I had visualized and made my choices only in terms of design. Now for the first time I laid a few collars one on the other so I could measure them by comparison. I hauled out the one that spread wide of the others, folded it carefully and laid it in a bag.

Not being quite sure how I should approach this awesome presence in blue, I held it out in an area somewhere between Hymie and the cop. Hymie looked from the bag in my hand to the policeman.

"Take, take."

Patrolman Lucas reached out for the bag, took off his helmet, and laid it in the helmet, which he replaced on his head.

"Don't leave any dirty collars layin' around in the gutter," the policeman said, closed his left eye for about five seconds, clapped his hand on the top of his helmet and swung off toward McKibbin Street.

My uncle said, "The only difference between this policeman and the policemen in Russia is that the Russian policemen demand what they get."

"No," Hymie said, "the only difference is that the American cop is smarter. He doesn't ask. He just looks at what he wants, and you'll have to remember that when you open your store."

Ten

We sold four collars that first day, and I was hoarse when I got home. My mother heard me ask for something and immediately got busy on a gogol mogol, a free-wheeling mixture of egg, milk, honey and butter. Because blending is vital to the efficiency of this concoction as a nostrum for the throat, she stirred and stirred for time almost unending.

As she prepared to pour it into a tumbler Uncle Herschel stopped her, went to the closet, brought out his bottle of brandy and was about to pour some into the mixing bowl.

"What are you doing?" my mother demanded. I think she was a little shocked.

"This will be good for him."

"Schnaps?"

"Why not? It will stimulate him and his blood."

"He's only a little boy."

"So? You think because he's a little boy this will bother him? Don't be silly. He'll love it, and he won't feel anything with all that stuff you just mixed up there."

She looked uncertainly from the bottle in his hand, to the mixing bowl, and to me. I grinned and said, "I'll like it, Ma."

She shrugged and said, "So!"

My uncle didn't measure what he poured into the bowl, but

I would say it was not excessive. I took the tumbler, sat down and tasted it sort of tentatively. It was good. My mother and uncle watched me as I tried to continue sipping with a nonchalance I didn't quite feel. I finished the drink and I felt an easing of the raw, rough edge in my throat.

"It was good," I said.

My mother smiled, and Uncle poured himself about an inch of the liquid and let it glide down his throat. Then I went to the Frieds', leaving Uncle with the Jewish newspaper and Mother with her preparations for dinner.

The next day when I got home, my mother was not there, and I knew Uncle Herschel would be on Seigel Street with the carton of collars. I took a huge bite of a buttered roll and set off for Seigel Street. Quite unaccountably for this time of year, the sun was bright and strong overhead, and before I had run half a block, my throat was dry with the heat and the crackling impact of the big, dry roll I was eating. As I got to the corner of Boerum Street, I saw Mendel's ice wagon. The rear of this wagon was always poaching area for us during the summer months, when we kids would assault the tail for the chips of ice that fell free as the iceman broke off chunks with his ice pick.

I reached up for a small hunk of the ice, and as I did I heard Muttel call me from down the street. I turned for only a moment, and the wagon stopped. The jar of iron tire on the cobblestones caused my arm to jog and slide off toward the left. I felt a sharp pain in my left forearm but ignored it as I swung around to tell Muttel where I was going. Then my left hand felt warm and wet, and I looked at it in some surprise. When I saw blood I was terrified. Holding up my hand, I saw that my forearm had been slashed open and that veins and other parts were bulging out over the cut.

Because I was facing Muttel, he saw the blood on my arm. He raced up to me, leaned over to inspect the wound and exclaimed, "Your guts are coming out."

That observation startled me, and I stuffed the veins back into my arm. "I got a handkerchief in my pocket," I told Muttel.

He searched my pockets and came up with a dirty handkerchief which I took from him and rammed against the wound.

"Gee," Muttel asked, "you gonna die?"

I ignored him and murmured, "I gotta find my uncle."

He trailed after me as I hurried up Boerum Street toward Seigel. I saw my Uncle Herschel hovering over his carton. As I approached, Hymie saw me and bellowed, "Now you're gonna sell. Here comes that wonderful salesman."

Uncle turned to look at me as I ran huddled over, clutching my right forearm. My head was down, but when I came closer and looked up I could see he knew all was not well.

"What's the matter?" he asked.

"I cut my arm on an ice wagon."

He took my arm. "Let me see," he said removing the handkerchief. The wound was open but it was no longer bleeding. Hymie came over, stared down at the cut and said, "Gah!"

"Hymie," Uncle said, "I'm going to take him to a doctor."

"Go, go. I'll keep an eye on your collars."

He remembered the doctors on McKibbin Street, and together we strode down that street toward the doctors' block. Muttel scuttled behind us nevertheless trying not to intrude on my misfortune. We rang the bell at the first doctor's house, but the lady who answered told us the doctor was out making calls and she didn't know when he would return. We had no better success at the second door, although it was my classmate who answered it. His father, too, was out making calls.

As we turned away, Uncle said, "Where does the crazy one live?"

I stared. "You want to go to him?"

He shrugged. "We won't listen to him."

I led my uncle to Dr. Padilsky's house on Cook Street, the only really clean looking house on the block. The girl who opened the door said the doctor was resting and would see no one. I translated for Uncle Herschel.

"Tell her," he said, "a doctor can't rest when an emergency comes to him."

I told her, but she stood big and bulky in the doorway.

"Go find another doctor. My doctor is resting and he can't be disturbed."

I pulled the handkerchief away from my arm, and she gasped audibly. For about two seconds she stared down, not certain what she should do.

We heard a voice behind her demand why she held the door open so long.

"It's a patient, Doctor."

"Didn't you tell her this is my resting time?"

"It's a little boy, Doctor, with a badly torn arm."

"And aren't there other doctors besides Padilsky?"

I answered that. "We tried two others. They're out on call."

"We have to see a doctor," Uncle Herschel called in Yiddish.

For a few seconds there was no response. Then we heard a really big sigh and the voice said, "Take them into my office. I'll be right down."

The girl led us through the reception room into the doctor's office and showed us where to sit on either side of a huge desk. Uncle leaned over to rest his chin on the head of his cane, and my eyes, open a yard wide, sought every title on the books in the huge glass-enclosed bookcase and in the frames on the walls.

Because the floor was carpeted we didn't hear the doctor as he came into the office. He was much more than disheveled; he was practically naked, judging from what he had worn the last time I saw him. Now he wasn't even wearing a vest. He had removed his collar and tie, and his suspenders hung down his back, causing his pants to droop almost sadly over his brightly hued carpet slippers. Once again the light struck his face, and I saw again how mottled his skin was.

Because I was nearer the door he stopped at my side.

"So, let me see this terrible wound."

I showed him.

"How did you get this?"

I told him about the iron tire on the huge rear wheel of the ice wagon. Then Uncle Herschel kicked the leg of the chair as he prepared to get up, and Dr. Padilsky looked up over my arm.

"You? What are you doing here?"

"I brought him here."

"You brought him here! This I'll have to remember. My worst enemy comes to me for help. You're a doctor, aren't you, or almost a doctor? What did you need me for? Why didn't you treat him yourself?"

"This boy is my sister's son but he's like my own son. I never treated my own children."

Dr. Padilsky stared at Uncle Herschel so long I thought he was working up enough anger to throw us out. Then he said "come in here" and led us into a room which was so white and so clean I was overpowered with admiration.

He pointed to a table, said, "sit up here," and kicked over a footstool so I could follow his instruction. Then he moved around with surprising speed and sprightliness for a man who just two minutes ago had shuffled in, dragging his suspenders behind him. He brought a basin to the table on which I was seated, a bottle, wads of cotton and a big roll of gauze. Then he poured from the bottle into the basin. The liquid gave out the vilest, most distressing smell. I had experienced it once before when that sick woman on our floor came home from the hospital. I remembered now. That smell had struck me the day after the visit to her home by the same man who was pouring it out for me now. Didn't he know any other medicine?

He held my arm over the basin and bathed it with the liquid over and over until I thought my unsupported back would collapse. Then he bandaged my arm and, having bandaged it, used some cotton to completely soak the bandage with more of that stuff.

When he looked up from what he was doing, he explained to Uncle, "We'll keep it open so we can catch an infection."

"Very smart," Uncle Herschel murmured, and for the first time I saw a tiny smile on the face of this terrible-tempered doctor.

"He'll have to keep his arm soaked all day," the doctor said. "I'll give you a prescription, and you take it to school. About every two hours you ask your teacher to let you go to the boys' room. Pour some of the acid right on the bandage. Don't take the bandage off, and if it comes off come right back to me. Understand?"

I told him I understood, and he turned away from us to return to his desk, where he wrote a quick scrawl on a pad. He asked my name and my address, tore off the sheet, folded it and gave it to me.

"What is your fee?" Uncle Herschel asked.

The doctor made a lordly gesture before he laid his hands on the desk. "My fee is fifty cents, but I never take a fee from another doctor or his children."

Uncle Herschel stared at him. I stared at him. Both of us thought he was laughing at my uncle, and I didn't like it.

"You're making fun of me," Uncle Herschel said, and I heard a quiet pride in his voice as he reached into his pocket.

The doctor held up his hand. Every gesture was primed with dramatic intent. "I'm not making fun of you. Fifty years ago all our doctors became doctors just the way you did. I knew you understood a sickness from the way you talked in the house of that encephalitis patient. I hollered, of course I hollered. I always holler. That makes me a better doctor. Only good doctors who have something to hide holler. If I see you in somebody else's house I'll holler again, and I'll probably call you a charlatan. Now, you know you broke up my afternoon nap, and I never let anybody do that."

He got up, walked by us into the hall and disappeared. We followed him, but by the time we reached the hall he was out of sight.

"Crazy," Uncle Herschel said.

"What is this stuff he put on my arm? It smells awful."

"Carbolic acid."

"Carbolic acid? Why did he put that on my arm?"

"The wound shouldn't get infected."

"But how will it get better?"

"By itself. The wound will close, and if the carbolic acid works you won't have an infection."

I was satisfied not only for myself, but also for the host of questions I knew would be hurled at me. I had already formulated answers to match every possible query. And the first one came immediately from Muttel, whom we found sitting on the doctor's steps. He bounded to his feet as we opened the door.

"Didja get a operation, Yank?" he asked.

"Nah, it wasn't that kind of wound," I said, quite lofty in my preparation.

"Phooey. You stink!"

"That's carbolic acid."

"Wow! Nobody's gonna wanna sit near you tomorrow."

"So! I'll sit by myself. I can't help it if I have to keep down the infection. That's why I have to use carbolic acid."

"Infection? What infection?"

"You know what infection is. It's like pus when you cut yourself. That white stuff, and you have to use peroxide on it."

"Is that what you've got?"

"Nah! That's what the doctor doesn't want me to get."

Mother was home, and when I came in behind Uncle Herschel she couldn't see the big grin on my face, but the thick bandage on my uncovered arm leaped across the room and filled her eyes with apprehension.

"*Oy!* What is that? What happened? What happened?"

"Nothing. It's nothing," Uncle Herschel said, "and before he becomes a father it'll happen over and over. He cut his arm and I took him to Padilsky."

I didn't know whether he spoke his name to take the edge off her concern, but it certainly was effective.

"To Crazy Padilsky? In the afternoon? He sleeps in the afternoon."

"So we woke him."

"Oh, I'll faint right away. Padilsky got out of bed to tend him?"

"Padilsky got out of bed to tend him."

"And Padilsky," I added, "wouldn't take any money from Uncle."

My mother turned to stare at Uncle Herschel.

"He thinks I know almost as much as a doctor."

As soon as I got to the school block the next day, I was enveloped by a pushing, *phewing* crowd of boys who alternately held their noses and asked the dopiest kinds of questions: what was that smelly stuff? what did your uncle do for you?

That second question, of course, I had to answer because I thought I saw Snotnose's lip curling, and I could almost cut the sneer in his voice.

"My uncle took me to Doctor Padilsky."

"What'd he do that for? I thought your uncle was a doctor."

"My uncle is like a doctor. He isn't a doctor because he can't write English good enough to pass the examination."

"From the way you was braggin' I thought he was a perfessor."

"I didn't brag to you, Snotnose. I didn't tell you anything about my uncle. Besides, my uncle does what every doctor does. He doesn't treat his own children, and my uncle says I'm like a son to him."

"I'd like to believe you. He probably didn't know what the heck to do so he took you to Doctor whatever his name."

"Betcha a million my uncle did so know what to do."

"Hah, wise guy, you're so ready to bet. How'd you prove your uncle knew what to do?"

"I don't have to prove anything to you. You're nothing to me."

"So, I'm nothing to you, but I still think your uncle didn't know what to do, Yankel."

"Oh, his uncle knows," Muttel chimed in. I looked surprised.

"How do you know what his uncle knows?" Snotnose demanded.

"How? I saw it on his face when he came out of Doctor Padilsky's office."

I felt Muttel had given him either the dopiest answer or the most inspired. His thought seemed to embrace the other kids like a mantle.

Snotnose was the first to recover. "What do you mean you saw it on his face?"

"That's what I mean—I saw it on his face. I can't explain it."

"Ah, you're nuts."

"I betcha a hundred million I saw it on his face."

I said, "Muttel means, if my uncle had to do it if we were on a desert island, he would use carbolic acid the way Doctor Padilsky did. That's what he means."

When we filed into our classroom I saw Mr. Samuelson's head go up like a bird dog's. He saw my bandaged arm and motioned me to him.

"What happened?"

I told him and showed him the bottle of carbolic acid I would have to carry with me to the boys' lavatory so I could soak the wound. The kids were watching my conversation with our teacher, and they smiled when Mr. Samuelson pointed to a seat at the end of the room. "You don't mind?" I did mind because no kid likes to be shoved into isolation even if he reeks from carbolic acid.

When I got home my mother hovered over me, buttered me a roll and poured a glass of tea. I ate and drank restlessly because I wanted to get over to the carton of collars on Seigel Street.

"Be careful. Mind the street. Look where you're going. Come back to soak your arm." These admonitions followed me into the hall, but I was not very mindful because I felt I was neglecting my uncle's business. I fled across Manhattan Avenue and up Boerum Street to Seigel. As I approached Hymie's pushcart and uncle's carton, I heard a steady tattoo on the sidewalk. Getting closer, I realized that Uncle was beating a *ratatat* with the ferrule on his cane to attract the attention of the women shoppers. He seemed to be succeeding.

I came up quietly behind my uncle, but he turned around instantly, and I knew why. So did Hymie, but he didn't turn; he winged around like something on an inspired, furiously motivated turntable.

"What the hell!" he yelled.

I just stood very still and waited for him to complete his explosion.

"You can't bring that stink around here. Nobody'll come near us."

"It's only carbolic acid," I said feebly.

"Only carbolic acid! I feel like I'm selling onions and potatoes in a hospital."

Uncle Herschel looked from Hymie to me, and Hymie explained what had inspired that outburst. Turning back to look at me, my uncle moistened his lips as he always did when exploring unknown or tricky aspects of a problem. Then he seemed to count the hairs in his goatee.

"I'm the one who'll make the sacrifice," he said.

"Why?"

"I'll lose a wonderful salesman."

"Git outa here before all the women start runnin'," Hymie bawled at me.

I was hurt; it was not easy to be a pariah, to be shunned, first by my classmates and teacher, and now by Uncle Herschel. I turned slowly and walked back home.

My mother was surprised and, I think, distressed to see unhappy lines on my face. "I stink, Ma. Hymie wouldn't let me near his pushcart."

"So you won't be near his pushcart."

"Can I go to the Frieds'?"

I waited almost breathlessly. To be denied access to the reading I looked forward to so keenly would be the cruelest test.

"Go, go."

"But I stink."

"You don't stink."

"But what will Mrs. Fried say?"

"She won't say anything. She smelled carbolic acid in her house before. She's a mother, she'll understand."

So I went to the Frieds' flat because I was eager to go and because my mother had many times come out a true prophet. Even so, I hesitated for just one instant as I came to the door, but I knocked and turned the doorknob as was our custom, without waiting to discover whether we were welcome.

Normally I just called hello and coursed right into the front room where Mrs. Fried always left the newspaper and *Collier's* for me. Today I paused at the door almost as though I had thrown in my hat and I was waiting to see whether it would be thrown back out. Mrs. Fried didn't turn from the stove, where she was slowly stirring a long-handled ladle in an oversized pot.

"You had an accident?"

"Yeh."

"What kind of accident?"

"I cut my arm on the iron tire of an ice wagon."

"Oh my."

"You knew I had an accident by the smell, didn't you?"

"Yes, but it isn't a bad smell."

"No?" I tried to crowd into that one word all my surprise and all my pleasure.

"No. It's a smell, but at least we know it's a clean smell. Go, go read the paper."

Eleven

When Uncle Herschel got home, he told us he had sold ten collars that day and some women had come back for more and others had promised to be back after they had consulted their daughters. At that rate, he speculated he would have to replenish his stock before the end of the week.

He told us even Lucas had returned to tell him how pleased his wife was with what he had taken out of his round hat, and Hymie had immediately packed up another collar for his daughter.

He looked at me because I had not spoken and he said, "In a few days the doctor will take away the carbolic acid, and then you'll be able to come back to Seigel Street."

"How many days?"

"The doctor will look at your arm."

"Can you?"

"I don't want to disturb his bandage. Later, we'll go over to the store to see how Sam is doing with the shelves."

I didn't hold this proposal suspect, but when my mother said "good, good," I knew both were conspiring to distract me, to take my mind off my distress at having been ostracized by the other kids and by Hymie.

We went to the store and when we saw a faint light there we

knew Sam was working on some phase of his contract with Uncle Herschel. He came to the door in response to the knock Uncle made with the head of his stick. He peered at us in the dark hallway.

"Who is it?"

From the way he held his hammer I knew he was ready to discourage any intrusion.

When we told him he moved away from the door, and we followed him into the store. The light in the store came from two very thick candles.

"You didn't expect us?" Uncle asked mildly.

"No, but I was expecting two men who came here this afternoon. They said they'd be back later, and later is now."

"Two men?"

"Two men. They didn't tell me what they wanted. They were both Jewish, but there was something about them I didn't like. I don't know what—maybe the way they were dressed." He paused to stare at Uncle. "You're dressed like a gentleman—you know, a white shirt, a bow tie and your shoes are always polished—and these men were dressed something in the same way. Their shoes had a high shine, and their shirts were white, but their suits and their hats and their coats! People who live around here don't dress like that, even those people who buy by Thorner. They were swells!"

"So what did they want?"

"I don't know, and they asked me a lot of questions I couldn't answer, mostly about what kind of storekeeper would rent this store. I asked them what business it was of theirs, and they only smiled. They said they were real-estate people, and they wanted to know what kind of business was opening up here. They didn't fight about it, and they went away."

"So why are you upset by them?"

"They came back in about a half hour, and this time they wanted to know if I could give them your address, and I said no, and they thought I knew your address, and one of them said,

'A smart man knows when to talk and when not to talk.' That's when I picked up a hammer and said, 'I know when to say "get out of here," ' and they went."

My skin was beginning to crawl a little, and I felt sensations on my spine and in my hair. When I walked down the long hall in our house, I always stopped about three feet before I came to the stairs because I knew there was a large space under the stairs where the janitor kept the garbage barrels. I always hesitated there so I could detect the sound of breathing, of a lurking human being or beings. For months now in the twilight, when I sat on the curbstone with Muttel and my other friends, we had talked about the Black Hand, whispering that one house down the block was where the Black Hand met and plotted their kidnappings and their other nefarious exploits. We knew they had to be members of the Black Hand because they wore such strange black suits and black hats and whenever I looked at them they stared back at me icily.

"Why would they want our address?" I asked a little breathily. "Do you know who they are?"

Uncle Herschel shrugged. "You know whom I know in this country. I don't know who these men are or what they want, and I'm not going to worry about who they might be."

Sam had been staring at my uncle as though he couldn't make up his mind whether he should believe him.

"Can it be you talked to these men and you don't remember what you said to them?"

Uncle shook his head. "The only stranger I talked to was a Russian about two weeks ago, but I didn't talk to him about what I was going to do and where I was going to do it."

"You think they're from the Black Hand?" I just barely whispered it.

Both men stared at me, but Sam recovered first. He laughed. "What does the Black Hand want with your uncle? Besides, the Black Hand doesn't bother Jewish people."

"What is this Black Hand?" asked Uncle Herschel.

"They're terrible people. They kidnap children and they make their fathers pay money."

"And you think they might want to kidnap me?" Uncle said incredulously.

I looked first at Uncle Herschel, because this notion as expressed by him was startling, then I looked at Sam. He, too, was staring at my uncle. Suddenly he let out a wild bellow which he permitted to simmer down to a loud cackling laugh.

"What do you say? Isn't that wonderful? The Black Hand is coming to kidnap your uncle! No use. We'll have to tell Callahan about it, to keep an eye out when the Black Hand comes visiting your uncle."

My uncle just waited for Sam to get over this fit of hilarity, but I was indignant, not only because I resented his laughing at me, but also because I felt that Uncle Herschel, too, was offended.

"Tell me," Uncle said, "when you have finished here, I'll have a lot of drugs to bring over. How will I be able to get all that here: drugs, bottles, jars?"

Of course I had the answer for him. I would round up all my friends, and we would form a safari like the natives in the Haggard novels I had read surreptitiously in the library.

"Oh that's easy," Sam said. "On McKibbin Street near Leonard there's a pushcart yard. Know where it is?" he asked me.

I knew.

"Go there and tell the man—I think his name is Kutarsky—you want to rent a pushcart for a couple of hours. That's all. Then you load your pushcart, bring the merchandise here and the boy can return the pushcart. Two hours will take care of the whole job."

Uncle looked at me to see that I understood, and when I nodded, he was satisfied.

"So, good," Sam concluded. "The job here will be finished on time, and you'll be able to move in here as soon as I'm finished."

We didn't answer immediately. We just looked around at what he had already wrought: one section of shelves nestled on one wall and lengths of lumber on the floor waiting to be processed.

"Come," Uncle Herschel said, "we'll go over to the pushcart yard."

"Tell Kutarsky I sent you," Sam said. "Sometimes he doesn't trust a new face he doesn't know, and he may not give you a pushcart."

"Is it too late to go now?" Uncle asked me as we came into the street. I didn't know but suggested we should go to look. I knew the pushcart lot on McKibbin Street and convoyed my uncle there without mishap.

There were pushcarts recessed in far corners of this huge lot shaded by many overaged, oversized trees. We walked to the center of the lot and looked around. We saw no one; we couldn't even spot a house or hut where a caretaker could be lurking.

Then, as we turned again, we saw a smallish man with huge eyebrows like an overhanging cliff. This I saw immediately and then I remembered him as I had seen him from across the street last year on election night.

That night he had raced from the lot to the street screaming I didn't know what, but I knew why. The big boys from the neighborhood had been stealing his pushcarts and rolling them toward Manhattan Avenue, where a huge bonfire had already begun to burn. The fire was about ten feet high, and any piece of wood not secured was instantly sacrificed to this election-night victory celebration. It didn't really matter who had won —I learned later that the boys who had been hustling wood to the fire had not known who had won or even who was running.

The boys had fled from his lot with twenty or thirty of the wooden conveyances, and Kutarsky had pleaded, cajoled, threatened all of them with no success. Cart after cart had disappeared and had been fed to the hungry flames around the corner. We little boys had danced up and down gleefully because Mr. Kutarsky was dramatizing his agony so vividly. Ever since, I imagine, he had regarded all intruders as enemies.

I'm sure he did not know me; indeed he hardly looked at me. But from the way his eyes were fixed upon my uncle, I thought he would never accept him as a friend.

"What you want?" he demanded.

"You speak Yiddish?" my uncle asked.

"Yeh, I speak Yiddish," Mr. Kutarsky growled, letting us know he might snap at any hand we held out to him. "What you want?"

"In a few days we'll need a pushcart."

Mr. Kutarsky's hostile gaze did not falter. "*You'll* need a pushcart?" He leaned so heavily on the "you" that my uncle grinned at him.

"Is there a law against my needing a pushcart?"

"You don't look like the kind of man who needs a pushcart. What do you need a pushcart for?"

Because Uncle hesitated and went to his goatee for consultation, I thought he was getting ready to tell Mr. Kutarsky to take his pushcart. . . .

"I'm opening a store on Cook Street in a couple of days, and I need a pushcart to move some merchandise from my home to the store."

"Where do you live?"

"Seventy-nine Manhattan Avenue," I butt in, not sure Uncle would remember.

Then for the first time he noticed me, as though I had been only on the fringe of his awareness until now. He took time to scrutinize me.

"Who are you?" he demanded.

I thought he was approaching me from the wrong end. "He's my uncle," I said.

"Hmmm. For how long do you want the pushcart?"

"About two hours."

"*About* two hours! I can't charge you about. About two hours can be four hours or six hours."

"Two hours."

"Two hours? Twenty-five cents."

I said, "Wait a minute, Uncle. Twenty-five cents is too much."

I really didn't know the going rate for pushcart renting, but I knew twenty-five cents was a lot of money. Why, for twenty-five cents I could buy five quarts of milk or seven or eight loaves of rye bread. Mr. Kutarsky turned to stare at me, angrily, venomously.

"Who asked you? Why don't you take your snotnose out of my business."

I ignored him. "Twenty-five cents is too much. Don't give him more than twenty cents."

He stared angrily at me, an impudent little boy butting in on a bargaining session between two adults.

"Who the hell asked you?" Mr. Kutarsky demanded.

"He's my uncle."

"So who cares if he's your uncle. You keep your nose out of this."

"What did he say?" Uncle asked.

"He said I should keep my nose out of it. Twenty-five cents is a lot of money for a pushcart for a couple of hours. I bet Hymie'll give us his pushcart for nothing."

"Hymie keeps his pushcart here," Mr. Kutarsky said owlishly.

"So what? He doesn't take his pushcart out on Saturday."

"Hymie wouldn't let you take his pushcart out on Saturday, and I wouldn't let you take a pushcart out on Saturday. Better you should go to schule."

"Why don't you rent a pushcart on Saturday?" Uncle asked.

I was surprised that he seemed perversely uninterested in the debate over the rental fee, suddenly taking up the question of religion instead. Mr. Kutarsky looked at him balefully as though he resented such a question.

"What do you mean why don't I rent pushcarts on Saturday? I'm a Jew, no? So a Jew should go to schule on Saturday instead of renting pushcarts."

"Why?"

"Why? Why? I just told you—because I'm a Jew."

"But why do you have to go to schule because you're a Jew?"

This blasphemy stunned Mr. Kutarsky. For a moment while he sought for words, he glared at Uncle Herschel.

"I go to schule to worship God."

"And how do you know there is a God?"

"How do I know? What are you, an atheist? How do you know you're alive?"

Uncle Herschel smiled mildly and fingered his goatee. "Touch your pulse and you'll know you're alive or you're what we call alive, but you haven't told me how you know there's a God."

"Because I believe it, that's why."

"That's all?"

"That's all."

"So when you go to schule you worship not what you know is but what you believe is."

I had to repeat to myself what Uncle said so I could understand what he meant, but Mr. Kutarsky was irretrievably involved. He refitted his hat on his head and said, "Mister, do me a favor. If you want a pushcart go to another yard. I won't rent you a pushcart on the Sabbath."

Uncle nodded. "We'll come on a Sunday and we'll pay you twenty-five cents."

As we left the yard I said, "We could have gotten that pushcart for twenty cents."

"Let the man make a living. What we won't give him won't make me richer, but it seems to mean something to him."

Well, it meant something to me too, but there was a note of finality in that last thought so I did not answer it. However, I told myself that soon, very soon, I would have to talk to Uncle about religion and about the way he just brushed off what other men were doing in the synagogue and about what they thought. We walked in silence—I know it was only a tentative kind of silence—for about fifty yards, and suddenly I had to ask.

"Why don't you believe in God?"

He gave his walking stick an extra dig into the pavement and turned his head toward me.

"I believe in God," he said.

"You do? But you smoke on the Sabbath and you never go to synagogue."

"I believe in God. I believe that there's too much order in the world and this order couldn't have happened without a Supreme Being. I pray to this Supreme Being. I talk to him constantly."

My eyes popped out and my tongue must have begun to hang out.

"You talk to God?"

"Of course. God is for everybody, not only for the people who go to synagogue. They have their own way of talking to God. I don't like their way. They don't treat Him as if He was a human God. They praise and praise and praise Him, even when their hearts are breaking over something that shouldn't have happened. Sometimes I get angry at God. I tell Him he makes mistakes, and once I asked Him, 'Who's your boss? I want to talk to Him.' He must have laughed, because I laughed, and I couldn't tell my wife why because she already thinks I'm a little bit crazy with my medicines and my cane and my polished shoes. . . ."

He trailed off and stared out to the street, to Manhattan Avenue.

"And if I talked to God like you, I wouldn't die?"

"No, how could you die? God is your father. Does your father like it when you talk to him, when you ask him questions?"

"Yes."

"Then God will like it. Just remember: your father will love you even if you don't love him, and God will love you for the same reason. I don't believe the synagogue is the only place I can meet God, and I don't believe He said I can't smoke on the Sabbath."

"And traif?"

"I don't know what traif is. If God made all of us, man and all the animals, why should He have made animals we shouldn't eat? I think taste should be the only reason for not eating something. I don't like meat because I don't like to eat the meat of another animal, even a kosher animal. In the same way I wouldn't eat grasshoppers, and I wouldn't eat spiders or snakes."

I stared up at him in awe and wonder. In a few minutes he had offered me so much to think about, expanded the boundaries of my mental and family circumference. I thought, How can I tell my father and my mother what Uncle Herschel has postulated for me this afternoon?

Three days later I asked my mother for fifty cents so I could visit Dr. Padilsky. She looked doubtful for a moment, and wondered if she should permit me to go alone into that lion's den. I guessed she was reluctant to go herself, because she was terror-stricken at his approach as were all the other housewives in the neighborhood.

I went, but not happily, to the office of Dr. Padilsky.

The big woman who opened the door stared at me until she saw my arm in the sling. Then she leaned out and looked behind and all around me.

"Where's your mother, little boy?"

If she had patted me on the head, I think I should have kicked her.

"Home."

"What do you mean home? She can't send you here alone. Doctor won't see you."

I drew myself up an inch or two. "Tell him I came here with my uncle the felsher. He'll see me."

"The what?"

"The felsher."

"What–is–that?" She said it slowly, deliberately, hatefully.

"That means he's nearly a doctor. Your doctor knows him. They worked together on a woman in my house."

That woman regarded me a moment as though I had said

something obscene. Then she stepped away from the door, and I entered the large reception room. Many chairs filled by many people stood at odd angles from the wall. I could judge only from their forms that each chair was different. In two or three spots, two people sat together on small sofas.

Everybody joined eyes on me, and I looked around uncomfortably for a vacant spot into which I could shrink or fade into a welcome anonymity. There were no empty chairs so I sought a wall against which I could lean out of the spotlight.

Far across the room I saw a bookcase and next to it a narrow, delightfully recessed niche. All eyes followed me as I hurried to its shelter, supporting my lacerated left arm with my right hand. Nudging myself into that welcome corner, I took a deep breath. I could sense that many pairs of eyes were still evaluating me not only as a patient but as a person, because I had attracted inordinate time and attention to myself at the door.

I pulled my arm out of the sling and lowered it; hanging in the sling was not a restful attitude for it. I flexed my fingers over and over. Then I looked at my hand and at my fingers. All this maneuvering made it possible to bear the continued scrutiny of almost fifteen pairs of eyes.

When the doctor's door opened, someone came out, and instantly a waiting person sprang to his feet and almost ran to the door. I didn't move toward that empty seat because I would have to share a small sofa with a girl about my age who had not given up staring at me since I came in.

The large lady in the long white dress came into the room, and I couldn't tell whether she was counting heads to see how many fees her doctor would collect or whether she was making the same kind of survey an usher makes periodically against the press from the standees. When she saw the vacant place next to the little girl she bent her finger at me, but I just stared at her.

"There's a seat over here."

I just continued to stare.

"Don't you want to sit down?"

"No."

Then she came over to me, perhaps because she was nearsighted and she wanted to review the expression on my face.

"Don't you want to sit down?"

"No," louder and more assertive.

She recoiled. "All right, you don't have to bite my head off."

I jockeyed my arm with my right hand, and I did not answer that last comment. I resettled myself in my niche, determined not to leave it until I could replace it with another that was as comfortable and as private. I was disturbed that I had nothing to read because I detested just sitting and staring.

Finally I had to settle for being occupied with a cold scrutiny of the faces around me. I had already decided I didn't like that girl who sat by herself on the double-seating sofa. I didn't like her face because it was so long and so sallow; I had to tell myself she was a sick child. I didn't like her long black braids, which spilled over on her chest; and I looked askance at her long ribbed stockings, which were puffed up on her skinny legs and knees because she was wearing long woolen underwear. The dress she wore to below her knees was made of blue serge and must have been scratchy. I knew, because the blue serge suit my father had bought me the year before was torture to wear when the sun was overhead.

There were no other children in that room; all the others were old, or so they appeared to me. "Old" began at twenty and anybody over twenty was really old. Two longbeards sat near their wives, who wore thin shawls on their heads. These two aged men, whom I would now place at forty or forty-five, began to rock as I sat down. Their eyes were closed as they swayed back and forth, but their lips moved with unbridled speed.

For a little while I watched them with the same fascination I had experienced in schule about three years ago, when I had become aware of the old men who stood right through the day on Yom Kippur, their heads constantly covered by prayer shawls and their lips moving furiously. They held prayerbooks in their hands, open of course, but their eyes were always closed. What astounded me was the regularity with which they turned the pages, so I got right up to them to check their eyes. And as they prayed and prayed, they rocked in an almost set pattern. After a while I counted to see how long it would be before they stopped rocking from front to back and began rocking from side to side.

The afternoon was long, and that man in there was distressingly overcareful or overconscientious. When that girl went in, I began to count because I had no watch. I got as far as fifteen hundred and six when someone banged on the front door and my curiosity about what kind of rude character would assault the doctor's front door made me lose count. It wasn't anybody important after all, and the knock wasn't even a knock. The newsboy had thrown the newspaper against the door.

It was almost five o'clock when the big woman opened the door for me to go into the doctor's office. He was still writing something in a book, so I waited near the door until he looked up.

"Come in and sit down," he said.

I came in and sat, and suddenly his head went up as if it were on a spring. "Where's your mother?" he bellowed. "Mrs. Cartney, why do I have to be bothered with children without mothers? Am I running a clinic?"

"My mother couldn't come," I said.

"What do you mean your mother couldn't come! What's more important than coming here with a sick child?"

"I'm not sick–"

"Who asked you, and what do you know what's bothering you–"

"I know what's bothering me."

"Oh you do! Now tell me what college you went to."

"I know what's bothering me. I cut my arm, and you bandaged it last week."

He stared at me, then moved the gas lamp closer to my face. "Ah, where is your uncle, the felsher?"

"He couldn't come."

"He's out maybe with a patient?"

He had led me into his examining room where he had begun to unfurl the bandages from my arm. I looked into his face when he asked me that question about Uncle Herschel's patients, but I would have preferred to kick him hard in his shins. Instead, however, I just shuffled my feet and didn't answer. After all, how did one sass back a doctor or a teacher?

However, my tormentor was not motivated in this way. He must have accepted my reluctance to talk as an acknowledgement that Uncle Herschel was actually practicing medicine.

He said, "Do the patients come to him or does he come to them?"

"He hasn't got any patients, but don't you worry—he's a good doctor and one of these days he's gonna be somebody big."

"Aha! Maybe a professor in a medical college for doctors?"

"Better than that," I exclaimed because he had needled me beyond all endurance. "You wait and see. You wait and see when he opens up his store on Cook Street."

"And what will he sell in the store on Cook Street?"

"What'll he sell? What do you think a felsher would sell?"

"I don't know." He was peering down at the wound on my arm. "Ah, very good. You were a good boy, and you did your homework. So what did you tell me your uncle, the felsher, was going to sell in a store on Cook Street?"

"Medicines," I snapped at him, "medicines."

His eyes lit up as if some internal combustion had been ignited by what I had just told him.

"You mean your uncle is opening a drugstore on Cook Street?"

"No. My uncle isn't a druggist, and he's not opening a drugstore."

"Then what kind of store will it be?"

"A medicine store. Like if you have a sore on your finger

you come to him, and he gives you a medicine to fix up the sore."

"And how soon will your uncle open this store?"

"Maybe in a month or two months. The store is being painted now and the man is putting in shelves and then my uncle has to make the medicines."

"So! When your uncle opens his store you'll have to come and tell me about it. Maybe I'll come and buy some medicine from your uncle."

He gave himself barely enough time to expel the last word so he could lay his head back and bellow out roll upon roll of thunderous laughter. I just stared at him, wondering what the devil he was laughing at and knowing that somehow there was a sinister connection between what he had heard about Uncle Herschel and this outrageous outburst.

Of course, I could not ask him why he was laughing, because I could not forget what I heard insistently in my home: a child must always be respectful to an adult.

The lady in white opened the door cautiously to look in; the doctor caught the swift movement in white.

"Listen to this," he exclaimed. "You know where I'm going to send all my patients for drugs from now on?" He paused so she could bring the rest of her into the room. "I'm going to send them all to his uncle, the felsher, who's gonna sell medicines in a store on Cook Street. Maybe in time I'll open up an office in the back of his store. Wouldn't that be easy? All I'd have to do is open up my door and holler, 'Felsher, give this patient number three.' "

He tied a knot on the bandage as he said that last word and stood off from me with his blousy woman in white, and together they howled over his perfectly hateful joke. For one moment I regarded them venomously until their spasm had run out. Then I reached into my pocket for my half dollar as the doctor said, "Continue to use the same prescription until you come back the next time."

I did not seem to hear what he said because his derisive laughter was still clogging my ears. I slapped the half dollar down on his desk and I said, "I don't like when you make fun of my uncle. He's a smart man, and you're a shithead."

I moved so rapidly out of the room I couldn't even guess what their reaction was to my assault. It was probably as unexpected to them as it was to me. I did not know how I would answer his detestable needling until that word came out, and when it did I was petrified. I ran through that waiting room as everybody stared at me, and I did not stop running until I had come to my block. Somehow I expected the doctor or his white shadow to pursue me down Manhattan Avenue, seize me and drag me to my mother to accuse me of having abused them. I looked back several times during my retreat and I was relieved when I got to my block without being intercepted.

Muttel and Sam were sitting on the curb in front of my house matching cigarette pictures. I could never join them because my father made his own cigarettes, but the other fellows got their cards from packs of Sweet Caporals, Mecca, Fifth Avenue, Hassan, Murads and other cigarettes their fathers and big brothers smoked. I sat down next to Muttel, and he knew instantly who was there at his side.

"Ooh! You stink," he greeted me.

I watched the cards being turned over and matched, then I said, "I just told Doctor Padilsky he's a shithead."

For about ten seconds neither Sam nor Muttel commented on that, and I was preparing to be indignant.

Muttel was the first to react. "You told Crazy Padilsky he's a shithead?!"

I nodded.

"You did like hell."

"I betcha million."

"Awright, I betcha million. How you gonna prove you called him a shithead? You gonna take us over there and say, 'You prove it, doctor, if I called you a shithead'?"

"Nah, I'm not going over there."

"So, how then?"

"I don't know how. He got me mad the way he was talkin' about my uncle and I was bustin' inside and before I knew what I was sayin' I called him that and ran."

"You think he's gonna get you arrested?"

"Arrested!"

"Sure, You can't go around calling doctors shitheads, Yank. Suppose if every time you went to a doctor and he made a mistake or you didn't like what he said you called him a shithead!"

"Awright, whose side you on?"

"I'm on your side, but my doctor ain't a shithead."

"Well, your doctor didn't say about your uncle what Padilsky said about my uncle."

"What did he say about your uncle?"

When I realized suddenly I was being led down a dark alley, I pulled up.

"Never mind what he said, and I still say if he's gonna say things like that about somebody's uncle then he's a shithead."

"So you didn't tell me what he said."

"Never mind what he said. I'm not afraid of him."

I had to say that boldly, because I did not yet know how deeply the man had been affected by what I had said and what reprisal he would seek. He might even appear at our flat to accuse me of having abused him in his own home, in his own office.

I went up to my flat with plenty of misgivings, told my mother the doctor had said the wound was healing nicely, ate my roll and butter, and hurried down the hall to the Frieds'. I was already late by a half-hour, but Mrs. Fried didn't seem to be aware of time. She offered me a piece of hot strudel, which she put on a dish, and I placed it on the carpet beside me because I loved to read on the Frieds' rug in the front room.

I hoped I could so immerse my thinking in the newspaper and *Collier's* I would forget my encounter with the doctor. I was wrong. My temerity embraced me on every page, and my concern grew with each item I read. For the first time in weeks I was so completely aware of the time that I left before Mrs.

Fried could warn me her family would be home soon. As I moved toward the door she said, "You must be hungry."

Everybody was home for supper that night. My mother had prepared a dairy meal (I had noticed we had been having more than the normal number of dairy meals during this last week) which featured hard-boiled eggs, herring, blintzes that my mother made with cottage cheese on two huge frying pans.

Uncle did not touch the herring but he ate a vast number of eggs and mountains of blintzes. My mother told him of my visit to Dr. Padilsky, and my uncle asked me an extraordinary number of questions about what he had said to me and what I had said to him.

I talked almost volubly about the throng in the waiting room and about that monstrous woman who defended the doctor's outer works, but I was understandably reluctant to discuss what had happened in my dialogue with the doctor. I responded to pointed questions in monosyllabic explanations, and I noticed my uncle looked quizzically at me as though he sensed I was withholding something from him.

Beginning to feel a little desperate, I wondered if I should tell them the whole story. After all, I had exploded impatiently only when I felt that man was abusing someone for whom I had already developed a rather large regard.

Suddenly we were all terrified, immobilized by a frightful scream outside our kitchen window, and we knew instantly that something dreadful had happened to Jennie's mother.

My father flung the window up and we saw Jennie, her arms stretched out to us, screaming that her mother had died. When my uncle moved toward the window, Mother stopped him.

"It's dark now. You'll fall. Go by the stairs."

He turned to the door, and I raced in front of him, making sure he could keep me in view as I plunged down the steps two at a time. I paused at every landing until he came around the bend.

On the street I waited for him to join me.

"Go for Doctor Padilsky," he said.

I began to breathe hard. "No."

He stared at me. "She needs a doctor."

"Can't I go for another doctor? Please, Uncle?"

"No. He's a good doctor and he knows the patient."

"But if I can't get him?"

"You'll get him. All doctors are home now."

"But if I can't get him?"

"Doctor Padilsky, and maybe later you'll tell me why you're afraid of him."

He just strode by me, letting me know he had already divined my secret from my reluctant conversation at the supper table and my unusual behavior here on the street.

I could not add to my rebuttal because he had already entered the house next door. I took a deep breath and looked around irresolutely. I could run away from home this very instant and cause the death of a very sick woman, or I could march steadfastly into the home of the doctor to tell him he was needed. I found myself running and sobbing because I was terrified. When I came to the doctor's door I paused. I knew I would not be able to speak if I rang his bell now.

After about twenty seconds or so I approached the door and rang. The reverberations were horrid and scary, and I waited fearfully for an unpleasant doom to strike me.

When the door was opened I saw an apparition in bedroom slippers, holding his pants with one hand and the doorknob with the other. At his back and sides hung the same suspenders I had seen on him the other day. The light behind him was dim, and the gaslight on the street was surely no help to him as he peered out at me.

"What do you want?" he asked.

I turned to one side so he wouldn't see my arm in a sling and said, "A lady sent me to get you. Her mother has sleeping sickness and she's dying."

He stared at me and then he hitched up one side of his suspenders. "Her mother is dying! So what do you want from me—I should help her to die?"

I opened my mouth, but no sound came out. How could I answer such a monstrous question? I thought he was a beast, but I did notice he had already slung the other half of his suspenders over his shoulder.

"Stand here," he said. "I'll come right away with you."

He closed the door in my face before I could tell him the address and the name of the patient so I would not have to escort him. But I did not have time to nurse my misgivings. Almost before I had pried my way through all of them the door was flung open, and he stood on the top step. He had wound some kind of neckerchief around his neck and was wearing a coat.

"Take me," he said.

Without a word I stepped off the stoop and turned toward Manhattan Avenue. We had walked a few steps when we came under the soft light of a gas lamp. I lowered my head, suspecting he might want to have a good look at who was leading him.

Alas, his eye and his memory were keener than I had hoped.

"Aha!" he said. "The shithead!"

I looked a little sidelong at him and I wondered if he would deliver me a good solid clout on the head.

"So! Tonight you have no name for me?"

"No." Just barely audible.

"Because you can't think of another name or maybe a better name?"

"No."

"So! Did you tell your mother and your father, maybe, what a name you gave your doctor?"

"No."

"No! Oh my! Then maybe you told your uncle, the felsher."

"No."

"What is all this 'no'? Then why did you say it in the first place?"

I seized this opening almost savagely. "Because you said all those nasty things about my uncle."

"Oho! That's how much you like your uncle. He must be a very fine man."

"He is a fine man."

I looked up at him almost defiantly, and our eyes met. He said "hmm" as we turned into the house. We walked up the stairs in silence, and when we came to the flat on the second floor, he knocked once briefly and strode in. Jennie's father was sitting on a wooden chair kneading his hands, and Jennie, a few feet from him, was crying softly into her arms.

Uncle Herschel stood by the door of the bedroom, smoking calmly, one hand on the head of his walking stick. As he walked by my uncle Dr. Padilsky asked, "Did you look at her?"

Uncle shrugged. "I'm looking at her now."

"Ah! You know what I mean."

"Would I have sent for you if I had examined her?"

Dr. Padilsky turned swiftly to look at Uncle's inscrutable face. Then he took out his stethoscope and applied it to the woman's chest. After moving it from area to area and listening hard, he laid it aside and raised her eyelids slowly.

As he folded his instrument he looked up at Uncle Herschel, and I saw my uncle shake his head slowly.

"Do you want to tell the family?" Dr. Padilsky asked Uncle.

Uncle Herschel shook his head and smiled dimly. "If I were the doctor I would tell them."

Dr. Padilsky strode into the middle of the room.

"Better listen. Your mother is as good as dead. Before the night is over she'll be dead. Now, not even God can help her. In her condition, God is kind to her to let her die so quietly, so quickly. If you want, I'll send a nurse. It'll cost you. You don't need a nurse. I'll come back around ten o'clock."

"They won't need a nurse," Uncle Herschel said quietly. "I'll be here."

I looked from Dr. Padilsky to my uncle. I was very proud of the strength and comfort his quiet assurance must have given those two unhappy, bereaved people.

Their faces were like stunned masks, their eyes glazed as they sat and waited for the twin gods to spell out a new life for them. Jennie had stopped crying. She just stared at Uncle Herschel and the doctor.

"She's still alive?" she asked.

"She's still alive, but only her pulse. She's now in a coma, and soon the coma will end." Dr. Padilsky spoke as though what was today or tonight no longer mattered, that the fuse was inevitably fading.

Then suddenly and irrelevantly he swung on me and leveled a long finger at my face.

"Felsher," he said, "you have a nephew who loves you a lot. He came to me today I should look at his arm, and we were talking about you, and I said something about you in a joke—"

"It wasn't a joke," I flared at him, but when I looked into Uncle's reproachful eyes, I quickly subsided.

"You know what he said to me?—if I think that way about his uncle I'm a shithead."

Uncle Herschel had not yet turned from me as he asked, "What is that?"

I said nothing. This is Padilsky's story, I thought. I wouldn't have told it, and if he felt the need to tell it let him explain. He did, and as I returned my uncle's gaze, wondering how he would react to my temerity, I saw the end of his mouth pucker a little.

"What made you say that?" he asked, but there was no anger or reproach in his voice.

"Because you're my uncle and he had no right to say what he did about you."

"Ah, what did I say? I was just making conversation with a bright boy."

"Sometimes," Uncle Herschel said, "a bright boy gets closer to God than His angels."

Twelve

I was impatient to go back to the store on Cook Street, and I could not understand how Uncle Herschel could wait so calmly for next week, when Sam had promised the store would be ready. I watched him at night after supper when he would begin to smoke his cigarettes in almost tireless succession, interrupting himself only long enough between cigarettes to pour from that everlasting bottle.

He never stopped to raise his glass to make a toast or salute anybody's health. The glass seemed to know the way, almost guiding his hand from the table to his mouth. Uncle Herschel made no comment about this drinking, which was by this time an accepted way of life for all of us. None of us thought it odd that he would follow three or four glasses of hot after-supper tea with four or five small glasses of that liquor.

When the day finally came the following week, he said to me, "After supper we'll go over to the store to see how soon we can move in."

I turned to look at my parents and my mother said, "Go, go."

I hurried to get my hat and coat and preceded my uncle into the hall. This was a journey of fulfillment. I was so entranced by this new phase of the adventure I could hardly restrain myself from prancing down Manhattan Avenue toward Cook Street; but I walked soberly as befitted the nephew of a felsher.

"Do you think he finished the store?" I asked eagerly.

Uncle Herschel tapped his stick on the pavement. "Sam is an honest man. He made a promise and he'll carry out that promise."

"And when will you start making up the medicines?"

"As soon as we move in."

"And will you let me help you?"

"Well, you have work to do from your school–"

"Oh, I can finish my work very fast and I can do a lot of things to help."

"We'll see."

That surely was not a satisfactory answer because I had to have supporting truth for the stories I planned to tell Muttel and Sam and the others. I would lead them into the store to show them where my talented hands had made progress possible, and they would gawk and marvel.

We were in the store almost before the end of my pleasurable reverie. Sam was in the back setting the screws in two big braces for a wide shelf. We had paused in the store proper to gaze in wonder and admiration at the newly painted bright green walls and the sharply colored shelves on the far wall. The shelving was such a vast expanse I marveled how Uncle Herschel could make enough medicines to fill it. I looked at Uncle to see how he liked what Sam had wrought. He made little noises with his tongue and he repeatedly flexed his lips over his tongue as though he were tasting what he was viewing. I wondered whether he was pleased or not. Then he raised his stick and stomped it on the floor.

"Good," he said, "very good."

"Tomorrow I'll clean the front window, and you can move in whenever you're ready," Sam said.

"We'll move in on Sunday."

"Why Sunday?"

"On Sunday I'll have help. This I can't do by myself."

"So good. You're satisfied, and I'm going to have a good tenant. Come upstairs, we'll have a schnaps for a good bargain."

Uncle's upper lip unfirmed as he said, "Ah, good, a schnaps."

I didn't know whether that invitation extended to me, but I clumped up the wooden steps behind my uncle, who didn't seem surprised that I was right at his heels. At the top of the stairs Sam kicked the door open and yelled, "Yetta, people are coming."

Yetta came into the kitchen from another room and waited, smiling, for her husband to tell her who followed.

"Yetta, this is the felsher who rented the store. He went to see your aunt in Bath Beach, remember? And this is the nephew. He's a good boy, a smart boy. I asked the felsher to come up to have a schnaps with me because I just finished the store and tomorrow he can move in."

Yetta bustled over to the table as Sam turned up the gaslight to a brighter white glow. She pulled out four chairs and disappeared behind a curtain as Sam lumbered toward the table, bearing a bottle and three glasses draped over three fingers. He set the bottle down with his left hand and flipped the glasses over with the three fingers of his right hand.

As he filled the glasses I was intrigued with speculation about that third one. I could readily account for two, but that third glass. . . . Yetta brought two dishes piled high with cookies and peanuts. Only in my Aunt Esther's house had I ever seen entertainment so lavishly dispensed.

"Take cookies, take peanuts," she said.

Uncle Herschel held his glass up to the light. Apparently he liked what he saw there. When Sam said "l'chaim," Uncle said "l'chaim" and Yetta said "l'chaim." She, too, raised a glass. She had resolved my doubt.

"L'chaim," I said and I reached for a cookie.

"Tell me," Sam said, "you're going to sell medicines here, but you're not a doctor and you're not a druggist. How can you do it?"

Uncle Herschel ran his fingers over his mouth to catch stray drops of the liquor and he paused to hold a light to a cigarette.

"I won't be a doctor and I won't be a druggist. If a man comes in and says he has a pain in his stomach, I'll tell him to go see a doctor. If the man tells me he's got an ulcer, I'll tell him to go to the shelf and find a medicine that will help him. I'll make signs and I'll hang up the signs: 'For Shampoo,' 'For a Cough,' 'For a Headache.' If a man brings me a prescription from a doctor, I'll tell him to go to a druggist."

"Oh, then you have nothing to worry about. You're really a smart man."

"I'm going to try to make a living so I can bring over my family."

"You hear, Yetta, how smart this man is?"

"I hear," Yetta said, reaching for the bottle to fill everybody's glass.

"Yetta, did I tell him those men were here again?"

"No, you didn't tell him."

Sam raised his glass and Uncle Herschel just flipped the drink into his mouth. I had seen him perform the same rite before, but I was still fascinated with each repetition.

"They were here again," Sam said, "those two men. They look like gangsters to me, even if they were nicely dressed."

"So what do they have to do with me?"

"I don't know. All I can tell you is they want to talk to you and they asked me over and over when you're going to move in. I told them I didn't know and I really didn't, but they are not stupid. The little one of the two looked around and he said, 'You're almost finished fixing up the store, so he'll be moving in when you're finished. When will you be finished?' I said, 'Maybe today, maybe tomorrow, maybe the next day.' 'Well,' he said, 'suppose we say you'll be finished by the end of the week.' So I said, 'Say, if you want to say. I'm not signing a contract with you.' 'So,' he said, 'when your man moves in we'll be here to talk to him.' 'So you'll be here,' I said."

"And that's all?" my uncle asked. I looked at him and I thought I saw he was only curious and not apprehensive.

"That's all. I told you about them before. You don't know them?"

"I don't know them."

"And you don't know what they want?"

"I don't know what they want."

"Then to hell with them. Let's drink to that. You'll have a lot of people coming here, each one with another crazy scheme, another big idea to make you both rich quick. Tell them all to go to hell. They're all vultures. They're always looking for a schlemiel with a little bit of money so they can tell you about a wonderful way to make a million dollars fast."

Uncle Herschel shrugged, "I'm concerned only with bread and some good liquor."

"A man after my own heart," Sam exploded, and he reached for the bottle. I leaned over for another cookie and a handful of the peanuts his wife had roasted.

On Saturday, the day before we were to move, I deployed my forces for the next day's undertaking. I met Muttel on the street and spread a handkerchief on the curb before I sat down because I was wearing my Sabbath suit. I approached the matter obliquely.

"My uncle's going to move tomorrow."

"Yeah?"

"We couldn't move today because we couldn't rent a pushcart on the Sabbath."

"Wow!"

"I'm going to pick up the pushcart around eleven o'clock."

"Kin I come with you, Yank?"

"I'll have to ask my uncle."

"Would you? Hah?"

"I'll ask him, but don't go blabbing to everybody you're going to help us move."

"No, I won't tell nobody."

"Won't tell nobody, what?"

That was Sam. He had a way of insinuating himself into the

middle of a conversation and asking a question that was most embarrassing to answer. I looked at Muttel, and I saw his hand over his mouth as though he sensed he had committed an irretrievable blunder.

"You can tell Sam," I said, "Sam's our friend, but nobody else."

"Okay," Muttel exclaimed, "me and him are going to help his uncle move into his new store on Cook Street."

"Gee whiz, can I come too? I'm strong; I won't tell nobody."

"Okay, I'll have to ask my uncle."

Sam smiled almost triumphantly and he rubbed his hands together.

When Uncle and I came into the street the next morning, Sam and Muttel were ranged in front of my house peering expectantly into the long hall. When they saw us, they braced their shoulders to demonstrate their readiness to take on any burden.

I said to my uncle, "That's Muttel and Sam. They're going to help us move."

Uncle glanced at them swiftly. "Good strong boys," he said, and I looked at him because I couldn't always be sure when he was serious or when he was laughing. All the lines in his face were sober as he replaced the cigarette between his lips.

We marched down the street and turned the corner at McKibbin. We knew where the pushcart lot was because it was not uncommon for boys to raid the carts even though the fruits and vegetables were covered and the covers nailed down.

Kutarsky, the pushcart landlord, watched us invade his island, waiting for us a little sourly, I thought, because I had haggled with him. However, he didn't appear to be intent upon Uncle or me. He pointed a stubby, dirty finger at Muttel.

"What do *you* want?"

"I'm with them." Muttel moved his head toward us.

"And what do you want?" to Sam.

"I'm with them, too."

Kutarsky spit in disgust. "A whole gang to rent one lousy pushcart for two hours. No wonder the country's goin' to hell.

Come on." He beckoned to us as though he was now ready to accept almost anything from Fate.

"Here y'are." He stepped back and waved at a mess of pushcarts. There were long, narrow, shallow pushcarts and short, square, deep pushcarts. Some had two big wheels, others three.

Muttel scuttled around the pushcarts, in and out like a termite. He was about thirty yards from us when he waved, hefted himself up on a small front wheel and hollered, "Here's a dandy, painted red and green."

Kutarsky glared at Muttel, and I signalled him back to us.

"What do you need this pushcart for?" asked Kutarsky.

"Packages," Uncle said, "a lot of packages."

"Then take this one." He laid his hand on a short cart which was at least twice as deep as the longer carts. Uncle looked at me, and I nodded my agreement. He held out his hand, palm up. "Pay now for two hours. If you use it for more, it'll cost you ten cents an hour."

Uncle gave him a quarter, pointing to a pushcart which was easily accessible, and I moved over almost majestically to take possession. No big-shot Roman ever took the reins of his chariot with greater pride. I ran my hand over the two handles which were firmed to the two sides of the cart and looked around like the engineer of a fifty-car train about to pull out of a terminal.

"Okay?" I asked, and Kutarsky answered "okay." I pushed forward on the cart, but it wasn't easy because the wheels were rutted into the earth. I pushed harder. Still the earth would not yield. Everybody watched me struggle to start that uncooperative cart, but no one seemed to know how to help me.

Kutarsky was the only one, however, who was impatient with me. He shoved me away from the handles, looked at my uncle and said, "Better let him be a doctor; a pushcart peddler he won't be."

"God has a way of choosing for us," Uncle said.

Kutarsky looked askance at Uncle Herschel for one brief moment; then he took a firm hold on the handles I had released, gave the cart a swift jerk toward his body, and then an equally swift stab forward. The wheels erupted out of the ruts, and in an instant the cart was leveled off, ready to go.

Again I returned to the handles, and this time the big wheels rolled forward in response to my pressure. Sam and Muttel ranged themselves on both sides of the cart while I pushed it into the gutter. They grinned up at me; they, too, were proud. Uncle remained on the sidewalk, keeping pace with us as we propelled our royal wagon.

Actually, we had only a short haul around the corner to my house. When we got there I said, "Muttel, you take charge of the pushcart. We'll go up and bring down the stuff."

My mother held the door open for us as we made up a safari to the pushcart. She advised us all the way down the stair well: "watch where you're walking," "hold the bannister," "lean against the wall," "don't carry too much or you'll hurt yourself," "don't lift too much," "don't jump down the stairs two at a time."

When we got to the street, my father supervised the packing of the cart. He was good at it. He had to be because we had many packages and we were beginning to wonder whether we would have enough room to take it all in one trip.

As we made our third trip down from the flat, Muttel, now the very proud custodian of the cart, hustled around to our side to push away three or four little boys who had crept closer to the cart to see what was being loaded. They resisted him until he said, "Get out of here or I'll kick you in your ass." Then they eased off when they saw so many larger, older people.

My father packed this trip so cleverly that we could look forward to space for our last load. This last one didn't take long, although we had to move it very cautiously—it contained packaged glass bottles. We bore it slowly down the stairs, sighing with relief when we reached the lowest landing. Outside I had to set my package on the ground; my feeling of tension had actually added weight to it.

I rubbed my hands vigorously before I reached down to heft

the package into the cart; then I led the way out to Cook Street.

We turned the corner to Cook Street and pulled up in front of the store. Sam stood on the top step of the stoop like a welcoming colossus. As Uncle Herschel started up the steps, Sam held out his huge hand and enveloped Uncle's completely. In his left hand Sam waved the key to the store, which he laid dramatically in Uncle's hand.

"Bringing gold into the store?" Sam asked.

Uncle didn't smile, although I thought Sam had made a good joke. "Would I need gold to lead an ass?" Uncle said, and Sam guffawed.

Each of us grabbed a package and hauled it into the store. Uncle directed us to lay the supplies on the floor near the window, saying he would need room to sort them. Sam watched the steady trek to and from the cart and he asked questions about each package that came in. Two packages, which my father had carried down, were too heavy for me. Muttel, Sam and I braced one among ourselves and staggered into the store under its load. Knowing its contents, we elected to lower ourselves to the floor and permit it to slide off our thighs. We repeated this operation on the other overweight carton.

I told Uncle I would return the pushcart and come back to help him. I beckoned to my friends and we went out to the street. I took my place at the two handles, while my friends laid possessive hands on either side of the cart. We wheeled it swiftly to the lot, where Kutarsky watched as I propelled it back to the spot it had earlier occupied. I turned to see if he approved of my handiwork. His eyes were watchful under lowered brows.

"Okay?" I asked.

"A pushcart peddler you wouldn't be."

"Who wants to be a pushcart peddler?"

"Good. Now get the hell out of here with your friends. I know your kind. You're probably looking around for the pushcarts you'll run out of here on election night."

"I'm not a thief."

"So good. So get the hell out of here."

"Wait a minute. You forgot you rented a pushcart to a felsher."

"I don't care if he was the Czar of all the Russias. Get out of here."

When we got to the sidewalk, Muttel suddenly turned and yelled, "You stink."

Kutarsky never stirred from where he was standing. As we walked away Muttel said, "You like the way I told him?"

"Okay."

"Okay? Did you hear what he said about your uncle? Your uncle's a felsher!"

"Ah, he's nothing. I'm not worried about him."

"Muttel's right," Sam said.

"Yeah," I said, "I'm going back to the store."

I left them, disturbed that I had not firmed a defense for my uncle, but my position was growing more difficult because I had to do battle with every ignorant peasant we ran into. I decided I would have to be selective. I could rebel against something another boy would say, but I was reluctant to raise arms against an adult. I knew how profoundly my parents detested such behavior, and I myself had not yet recovered from my impulsive assault upon Dr. Padilsky.

When I came into the store, I saw my uncle bare-armed, without his coat, for the first time. Sam had not left; his sleeves, too, were up to his elbows. Together they had torn open all the packages and disposed of their contents. On the shelves they had stood up all the assorted bottles and small boxes that would apparently hold the dry preparations. All the large boxes and containers and bottles were in the back room.

"Good you came," Sam said. "Help me carry out all this garbage."

He had brought in two huge burlap bags into which we stuffed papers and empty cartons, upon which we stamped to make them pliable. Together we carried the bags to the side of the house for the garbage collector.

"Who's your garbage man?" I asked him.

"Willie the wop."

"I know him. He used to be on our block. He never bothers the kids when they play on the block, but the man we got now—he's murder. If we sometimes threw a ball in his truck, Willie'd get it for us, but the man now—he hates us. He won't even let us give his horse an apple or a carrot."

When the kids were outside, the clatter of oversized, iron-rimmed wheels could be heard all the way down the block from below McKibbin Street, because the horse that drew the two-wheeled garbage wagon seemed to sense he was approaching a pleasant experience. He was. When Willie rode in on the foolishly narrow seat of the wagon, which looked like a scoop without a handle, we kids scooted around the garbage looking for discarded apples or carrots.

The operation on the garbage man's cart was always a marvel of dexterity. Imagine! He would heft the garbage can to the top of the big wheel, brace it up there with one hand while he clambered up on the wheel, and dump the contents of the can into the wagon. If one house had five cans, he repeated this stunt five times. He must have been very strong because the cans seemed to flip up to the top of that wheel.

Even more exciting to us was the precision with which his horse responded to his "yup." The animal would go on to the next house and with an uncanny assurance, range the wheel right alongside the garbage cans. He was never off the mark, and his sense of tolerance was amazingly fine.

When Sam and I came back into the store, Uncle showed us where he wanted us to place the various ingredients with which he would work. Sam was constantly astounded as he tried to make out the long Latin names on the boxes and bottles.

"How do you know what to do with all this?" he asked.

Uncle, who had been bowed over several of the cartons, straightened his back.

"How do you know where to put a shelf in that big thing you built out there?"

"How do I know? I measure! How else would I know?"

"Ah! Exactly. I measure. I've bought the tools for measuring, and I'm going to use them to measure quantities for everything I prepare."

I was beginning to be awed all over again. "You must have a big book in which you keep all these measurements," I said.

He held a light to a cigarette. Sometimes at home I would count the number of cigarette butts in a dish and marvel, because my father smoked only one cigarette after supper. Here he had no dish, so I couldn't know if this cigarette was perhaps his tenth since we had come here.

"I keep them here," he said tapping his temple.

"And you never get them mixed up?"

"Does your mother remember which ingredients go into something she cooks or bakes?"

"But how many things does my mother know how to make? With all these shelves, you'll probably have a hundred different kinds of things."

I had started to say a thousand but had quickly reduced it to a hundred because I thought a thousand would sound silly. Uncle nodded.

"I'll have a lot of different things."

"And you won't get them mixed up?"

"I won't get them mixed up."

"But why don't you write them in a book? That way you wouldn't have to think about it at all."

"That's true, but that way I could also lose everything I know, no? Suppose I should write all the formulas in a book and I should lose the book or somebody should steal the book? To whom would I complain? God would tell me I'm a fool who didn't protect what belonged to him."

"You could put it in a safe."

"If I had a safe."

"Mister," Sam said, "maybe I should hold my mouth because you weren't talking to me, but you have a family. You said you want to make enough money to bring your family over. Don't you want to leave for them everything you know about these drugs?"

Uncle waved at him. "My family! Ach!"

Sam didn't look at my uncle; he looked at me, but I couldn't and wouldn't enlighten him. He continued to tear open packages and set boxes and bottles on the floor and the old wooden table we had found in the back room. For about five minutes nobody spoke, and the only noises we heard were tearing and ripping. Every now and then we were alerted by a glow, when Uncle's newly lighted match brightened the room. I think I looked up each time but, I guess, only as a reflexive response to the light popping off the match end.

That was why all of us heard the peremptory knock on the door. All three turned to look toward the sound, but it must have been Sam's experience that inspired him to go to the door.

Thirteen

We heard him say, "Oh, you're here again."

A voice, a bright, cheerful voice, told him, "Why are you surprised? I told you we'd be here when he moves in. Is he here?"

"He's here."

Then we heard a many-footed approach, and I knew there were at least two. They came to the door and they paused on the threshold as though reluctant to invade a sanctuary.

"Felsher," Sam said, "this is the man I told you about. He came to see you."

Uncle took the cigarette out of his mouth and inclined his head toward the man and his companion, who was so tall his head seemed to disappear over the top of the door.

The shorter man (he was actually no taller than my uncle, which indicated that his design was really short) smiled pleasantly at Uncle and at me.

He said, "I see you talk Yiddish, and that makes me very happy because I don't have much opportunity to talk Yiddish since my father and mother died. My friend behind me doesn't speak Yiddish." (I couldn't see his friend's face, but later, in the larger room, I could see why he spoke no Yiddish.)

"I'd like to come in to talk to you, Felsher," he continued.

Uncle looked out toward the store. "Maybe there would be more room in the store."

The short man turned, said, "Back up, Horse."

My ears almost flipped. Could it be that he had called that big man "horse"? Could it be this big man was responding like an actual horse? There it was. Horse backed away from the door, Sam and the short man turned to follow Horse into the store, and Uncle and I closed the rear rank.

"Felsher," the short man said, "my name is Maurice, but you can call me Moishe. I like that name better."

"I had an uncle whose name was Moishe," Uncle said, and from the way he was caressing his goatee I knew he was not impressed by his Uncle Moishe or by this Moishe.

"My friend's name is Charlie, but we call him 'Ferd,' but only because he's so big. Charlie," he added in English, "say hello to the felsher."

I almost liked Moishe because I appreciated how he had defined "*ferd*," which in Yiddish means "horse" literally but is also used to characterize someone as a fool, a dolt, impossibly inept.

Charlie waved his hand at Uncle and said, "Lo!"

Moishe nodded when these formalities were complete, as if he were clicking off another duty on his list.

"You know, Felsher, I've been waiting a couple of weeks to talk to you. Can we go into the back room where we can talk in private?"

"You have something you want to say to me in private?"

"Yes."

"What do you have to say to me in private?"

"Well, that's what I want to talk about in private."

"You just said that."

"Felsher," Moishe said a little more slowly, now as though he were picking over the words he was planning to use. "I want to talk to you about a way you can make a lot of money, but I want to talk to you about it in private."

"Talk," Uncle said.

Moishe stared at him a moment, perhaps feeling frustrated. Then he looked first at Sam and then at me.

"You want to know who they are," Uncle said. "This is my landlord and this is my sister's boy."

Moishe reviewed what he had seen before when he had looked at Sam and me. Then he said, "I still want to talk to you in private."

"Why?" Uncle asked. I began to sense in this bland one-word question a quiet resistance, as though my uncle did not like being pushed.

"Look, Felsher, I'm trying to do business with you. . . ."

"What kind of business would you want to do with me? Are you a druggist? . . ."

"No, I'm not a druggist, Felsher."

"Then, what—?"

"Ah, you make it so hard for me, and I'm trying to be patient. I'm not pushing you. I just want to make you a business proposition."

"So, make—"

Moishe slapped his palms on his thighs. To this Sam responded, "I'll wait on the street. Maybe he's right, Felsher. If he wants to do business with you and if the business is private, why should the whole street know about it?"

As Sam turned to go, Moishe touched his arm. "You're a smart man. Maybe I'll be able to do business with you, too, someday."

Sam closed the door, and Moishe pointed to me. Uncle shook his head.

"You have a witness, I have a witness."

Moishe stared down at the floor a moment. Evidently Uncle had posed him a problem he had not anticipated. He looked swiftly at me and then at Horse, who stood like some awesome giant to the right of me.

"Children talk," Moishe reminded Uncle.

"Even walls talk."

Moishe shrugged and said, "You're the boss. He's your nephew."

I straightened my shoulders because that statement implied so much that could make me proud. Moishe looked around as if he were deciding what his next move would be, and Horse remained huge and imposing.

"Felsher, you're a businessman and I'm a businessman and we can talk because we have this one thought together. We can hold hands together and make a lot of money."

"You say something interesting because I'm curious to know how we can make money by holding hands."

Moishe looked over at Uncle as though he were sensitive to the overtones in what Uncle had just said. I even thought he was looking for a smile on Uncle's face.

"That isn't too hard to understand, Felsher. You and I have two hands. In each hand we hold something that the other wants. Understand?"

"I understand that you want something from me and you're trying hard to convince me that you have something I would want."

I took a deep breath as I tried to follow Uncle's thinking, and I knew that Moishe had the same problem because he did not answer as swiftly as he had before. Instead, he smiled and shook his head.

"You're going to be a hard customer," he said. "Everybody knows that one thing everybody wants is money."

"I think you're safe in saying that."

"And most people would love to get their hands on a lot of money."

"Um—most people."

"You too?"

"No."

"No?" incredulously.

"No."

"You like to play with words, Felsher. If you're not anxious about making money, why are you opening this store? Why did you buy all this stuff, and why are you breaking your back to put all these ingredients together?"

"A person has to work. Work is important for living. I cannot be idle. I love what I'm going to do, and that's one reason why I bought all these ingredients, and that's why I'm going to work hard to make up all these different packages and bottles."

"Good. I agree with you: work is very important, as you say. But you said that's one reason. What is the other reason?"

"I'm an animal. In order to work I must eat, and I must have a place to sleep and rest. For all these I need money, so my other reason is the money I hope to earn when I sell what I make up here."

"Fine. So you need money to live, but why should you live in a slum? Why should you live in a flat that has a toilet in the hall, that has only cold water, that doesn't have a bath, and that has only gas light? There are houses in Brooklyn which have hot water and bathrooms and electric lights. Why shouldn't you have enough money for all these luxuries?"

"They're good luxuries, and some day I'll have all of these."

"You want to bring over your family as soon as you can and give them all these luxuries?"

"Soon, soon."

"Why do you have to wait, when you can have them as quickly as you wish."

For the first time as this dialogue continued, my uncle stopped.

"You must be pointing at an apple," he said.

"What do you mean?"

"You didn't spend too much time in Hebrew school?"

"I went to Hebrew school until I was bar mitzvah."

"Then you must have heard the story of Adam and Eve and the apple. . . ."

"They weren't supposed to eat the apple?"

"Yes, that's it."

"What's that got to do with what I'm saying to you?"

"You were talking to me like the serpent in the Bible, but you haven't shown me an apple."

"And what does that mean?"

"It means you're trying to persuade me that I should live better than I'm living and you'd like me to live better. That costs money—more money than I have now and more money than I'll make very soon. So you tell me about a place that's better than the Garden of Eden if I'll only bite into the apple, but that's all you tell me."

"I wanted you to know what you will be missing if you don't accept my offer."

"Ah! Your offer. You're beginning to let in a little light."

"All right, I'll let in a lot of light. I told you at the beginning that you have something I need and want and I have something you ought to need and want—you know—a bath, a toilet, electric light. Now we're coming down to it: what do you have that I want and need?" He paused as if to make his point dramatically. "You have alcohol, pure, grain alcohol."

"I have alcohol."

"That's what I want to buy from you."

This statement was blunt enough, so Uncle apparently had to review it slowly and carefully in his mind.

"Now this I have to understand clearly in my own mind. You say you want to buy the alcohol from me. Why can't you buy it where I bought it?"

"They won't sell it to me."

"Why?"

"Because I can't tell them I'm going to use it for medicinal purposes."

"Oh! And for what purpose are you going to use the alcohol?"

"Why do you have to know?"

"Why do you need the alcohol?"

"I'll be honest with you. . . ." He paused and studied Uncle's face for any trace of humor or ridicule. "I don't think I have to tell you that alcohol makes a good base for all liquor—fast. We don't have to wait for distilling, for fermentation. We cut your alcohol, and from one of the five gallon bottles we can make a lot of good liquor after we flavor it."

"If that's such a good idea and you're a good businessman, why don't you go to where I bought this alcohol and tell them what you want to do? Then they'll sell you all the alcohol you need."

I thought this was an eminently logical piece of reasoning and I turned to see how Moishe accepted it. He was staring at Uncle with an odd expression on his face. I could sense that he was puzzled by something Uncle had said; he kept licking his lips as if he had tasted something unpleasant.

"You know, Felsher, I've been trying to make up my mind if you're laughing at me or you just don't know. I think you just don't know. How long are you in this country?"

"Four weeks, five weeks."

"All right, now I understand. I would have to explain to these people why I wanted the alcohol, and I couldn't, because then I would have to pay a tax—a large tax on every bottle of liquor we make and sell. Now do you understand? If we don't pay a tax, we can sell a lot cheaper than the people who pay the tax, and we can make a lot of money. If we make money, you make money."

"I'm trying to remember if we had people like you in Russia. In Russia, only the government made liquor."

"What do you mean people like me?"

"People who break the law."

"Oh, come on, Felsher, everybody breaks a law every time he turns around, there are so many laws."

"Then we live in a terrible world."

"It could be. I don't have to tell you—you're not a child, and you're a bright man. My father used to say, 'God, heaven, and swindle.' I never knew just what he meant, but I can guess. Everybody's waiting just around the corner to swindle you. I don't want to swindle you, so I was open and honest with you. You asked me what I needed the alcohol for and I could have told you a fancy story and maybe you would have believed me, but I tell you the truth and you're ready to throw the whole deal in my face."

"Don't be so upset. I didn't send for you."

"I know you didn't send for me, but this is so perfect. You buy the alcohol, we'll buy the medicines from you so your books can show you need the alcohol, and we'll give you a tremendous profit on the deal."

"But you will be stealing from the government, and I will be stealing from the government along with you."

"Ah! If you knew how much the government collects in taxes from the sale of liquor, you wouldn't get excited about the little nothing we're going to take when we make the liquor ourselves."

"Moishe, it may be hard for you to understand: I don't want to get rich in a big hurry in your way. Do me a favor. I'm not an ambitious man. I'm happy in what I'm doing, the way I'm doing it. Leave me alone. I appreciate the fact that you came to me to offer to make me rich. Just think it was a mistake and look for some other way."

"You don't understand, Felsher. We didn't make a mistake. We knew all about you as soon as you left that store where you made that order. We had it all carefully planned. We didn't just happen to come here. We came here because we knew you would have what we wanted. There is no risk for you. We take all the risks. This is only the beginning, Felsher; soon we'll help you open a really big store on Broadway, and you'll be able to order a lot of alcohol for us. Besides, nobody will know where we're getting this alcohol."

"I will know."

"So! So you'll know. What's the matter—you worried about going to heaven?"

"I have read in the Talmud that a man cannot assemble riches from theft."

Moishe made a wry face. "Tell me I'm a thief, but don't tell me what you read in the Talmud. I heard enough of that stuff to last me a lifetime."

"I didn't know. You're a thief."

"I'm not going to steal from you."

"That isn't a very big consolation for me because the Talmud also says 'a partner in robbery is also a robber.' "

"But I'm not asking you to be my partner."

"You will just pay me to be quiet."

"You're not an easy man to talk to, you know that, Felsher. You twist whatever I say, so I don't know what I said."

" 'He whose hands are smeared in robbery will call upon God but will not be heard.' "

"From the Talmud?"

"From the Talmud."

"Do you believe in God, Felsher?"

"No."

"Then why do you keep throwing God and the Talmud in my face?"

"Because you can't brush off the wisdom of the men who wrote the Talmud."

"But they believed in God."

"I don't believe in their picture of God."

"Then you do believe in God."

"In my own way. I don't believe in a vengeful God. I don't believe God intended for us everything the wise men lay out for us, but their wisdom is true wisdom."

"You know, Felsher, you got me tied in a knot, and I'm not succeeding in what I came here to do; but this is different, because for the first time I'm almost enjoying what I'm doing."

"You never enjoyed stealing before."

"Not like this. Here I come to you to make you a proposition that will make both of us a lot of money, and you tell me what the rabbis said about stealing three thousand years ago. And who said anything about stealing? Usually when I come into some place and make a proposition, the person understands he'd better or else."

"Let me tell you another story, my friend."

"From the Talmud?"

"From the Talmud."

"You know, my big friend is beginning to wonder why I haven't told him to break up your store and throw a couple of chairs through that big window you have out in front. . . ."

My uncle and I glanced at the big friend, who had folded his monstrous arms across his enormous chest and he had begun to rock on his heels, I thought, a little impatiently. I knew he didn't understand Yiddish and I suspected he was wondering why Moishe was talking so amiably to someone who was foiling his project.

"Don't threaten me, my friend," Uncle said, "because I have only a few worldly goods and days to lose. You have a great deal more to lose. Listen to this: in a village in one part of Palestine there was an inn. The innkeeper had partners who lived a little distance from town. Every morning the innkeeper would wake his guests very early, show them the best road, and advise them to set out immediately so they would not be oppressed by the heat of the day. His guests were delighted with their kind host. They followed him down a dark road, where they were held up and robbed by the innkeeper's partners. Once a rabbi Meir stayed overnight at the inn. He rode a splendid animal and appeared well-to-do, and the landlord rubbed his hands in gleeful anticipation.

"However, when he offered to go with this guest before dawn, the rabbi said he had to wait for his brother Kitov. When the sun rose, the innkeeper came out to see if the guest's brother had come but found instead that the rabbi had mounted his ass. He said, 'Where's your brother, Kitov?' and the rabbi said, 'The light of day. It is written: "And God saw the light, Ki-tov: it is *good.*" ' "

"Felsher, I think you were surprised by the deal I offered you."

"If you think I haven't seen thievery and swindle before . . ."

"I don't want you to give me an answer right away—"

"Oh, I can give you an answer right away."

"No, I don't want an answer from you now. I'll be back."

"I'm not an innkeeper."

"Innkeepers are all poor slobs."

"There must be other places and other people who will welcome what you asked me to do. . . ."

"Felsher, I'm not interested in other people. I want to do business with you."

"You'll have to wait."

"We'll wait. We're very patient people, but don't make us wait too long."

"Just remember, I'm not opening this business to help you in what you are planning to do. I'm going to make up medicinal preparations and I'm going to sell them."

"Whether you like it or not, we're partners. I've just declared it."

"I will not be your innkeeper."

Moishe held out his hand and my uncle shook it almost warmly. I was surprised because in my thinking an enemy, a declared enemy, was somebody you hated, certainly not anyone whose hand you shook.

"Good-by, Felsher," Moishe said. "I'll be back in about a week, after you've had time to set yourself up nicely here. You have a good answer for me so we can start doing business fast together. Don't forget, I'm offering you a good life with a bathroom in your flat."

"I don't want to be a partner in your robbery."

"Good-by, Felsher." Moishe waved to him, clucked at me, and said to the colossus at his side, "Let's go."

When they had closed the door, I stared after it, but when I turned around, I saw that Uncle had already begun to busy himself with a design of his own.

I said, "He wants you to steal from the government, doesn't he?"

"Yes."

"Are you going to do what he wants you to do?"

"No."

"Because you're afraid you'll go to jail?"

He was bowed over what he was doing, and for a moment I wondered if he had heard me or if I should repeat what I had said. Then he straightened up and turned to me.

"I'm not afraid to go to jail," he said. "There is something more important in a man's life than being afraid to go to jail. A man can live with being in jail or with having been in jail, but it isn't easy to live with the thought that you've been a thief. Animals steal from each other and never think that it isn't right, but when animals steal, they steal because they are hungry. If I were so hungry, or if my family were so hungry that we had to steal, I would beg, because we are taught that it is holy to give charity. It is sinful to steal: not only against God but against yourself."

I wanted to ask other questions because I had not completely grasped or understood the relationship between my uncle and the alcohol Moishe wanted. The element I did not hitch onto involved the taxes Moishe would normally pay and wanted to avoid. I started to ask this question as the door opened. I think both of us responded nervously to the creak of the hinges. We were relieved when Sam's big bulk spread over the threshold.

"They went?" he asked.

"They went," Uncle said.

Sam edged forward into the room, pausing on the lintel separating the store from the back room. He leaned confidentially on the jamb.

"I wouldn't trust those fellows," he said. "I don't know if you know what a gangster is, but these fellows look like gangsters to me. . . ."

"Like the Black Hand?" I asked, and my eyes opened wide.

"Nah, there are no Jews in the Black Hand. This little guy is a smart little gangster, and he carries the big guy around with him for protection."

Uncle nodded as I listened breathlessly for what else he might reveal. I was already wondering how much of the dialogue I would dare repeat to Muttel and the other fellows.

"What did they want?" Sam asked.

As the question came to him Uncle reacted as he had to what I had asked him a few minutes earlier.

"They are thieves," he said finally.

"They wanted to steal from you?"

Sam was outraged. He even prodded himself away from the door as if he were preparing to do battle.

"If they wanted to steal from me," Uncle said, "I would laugh at them. What can they steal from me?"

"Then what?"

Uncle told him, and I watched Sam's face as Uncle outlined the grand scheme to him. At first his eyes widened, then slowly they narrowed.

"Pigs!" he said. "Why don't you go to the police?"

Uncle shook his head. "I'm green in this country. For me to start complaining about an American citizen a month after I come here is not good. What can I prove? He'll deny he ever talked to me."

"The police would know what to tell you. I don't."

"I don't need the police to ask questions about what I'm doing here."

"Do you have anything to be concerned about in what you're doing here?"

"No, of course not."

"So?"

"So, if I have to explain to a man who knows and understands what I'm doing here, there will be no trouble, but if I try to explain to a policeman and he doesn't understand what I'm saying—"

"Then you're going to let that man swindle you?"

"No!"

"Well, how will you stop him?"

"My God will show me the way. I have an agreement with

my God. Usually, I don't bother Him and He doesn't bother me. We get along well."

"But if your God *and* you need help, you let me know."

"What will you do?"

"What will I do? Have you ever noticed that God helps the man with the biggest fists?"

Actually, I had not noticed his hands before, but when he made his right hand into a fist and held it up and when he straightened his big back to its full height, Sam was something spectacular, awesome.

Uncle and I went home shortly after this conversation. We told our story to my family, and they sat through the evening meal and listened breathlessly.

"What are you going to do?" my mother asked.

Uncle laughed. "What can I do? I'm going to do nothing."

"But they'll be back."

"They'll be back. I can't do anything about that."

"But they'll want that alcohol. What will you say to them?"

"I'll say what I said before. I'm not going to break the law because I have too much to look forward to in America."

A kind of sodden gloom permeated the air of the room after that. Everybody was reading or doing homework, and the silence was almost eerie.

At last, when I had finished my homework and I returned to reading, Mother poured tea for the adults. Once more, this ritual of steady drinking continued until my father got up and moved toward the bedroom. Then my mother collected the glasses and saucers to wash and I rolled out my folding bed, which I would shortly open in the kitchen.

Fourteen

Uncle was up early the next day. He washed at the kitchen sink, then retired to the front room to shave with his long straight razor. I had never seen a straight razor in my home. Before the invention of the safety razor, men bought shaving mugs and left them with a barber. Every barber kept his customers' mugs on long shelves in the barbershop, and when the men came for their shaves he would lather each one from his own mug. My father went to the barber twice, sometimes three times a week and came home perfumed, smelling exotically of some dusky, murky face powder. About once a month I went with him to have my hair cut. I always came away with horrid little bits of shorn hair clinging irritatingly to my neck and face, because the barber had doused every part of my head with a sticky ointment that gave off an exciting smell so different from the smells I normally inhaled at home, in the hall, and at school. My hair, stiff as concrete, was planked against my skull by that ointment, but I didn't mind because I was the only one in my class whose hair was curly and unruly.

Uncle told us he would work all day in the store making one preparation at a time. I asked him how he would tell one preparation from another on the shelves. Uncle smiled and said he would know, that it would be as easy for him to know his preparations as it is for a father to know his own children. But, I persisted, what if Uncle wasn't in the shop and I was there and a woman came in to ask for a preparation to relieve her corns? How would I know?

I think Uncle looked a little confused for the first time.

"I should have labels, shouldn't I?"

"How can you be without labels?" my father asked. "Everything in this country has a label, and it's good that way."

Uncle was convinced, and there was no further talk about labels. I asked him if he wanted me to peddle the rest of his dress collars on Seigel Street, but he told me not to be concerned about them. He could return them to his cousin.

When Muttel and Sam asked questions the next day about Uncle's venture, I was unhappy because my lips had to be sealed about our two visitors. I recited for them just what we did after they left and outlined for them the magnitude of Uncle's undertaking. I was amazed that they asked only one question: did I think my uncle would become a rich man? Of course, I told them I was certain my uncle would quickly make his fortune there and would open other stores around the city and around the country, where they would make and sell preparations according to his formulas.

"How is it that your uncle can make medicines when only a druggist is allowed to do it?" Sam asked.

"I don't know," I said, "but he's allowed to because he knows what he's doing."

"Well, my father said if anybody goes to him instead of a doctor, he's a shithead."

"Well, your father don't know everything." Muttel rushed in to defend me. "His uncle knows more than your father, and if I get sick I'm gonna use his medicine."

"Well, my father said he'll bet your uncle a million dollars he can't cure consumption. My uncle had consumption, and the doctors couldn't do nothin' for him and he used to drink hot milk all day, and nothing helped him. One day he just croaked."

"So what," Muttel said. "I once had an aunt who died because she had too many babies."

"How can you have too many babies?" Sam snorted. "My grandmother had sixteen babies, and she had two baby carriages —you know, when the baby isn't born and it's born dead—"

"Ah, you're talkin' through your hat. What do you know about babies? How many brothers and sisters you got anyway?"

"Wait, I got to count. Six—no, seven. One's married, and I always forget about him. But that don't mean we don't know nothin' about medicines. Once when my father wanted to get something for his corns he went to a druggist, and the druggist gave him something that was no good, and my father went back to that druggist and he said, 'If you don't give me my money back I'll throw this crap in your face,' and the druggist gave him his money back."

"Well," I said with deep dignity in my voice, "nobody's going to throw any medicine in my uncle's face, because he's better than a druggist. He's a felsher."

That afternoon when I came to the store, I found that Uncle had filled many bottles of three varieties, which he had spaced generously on the shelves to avoid confusion. I asked him how I could help, and he assigned me to hold the funnel for him as he poured a liquid preparation from a large beaker. I could see that my two hands were necessary so that he could concentrate his two hands on the beaker. This reduced his effort and the time he would have to spend pouring into the beaker, which previously he had to support with one hand.

Then I carried the bottles into the store and, at his direction, placed them with others of the same contents. This, of course, troubled me, and I returned to the question I had asked yesterday. Uncle stood with me in front of the shelves and he pointed to each row of bottles.

"This is for the hair, and over here, these bottles are to bathe the eyes, and these bottles are for the skin."

I stared at them as I tried to associate a color with a word. One liquid was white, another green, and the third a deep amber. I went back to the room and tore three narrow strips from the wrapping paper we had not yet disposed of. Then, on each strip I wrote one word: "skin," "eyes," or "hair." I laid one of these labels on every shelf, creasing it enough so I could set two bottles on each strip. Then I called my uncle. When he read what I had inscribed on the papers, he smiled that soft, gentle, proud smile I was beginning to know—the same patient smile he had turned on Moishe and his big guard.

"Now I will never get lost among my bottles," he said, and I knew he was not patronizing me. "Make more for my other preparations."

I was very happy and I was very proud, because for the hour that followed, he dictated to me the names he wanted me to print on the narrow strips of wrapping paper. There were many, but I did them all before we went home.

I don't know why I felt as I did—Moishe and his guard were certainly trouble for my uncle—but somehow I rather looked forward to their coming the next day. I didn't talk about them to my uncle, but I suspect he too wondered if they would appear on our threshold. We worked so diligently that afternoon that by five o'clock we had filled every bottle my uncle had bought and each little jar into which he had prodded an assortment of salves.

We stood them up on the shelves and we labeled each item, writing on the gummed labels Uncle had bought from a stationer on Graham Avenue. While I stood in the store staring bemused at the bottles, wondering if I would ever get to know them all by their contents, I heard my uncle splashing around in the sink and I knew he was washing up to go home. I, too, went to the back of the store, because my fingers were gummy and sooty and I wanted to remove that icky feeling.

As he dried his hands and he watched me slap the soap around to churn up a lather, he said, "You're a good boy, and if I can't give you a reward for everything you've done for me, I'll talk to my God for you. He'll listen to me."

I permitted myself to look a little askance at him because I thought he was talking a little lightly about the God my father worshipped—the only God I knew—who was not addressed so readily and so out of hand. Yet how could I argue with this man, whose tone was so serious and whose attitude was so sincere.

"I don't need anything, Uncle," I said.

"Wait, you'll yet see."

I didn't retreat from this assurance but just let it glide by me. I dried my hands and went to the door, thinking to open it to the light in the little vestibule so Uncle could turn off the lights in the back room and in the store.

Sam stood in the tiny foyer, preempting every inch of its space.

Startled by his presence, I said "oh," as though I had opened the door on an apparition.

He laughed. "What are you afraid of? Devils? I was just coming in when you opened the door."

I retreated from the door and Uncle said, "Come in, come in. We were just getting ready to go home."

Sam almost laid his head on his right shoulder to get an overview of what Uncle and I had wrought in the past few days. He clucked his teeth and walked toward the shelves, leaning forward to read the inscriptions on the labels.

"Are these for sale?" he asked.

"Of course."

"Then give me this one."

He reached for a bottle whose contents were amber colored.

"That is for the skin," Uncle told him.

"How much?"

"Twenty-five cents."

Sam stared at him. "This is how you'll make a living? Twenty-five cents! For twenty-five cents you can't fill up that bottle with piss. You got to charge for what's in the bottle, the bottle, and your time. You're selling this for fifty cents."

"Fifty cents is a lot of money, Sam."

"A woman who pays you fifty cents will be convinced this bottle will help her skin. For twenty-five cents she'll think she's getting piss. She won't eat for a couple of days, and she'll buy a little meat, but she'll be here. And if she thinks it helped her, and if it has a good smell, she'll tell all her yenteh friends, and you won't have enough bottles to take care of all your customers."

Uncle stared at Sam, then at his bottles, and I suspected that Sam had suddenly enveloped him in doubt and uncertainty, not about what he was ladling into the bottles, but about his sense of values in this whole venture.

"Then am I being honest," he asked, "if I sell something for so much to poor women and men who need it so badly? You say I charge them a little if I ask twenty-five cents, but the bottle costs me less than a penny, and the drugs I put into the bottle cost about two or three cents. How can I ask more than twenty-five cents for such a bottle?"

"Don't ask me how you can. You *must* charge more, because the women will think you're selling drek, because for twenty-five cents, they'll say, you can only afford to package drek."

"Is everything in America such a swindle?" My uncle's voice carried an overtone of sadness.

"Swindle! *Ho! Ho!* You talk like a child. This is business, good business."

"Then maybe I'm not a good businessman."

"A good businessman worries only about making a good profit."

"Then maybe I'm not a good businessman. People are important to me, and if a woman tells me she doesn't have the money for one of my preparations, I'll have to give it to her."

Sam stared at Uncle. He couldn't believe what he had heard. Then he turned to look at me as though he needed confirmation from me. I stared blandly back because in the first place I did not want him to feel I agreed with him and in the second place because I sensed my uncle had made a rather startling pronouncement. So Sam just shrugged his shoulders as if to say this was my uncle's business and he could run it however he pleased without interference from him.

Fifteen

Only one fact disturbed me. If I would go regularly to Uncle's store, I would have to give up the one activity which until a month ago had meant more to me than any other. I would have no time for reading in Mrs. Fried's front room and I would have even less time for afternoon and weekend excursions to the the library. I regretted this loss but felt compensated by the excitement of the new adventure in Uncle's store.

When I got home the following afternoon, I buttered a big roll and told my mother I was going to the store and hurried down Manhattan Avenue.

There were some changes in the store and in the back room. On the shelves Uncle Herschel had pasted names for the preparations, carefully lettered in Russian. I was intrigued and charmed by the odd configurations, and, for almost a half hour, Uncle patiently read them to me and corrected my pronunciation of these Russian words while I tried to memorize them. I saw similarities between the lettering and the words, and after Uncle left me I went over the words until I thought I knew them.

In the back, Uncle had effected an order that had not been there the day before. From my reading, I reflected that what I saw here might be characterized as shipshape. Everything had a place of its own on the shelves—all jars, and bottles, and boxes, funnels and measuring devices. Nothing anywhere on the floor—I rejoiced in the neatness I saw around me. On the solitary chair sat a Hebrew volume with a bookmark in its middle. I tried to read it but gave up immediately because there were no markings in the text for vowel sounds.

"Did you have any customers today?" I asked.

"If you mean did I sell anything, the answer is no, but at least ten people came in to sniff the air and to ask what I was selling. That was good because these ten will talk. Perhaps others will come in tomorrow, and soon the curious ones will come in to buy."

"Maybe even Doctor Padilsky."

"Maybe."

He smiled, and I thought how happy that would make him. Looking around for something to do, I decided, I'll sweep the store.

Uncle pointed to the broom that stood in the corner, and I wrestled it around the store, hunting down every speck in every recessed area until I had assembled a pitiably tiny heap. I hustled the pile toward the door, out into the vestibule and onto the top step of the stoop. I brought the broom back and from the backswing came around in a huge arc. I dispersed the dust, but as I completed my follow-through, someone said, "Whoa, boy. That ain't the way to meet customers."

I looked up. Moishe and his huge retainer stood three or four feet from the stoop, whence they had retreated as I began my downward sweep. I stared at them and thought, More trouble for my uncle. Customers, I sneered inwardly, customers!

"Is your uncle in there?"

I wanted to lie to him, but I knew he would say he'd wait and come into the store. I hated him and could not talk because I was afraid I would say what was on my mind, so I just moved aside.

Moishe and his large shadow, Ferd, mounted the short step into the store, but I ran on ahead of them and exploded into the back room.

"Those men are here again," I exclaimed.

Uncle was not agitated. He raised his head from the Hebrew text he was reading, unclipped the glasses from the bridge of his nose, stuffed them into his vest pocket and got up, unperturbed, to greet what I would call unwelcome guests.

Moishe came forward, his hand extended cordially. Uncle took his hand and shook it with surprising friendliness. I wondered if that act was part of being an adult, because I didn't feel quite the way Uncle did. If I disliked someone, I made no pretense about it; I evaded him, ignored him, told him very plainly I did not like him. I couldn't say right off how my uncle felt about this character and his cyclops, but I suspected there was no affection in that handshake. I compared it in my mind to the handshake of two men in a boxing ring just before they try to knock each other's brains out.

Moishe said, "I didn't know if I should call you Rabbi or Doctor."

My uncle smiled almost as though he were talking to some precocious child who had just said something cute but impertinent.

"I'm not a rabbi and I'm not a doctor."

"It doesn't matter." He looked around at the shelves. "Ah, you're doing fine things with your store. I'll be happy to be associated with you."

Again my uncle smiled, but this time he shook his head.

"Why do you shake your head?"

"Because you have a short memory, because you don't remember what I said to you the last time you were here."

"Oh, I remember. That's why I'm here–to give you a chance to forget what you told me or to change your mind."

"You're like a child, my friend. I have no intention of changing my mind."

"Maybe I ought to go over this with you again. You don't seem to understand what a wonderful thing this would be for a man who has no money, who just came over, who wants to bring his family over, who wants the best for himself and his family."

"Don't waste your time and my time. I know all your arguments. I've thought about them, and my answer is still the same: I'm a guest in this country, and for me to steal from my host goes against everything I know and everything I've learned and everything I feel. The Talmud asks, 'How can a man bless God over bread which he has made from stolen flour?' "

"Oh, come on! The whole world lives by it? You think the big wheelers and dealers are pure and holy? You think the big merchants don't steal from each other, from the poor slobs who work for them? You know how many hours a day a man works? Twelve hours, and what does he get for it? Bubkiss! That's what he gets. He makes just enough so he can come to work the next day. Is God looking out for those poor slobs! Like hell He is. What's it gonna get those slobs? A place in Gahn Eden? Let them work for it. I want my Gahn Eden right here, while I'm still alive—"

"I'm not concerned with Gahn Eden."

"Then what? Why are you so stubborn about such a little thing? All you have to do is buy the alcohol—that's all. We'll take care of everything else."

My friend, even if I wanted to steal from the country in which I'm now a guest, I would not ally myself with you."

Moishe looked almost hurt. "Why do you say anything like that?" he demanded. "After all, I came to you with this proposition. Why should you be afraid of me, if that's what's bothering you?"

"What I'm saying is that you should leave me in peace. I don't want to become your partner because I don't want to steal from America. Even if I should want to, I wouldn't need partners—"

"Oh, but you *do* need partners. How could you explain buying so much alcohol?"

"I'm not buying so much alcohol. I'm buying only what I need."

"You're a very stubborn man, you know that, don't you?"

"When there's something worthwhile to be stubborn about, then being stubborn is a virtue."

"You know, Felsher, I'm a practical guy. When you talk about virtues and the Talmud, I get lost. I ain't got the knowledge or the patience to listen to you and try to follow you."

"Then why don't you go away and leave me in peace? I'm trying to start a little business here—"

"That's the trouble, you see. You think little. You *are* little, but you won't let us show you how to become big and rich. Why, you can open branch stores, and pretty soon we'll show you how to open a factory."

"All this so you can get my alcohol?"

"All this so we can get your alcohol. Even if you can't see how much we can make out of this together, we can."

"Moishe, don't think I'm not grateful to you, but you don't seem to understand my problem. I don't want to be rich. I have only one thought in mind, and that thought does not include you. So again I say to you, thank you very much. I don't want to be your partner. I don't want to become a rich thief. Please go away."

"We can't go away this way, Felsher."

"Then how can you go away?"

"Only if I have an agreement with you."

"No."

"I'm sorry you're saying that, because you're a nice man and I like you."

"You know, strangely enough, I like you too."

"We like each other, and you won't let me take back an agreement to my people."

"I'm sorry."

"You don't know how sorry I am, because we'll have to do things here you won't like."

Uncle stared quietly at Moishe for so long that the gangster began to stir a little nervously. "I've lived through pogroms before," Uncle said.

This dialogue disturbed me because I heard very plainly a threat in Moishe's words and in his tone. I was very far from the door—practically on the other side of the room—and as I measured the distance, I knew I would have to get by both Moishe and the enormous Ferd. I could run for the door so I could get help from the police, from a passerby, or from Sam. I started to edge around the side of the room, but my movement was not unnoticed. Moishe pointed a finger at me.

"Stay there!" he ordered. Then he turned to Uncle. "I want to tell you very quickly, Felsher. We operate on this thought: what we can't control, we destroy. If I give my partner the word, he'll smash every bottle on your shelves, and you won't be able to start again because we'll be back over and over until you give in and join us."

"If you destroy me and my store, what will you gain from it?"

"Only this: whatever we need, we control. We can't let anybody stand in our way when we run our business. This is our policy."

Uncle turned and looked sadly and speculatively at rows and rows of filled bottles, which represented to him a sort of down payment on his destiny, on his fate and the fate of his whole family. I watched him and I thought for the first time, Why doesn't he give in? He could even refuse to take the money for the alcohol to live with his conscience. To give up all this which he had materialized from his many years of experience was wrong, foolhardy.

"Don't let them smash all these bottles, Uncle," I said.

Everybody turned to look at me, and I was a little shaken by my temerity. However, because I had made my own opening, I raced in almost headlong.

"Give them what they want," I urged, "otherwise they'll smash all these bottles, and you spent so much time mixing all that stuff . . ."

Moishe beamed at me, and even the monster at his right managed to relax his tight lips.

"You see," Moishe said, "that's a smart boy. He's an American, and he knows the way Americans do business when they have to."

Uncle wasn't listening to Moishe. He took a cigarette, held a light to it and took a long, long drag on it. It seemed long seconds before some of the smoke flowed from his nostrils. He reached up to his goatee and smoothed it down. I waited impatiently for him to say he would agree to the gangster's proposition.

"Why do you think I should give them the alcohol?" he asked me.

"Because," I poured in vehemently, "you worked so hard on those bottles, and you want to bring your family over. You don't have to do everything he says. If he wants the alcohol, give it to him, but you don't have to take the money. Please, Uncle, don't let them smash all these bottles. Then everything will be gone, and what will you be able to do?"

"You see!" Moishe exclaimed, and there was a hateful overtone in his voice. "You see! This kid's got a good head on his shoulders. Why don't you listen to him? Why don't you follow the kid's advice?"

Uncle continued to look down at me; the smile on his face did not recede. It was almost as though he were talking to me about whether we should go home for an early supper or stay in the store for another hour.

"Did you listen to what I said to this man from the Talmud?"

"Yes, I heard you, Uncle, but I think even those rabbis would tell you to sell him the alcohol so you could save the store."

Uncle shook his head and the look on his face was sad, as if he were disappointed in me, or possibly in himself because he had failed to convey to us the essential meaning of honesty. He turned to Moishe.

"You're a Jew, so I don't have to tell you the meaning of a pogrom. If you have it in your heart to make a pogrom on another Jew, I'm not strong enough to stop you."

Moishe said, "Is that your last word?"

"That's my last word."

Sixteen

I sidled over to the door of the back room because I remembered my uncle's cane. I seized it as I heard a vast crashing of glass as the mastodon flung handfuls of bottles to the floor. I concealed the stick behind me and I raced toward the vast back of the despoiler and slammed the head of the stick as hard as I could on this broad target. It must have stung him, because he was moved to speak for only the second time in as many visits.

"You son of a bitch!" Ferd hollered at me.

I retreated a step or two and got ready to flail at him again. This time I wanted to get at his head, at his face. I was suddenly seized by a righteous fury. Perhaps my uncle's persistent reference to this transaction as a pogrom had infuriated me. I resented the constant implication that the descendants of the Maccabees would not fight back. I don't know what had happened to my uncle. I knew I had left him behind me as I had rushed by him on my first attack. Now the huge Ferd advanced, intending to take the stick from me. I watched him warily. I was not afraid. I wanted only to hurt this animal.

But I had forgotten about Moishe. He slipped up behind me and grabbed the stick.

"Gimme it!" Ferd shouted. "I'll bash his head in!"

Then I heard my uncle behind me holler "*Schmah Yizroel!*" I heard a big splash. I spun around and I saw that the splash was into Moishe's face. He screamed with a sudden agony, dropped the stick and he grabbed his face.

"My eyes, my eyes!" he screamed.

I turned away from him for one second. Uncle Herschel was standing on the threshold of the back room. In his hand was a beaker, which he had just emptied into Moishe's face, but on his face was an expression I had never seen there before. There was fury in it, and righteousness, and the kind of fear a man has only of God. I guess I had imagined this last because of what he had hollered as he flung the liquid into Moishe's face.

"My eyes, my eyes," Moishe moaned as he began to stagger blindly around the room. Ferd caught him and held him. Moishe shivered in the giant's arms. Then I heard the gurgling sound of a liquid being poured, and I knew my uncle had gone for a refill of that destructive compound.

Ferd had propped Moishe up against the wall, but his eyes had not left Uncle and me for a second. We had disposed of one—the smaller monster—but now the super avalanche was bearing down on us, and I began to wonder how we would fare against this renewed menace. I glanced at Uncle Herschel. His lips were compressed, but he was steady and calm; the hand that held the full beaker did not shake.

e watched Ferd take a huge bandana from his pocket and fold ı carefully. "I'm gonna take you apart first. Then I'm gonna take this stinkin' store apart," he growled.

He held the folded bandana in his left hand, ready to protect his eyes from Uncle's burning liquid. Ferd advanced slowly upon us. He was so intent upon vengeance that he did not see or hear the welcome apparition at the door.

Sam stood there for about two seconds, appraising the situation, understanding the impasse and deciding how he could best help us. Then he covered the distance to Ferd so swiftly that the big lackey did not know what had seized him by the collar and pants. He yelled, "Leggo, leggo, you bastard," as he flung the bandana from his left hand and fought to twist out of Sam's strong grip. But in five seconds Sam had propelled him furiously toward the big storefront window.

By this time the monster understood Sam's intent, and he tried to brake the impetus with his heels; but his own momentum impelled by Sam's huge body was too much to stop. Two steps from the window Ferd screamed, "No, no, you bastard," but this appeal did not inhibit Sam's mighty forward thrust. In the last few steps Sam heaved that furiously racing body at the shop window. Ferd was quite irresistible. He took the glass with him as he flew through to the sidewalk.

Then followed one long moment of silence. Uncle and I stared at Sam, marveling at the heroic fury of his onslaught on that Philistine, and the incredible strength in those carpenter's arms. He clapped his hands as if to scatter the dust of battle and then moved toward the shattered window to look at the wrecked gladiator. A good crowd had begun to gather to gape at the huge man lying senseless on the sidewalk. Uncle Herschel and I walked with Sam to the window; I was awed by the sight. That man did not stir.

"Is he dead?" I asked.

"I'll look," Uncle said and as I turned to him he gave me the two beakers he had been holding. I wondered about the two beakers, but it did not occur to me to ask at that moment. We watched Uncle Herschel squeeze through the crowd and kneel beside the fallen Ferd. For about ten seconds he held Ferd's wrist; then he laid it down and came back into the store.

"He'll be all right," he told us. "He was stunned by the fall."

Then we heard Moishe stir behind us. We had forgotten all about him.

"What did you do to him?" Moishe asked softly.

Uncle looked at Sam and said, "He fell through the front window."

"Fell?" There was an unspeakable overtone of bitterness in his voice. "Sounded more like he got thrown through that window."

"Thrown? Who could throw such a big man through the window?"

"I don't know. You blinded me. How could you do such a thing to me? I'm a Jew, and you're a Jew. How could you blind me?"

"Your eyes were no good to you. Now you see that one Jew shouldn't hurt another Jew, that one human being shouldn't hurt another human being. But with your eyes open you were willing that my bread and butter should be torn from my mouth, that I should never see my family again. All this because you wanted to make more money."

"Yes, but you made me blind. How can you compare the two?"

"And your partner is half dead."

"We didn't want to harm you or your boy. You made us."

"That wasn't it. You fought an old man and a young boy—two big strong men. You should have known I would fight back with what I knew best—chemicals."

"For God's sake, that's what makes it unfair! You acted like you were gonna fall on your face, like you had no fight in you."

Uncle smiled at the querulous tone in Moishe's voice, and I was still angry enough to want to bash him over the head with Uncle's walking stick. I couldn't relate to this calm conversation with a man who only minutes ago had tried so hard to do us in. An enemy is an enemy—someone to be fought into the ground.

"You had no pity on us," Uncle said mildly.

"Mister," Moishe exclaimed almost petulantly, "you weren't a man to me. This is a business deal I had to finish. You stood in the way, and we had to get you out of the way."

"So now you're blind."

"Goddamn it! Don't keep telling me that, and don't think for one minute my people will let you forget this!"

"But what will they do with you—a helpless blind man? They'll probably discard you like a torn bag."

"That happened only because I let you talk and talk the way

you're doing now. That's why you were able to hold on for so long and you were able to get that acid to throw in my face. Don't worry about me, Mr. Felsher. I got friends, and when they hear what you did to me, they'll come here and take this place apart."

"Ah," Sam suddenly pitched in, "why don't you get the police in here and arrest these two? They can get ten years for what they tried to do."

"Who is that?" Moishe demanded. "Another guy who talks big—"

"Shut up, you little snot, before I throw you on top of your friend out there on the sidewalk! You're a disgrace to our people, and if the felsher made you blind it serves you right. Now don't say another word or I'll make you dead!"

"No police," Uncle said. "I couldn't stand the shame of bearing witness against another Jew for a crime like this. Moishe, you didn't expect this blindness?"

"Oh, what a stinkin' question that is!"

"And blind, you are of no value to your present employers."

Moishe didn't answer.

"If it could happen, what would it be worth to you to have your eyesight restored?"

"Ah, to hell with you with your questions!"

"You're not interested in seeing again?"

"I say shut up, damn you!"

"You haven't answered my question, Moishe."

"And I ain't gonna answer your damn question. Go ahead, gloat. You got the upper hand now. You're big now, and I don't know what you did with my partner. But you can bet I'll leave here, and when I come back things are gonna be different."

"You stupid thing!" Sam exclaimed, and his huge hand tightened on Moishe's collar. "You came into this store to ask this good man to break the law. He wouldn't do it, so you threatened him and you started to break up his store. He threw something in your face and made you blind, and I threw your partner through the store window. If the felsher won't make a complaint against you, I will. He's a good man. I'm a peasant who owns this property. I'm going to the station house to tell them what happened and make a complaint against you. Go out." He waved to me. "Callahan should be someplace on the avenue. Bring him back here."

"Yeah, I ain't afraid of your arrest. I'll be out on bail in an hour," Moishe snarled.

"Not if we swear what you wanted to do here."

"Moishe," Uncle said, "I think you have suffered enough for your wrong thinking. Come with me. I'll relieve your blindness."

I had not run for Callahan as Sam had instructed because Uncle Herschel had said he did not wish to make a complaint against those two with the police. Now, however, I was even more intrigued by his invitation to Moishe, so I hurried behind Moishe and Sam as they walked into the back room.

Uncle turned on the water. "Splash the water into your eyes," he said. "As much water as you can get into your hands."

Moishe splashed and splashed great handfuls of water into his eyes, his actions frantic with hope. Uncle watched but he did not add to the first instruction. After a few minutes Moishe raised his head and opened his eyes. For a moment, his eyes were fixed upon the wall.

"I can see," he whispered.

"Oh, you'll see," Uncle told him. "I had to blind you fast so you wouldn't hurt my nephew or me. I was going to do the same for your friend—"

"Yeah, Felsher," Sam suddenly demanded, "I remember now, you had two of those glass things in your hands after I threw that guy out. Why two?"

"I can see," Moishe whispered again, as though he could not believe the miracle.

Uncle Herschel said, "When I ran back for more of the chemical, I knew that big man would be prepared for me and he could easily cover his eyes for one shot, but he would have to bring his hands away from his eyes to see where I was and grab me. That's what the second beaker was for."

I glanced swiftly at Sam's face to see how he was affected by Uncle's strategy. He was grinning, and I knew that he had packed into that grin a mass of appreciation and praise. My heart was full. I was delighted and I could think only how I would phrase this story for Muttel the next day.

Uncle watched Moishe as his stooped back gradually straightened. His dripping hands were still at his eyes, which he opened and closed over and over again.

"Do you owe me anything?" Uncle Herschel asked him.

Moishe stood up now and, in response to Uncle's question, turned to face him.

"What do I owe you? You made me blind, and now you made me see."

"I could have left you blind."

"Not a guy like you. You're too deep in the Torah and the Talmud."

"Will you take your friend and go away?"

"I don't know, Felsher. I take orders; I don't give them. And the guy who gives me my orders never heard of the Talmud."

"Then he must have heard of the police," Sam said.

Moishe glared at him. "You don't scare me, mister. We're bigger than you are, and don't you forget it. You can go to sleep one night and find your house burned down to the ground."

"Listen, both of you. What have we got to fight about? Moishe, tell your master I'll never give in to his demand. I'm not righteous. I just want to be left alone to make a small living from what I can do best."

"You're a very stubborn man."

"That too."

Moishe walked by Uncle Herschel and Sam to the front of the store. He looked out for a long time.

"Look at that big ox," he said, and, although we knew he was talking to himself, we went to look with him.

The big ox was on his hands and knees, his head drooping as though he could not yet raise it. He shook it over and over. The people who had come around him gaped at him and from him to the huge hole in the store window. Ferd's head remained bowed over his hands, not because he was undecided what to do, but because he could not do it.

"How do you like him?" Moishe asked. "My stinkin' body-guard that's supposed to protect me! Look at him. Big, he is, but stupid, he is too."

"This wasn't your day," Sam said mildly.

Moishe looked at him, sniffed and shook his head. Then he reached down for his expensive pearl-colored fedora. He slapped it against his thigh and, without another word or even a glance at us, tramped out of the room.

He paused a moment when he got to his partner.

"C'mon, let's get out of here," he said, and I heard a deep sneer, almost a snarl, in his voice. The big man shook his head; he was clearly hurt. He made no attempt to raise himself from the ground.

"C'mon, cut out monkeyin' around!" Moishe demanded harshly.

He leaned over and tried to heft him to his feet, but Moishe could no more stir Ferd than a flea could raise a dog.

"All right, you gonna spend the night here? What'll we tell a cop if he comes along and sees you in all that glass?"

Neither concern nor fear could motivate this horse to his feet.

"I'll be right back," Sam said.

I watched Sam push Moishe gently aside, clutch the giant around the chest and elevate him slowly to his feet. For a moment Ferd rocked on his heels and ran his hands over his eyes. Sam propped him up but did not release him.

"What hit me?" he asked. The words seemed to roll out of his mouth.

"Come, let's go home," Uncle said. "Your mother will be wondering what happened to us."

As we walked slowly down Manhattan Avenue, I tried to attune my steps to the rhythmic tapping of his stick. I thought he felt strong and proud today, because he had asserted himself over the two ruthless men in a way I had felt was completely unlikely for him. Now as I review it, what more natural weapon could Uncle Herschel have employed, steeped as he was in the mysteries and uses of chemicals?

"You know what?" I blurted out to my mother as Uncle and I walked into the flat.

Mother turned from the hamburger she was preparing to bake in the oven as a meat loaf with hard boiled eggs in the middle.

"There was a big fight in the store, Ma."

I had teetered from one leg to the other, anxious for an opportunity to tell this story which I suspected Uncle would be reluctant to relate. I did not look at my uncle Herschel so I would not risk the hazard of his disapproving eyes.

"What do you mean, you had a fight in the store?" my mother asked, looking fearfully from me to her brother. Uncle turned up his palms at me. Go ahead, his hands indicated, if you have to be a blabber mouth. I told my story vividly, I think, reviewing each incident in detail, enlarging upon two: Uncle's involvement with the chemical he threw into Moishe's face and the manner in which Sam devastated Moishe's companion.

My mother had taken her hands out of the huge wooden mixing bowl and had turned completely to face me so she would not miss a single word, a single thought.

When I paused briefly to swallow and to take a deep breath, she said, "These are murderers."

"I'm not afraid of them," Uncle said. "What can they take from me?"

"Your life."

"Nu, I've had an interesting life. If it's meant they should kill me—"

"No, Ma," I broke in almost breathlessly. "Uncle's only making believe. He wants to live. He fooled me, too, until tonight.

When those men came to the store today and once before, Uncle talked like he would just lie down and die as soon as they told him to. That's what I thought, but I was wrong. To your face, Uncle is sometimes soft, but he doesn't stay soft all the way. He never said anything to me about that medicine he threw into Moishe's face and made him blind. Then he went back and he got two glasses more—one for each hand—for the big man. Don't worry, Uncle isn't going to die so easy."

My mother looked uneasily from me to Uncle Herschel. She wanted him to confirm what I had enunciated so boldly.

"Don't worry," he said, "the Moishes are not yet ready to take over the world so long as we can get to a little back room."

"So thank God it ended this way," my mother said. "You remember Mrs. Teitelbaum, the lady you examined with the sleeping sickness—she died about an hour ago. The funeral is tomorrow."

Seventeen

We were many days clearing up the sticky, gummy mess the big animal had left us in that first big sweep of his arm. Sam was marvelously helpful. He came in with a huge bucket of water and a cake of brown soap. Holding a stiff brush by its long handle, he soaped up the floor and rubbed vigorously at the overlay of goo. Some of it yielded, but clumps which had dried resisted his sternest efforts. When his wife Yetta came down to survey the damage and direct Sam's efforts, she watched him a moment and said, "Let me."

She pulled the handle out of the brush, got down on her knees, and applied the brown soap to her brush. Then she leaned in on the unyielding spots, and they began to dissolve.

"This is really a woman's work," Sam said.

"It's a woman's work because you're afraid to get down on your knees," Yetta retorted. "You can't push around stubborn dirt from the far."

"So good," Sam said. "So finish already."

"I'll finish, I'll finish," she told him.

In ten minutes she stood up, said "I'll be right back," and returned with two thick rags. With one, she dipped into the hot water and rinsed away the heavy accumulation of soap. With the other, she mopped up the water.

When Yetta had finished, Sam carried the bucket to the street, where he tossed the slop into the gutter, while she gathered up all the implements he had requisitioned from her washing closet.

Uncle had stood off to one side, smoking one cigarette after another without speaking. As Sam and Yetta smiled over at him, he said, "What can I say? You are good people. I come into your store and I give you so much trouble—a big broken window and all this on the floor—and you come back to help me. If you believe in God, He'll reward you."

"We believe in God, Felsher," Sam said.

"Then all I can say is, please thank your God for making you such wonderful people."

The huge glass window was fitted in late that afternoon, and the procedure attracted a throng of kids just dismissed from school and adults, who watched breathlessly as four large men maneuvered the oversized pane. As they moved back and forth from their wagon to the store, the workmen had to admonish the kids who wanted to get close enough to really enjoy the spectacle. They threatened the kids they would kick their asses if they didn't move, and the kids responded by pointing to me in the store and demanding to know why they couldn't watch from where I was standing.

The workers hardly looked at me, but when they were ready to move the glass, they used their large carrying cloths to sweep through the encroachers and beat them back into the gutter.

Instantly they were saluted by indignant young voices. "You stink, you lousy bastards."

The workers responded with baleful looks, one or two muttering as they set their shoulders to the huge piece of glass they were preparing to place in the window frame.

I turned away as they began to hammer in the little retaining nails needed to hold the glass in position until they could apply the putty all around. My uncle had gone into his little back room, where, I knew, he would be preparing the mixtures to refill some thirty bottles the monster had destroyed.

I watched him measure quantities and stir them into the brew he would later syphon into the bottles. I reached up for the syphon, poked the throat into a bottle, and waited. We were not too long in filling the twelve bottles of hair tonic. Then we turned to the other mixture—a cough syrup—which had made the spillage so thick and gummy. I didn't know why this mixture was so long to prepare. Uncle Herschel stirred it endlessly —much longer than a ten-year-old can endure.

Once, he looked over to me as I shifted restlessly from one leg to the other. He smiled, but didn't lose one stroke in his rhythmic swirling. "It's much easier for an older person to be patient," he said. "You count, and tell me when you reach five hundred."

I was surprised when he paused long enough to hold a match to a fresh cigarette just as I had begun to count softly. He appeared to pay no attention to me, but once he said, "How far have you counted?"

"Two hundred and fifty, now."

"Good, go on, go on, and when you come to five hundred you say, '*selah.*' "

"*Selah?* What does that mean?"

"It means I should stop."

I took up the count more diligently now. Having become completely absorbed in my task, I forgot my restlessness. As I reached four hundred and ninety nine, I took a big swallow of air and exclaimed, "Selah." I grabbed the funnel and shoved it into the throat of a bottle. Uncle Herschel ladled the liquid into the funnel. The movement was rapid now. One full ladle filled a bottle and more, so those we had set out for this mixture were soon filled.

He wrote one label, reviewed its English name with me and began writing the Russian name on all the labels, while I filled in the English equivalent in my finest script. We laid them out to let the ink dry, then went back to the first we had written and pasted them on the bottles.

Our window was in by this time, Sam and Yetta had retired

to their flat, and Uncle and I had refilled the shelves that had been so cruelly emptied yesterday.

We stood back to survey what we had accomplished. After a minute Uncle said, "Now we can go home."

Just like that, I thought. One day after living through a near disaster, and he behaves as if he had sold thirty bottles instead of losing them to the vicious onslaught of a hooligan.

As we walked down Manhattan Avenue, I said, "Uncle, don't you feel terrible about what happened yesterday?"

He turned to look at me as though I had said something precocious or maybe childish. Then he shook his head and spread his mustache with his left hand.

"I can only be grateful that nobody was hurt," he said. "Some terrible things can happen in a pogrom."

"But this wasn't a pogrom, Uncle," I said.

"How do you measure a pogrom?" he asked. "Even if one Jew is set upon as I was, I would call it a pogrom. If many Jews are destroyed, then it's a large pogrom."

"But suppose those two men come back?"

"I can only imagine what will happen. They may break up the store, they may even kill me, but I will have the final satisfaction."

"What satisfaction?"

"They will not get the alcohol."

"But is it worth all that, Uncle? It's terrible."

"You are right. It is terrible, but a man must live by what he believes, by what is important to his heart. I will not steal. Maybe I can beg if that becomes necessary, but I will not steal, and I cannot steal from a country that has just allowed me to come in. Here I can live where I wish and go into any business. In Russia I could not become a doctor because my brother was a doctor. In Russia there wasn't much work I could do. I could become a tailor, stonemason or carpenter, but that kind of work was not for me. They would never permit me to open this kind of store."

I was silent after that. What he had said impressed me very

deeply. I could imagine myself as a child in Russia. What could I do? Where could I study? What could I look forward to? I stared at Uncle Herschel; he seemed so serene as he walked by my side, dropping his stick rhythmically to the pavement.

My father had not yet come home, and my mother was preparing the evening meal. She offered us rolls and butter and tea, but we told her we would wait for my father. In September I would be introduced to the study of Hebrew and Jewish history, for which, I knew, I would have to give up all my afternoon freedom in the library and on the street.

Uncle Herschel sat at the kitchen table where he could lay out the daily *Forward* my mother had bought that afternoon. I went into the front room to work on the irritating arithmetic problems, so meaningless to me, before I could relax with the narration in my history text and the descriptions in the geography book.

I heard my mother say, "They are sitting shivah in the Teitelbaum house."

My uncle rustled his paper and, I imagine, looked up. "How is it in America for a shivah?"

"We go. We bring cake and fruit."

"Good. Then we'll go."

"When we eat, we'll go," my mother said.

I came into the kitchen. "I never went to a shivah," I said. "Can I go, too?"

My mother looked up, and I could see in her eyes, a mingling of pride and wonder. "Yes, my son," she said, "you can go."

I did not know what to anticipate in a shivah. I had heard stories from boys on the block and in the schoolyard about the excitement of visiting the home of bereaved family and about the huge assortment of cakes and cookies and fruit and candies that were served to the visitors and mourners.

At the supper table my mother talked about the funeral services that were read in the home of the bereaved and the old men who sat up all night with the corpse reading the psalms aloud.

When they came home from the burial grounds on the other end of Staten Island, Jennie told my mother how bitter the journey had been, how one horse went lame, and how one wheel of the carriage in which she sat had come off. They had to wait for hours for the blacksmith and wheelwright to repair both areas of damage.

My mother had gone to the home of the bereaved and, together with another neighbor, had cooked a large pot of chicken soup and another pot of gefilte fish.

"How could a neighbor do less?" she asked, but nobody answered. After she washed and dried the dishes I stacked them away. She looked at my father, whose head was beginning to droop, and said, "Sit here. We'll go, but we won't stay long."

My Uncle Herschel and I waited at the door for my mother to drape a shawl around her shoulders before we walked slowly down the stairs and up the two flights to the Teitelbaums'.

We did not pause to knock at the door. One didn't knock at the door of a bereaved home; one just walked in. We were not the first callers. At least ten others sat in every available chair, and Jennie and her father sat on two boxes. Neither wore shoes.

Everybody turned to look at us as we came in. We could see instantly that there were no chairs, but my mother did not even look for one. She walked immediately to where Jennie sat with her father in the front room, against a wall, between two windows. In my child's mind they appeared to be sitting on thrones surrounded by their retainers.

All the attendants in this house of mourning were either staring down at their hands, which they had clasped in front of them, or out into space. Their eyes appeared glazed as they focused upon some object or area in the room. I tried to follow the line of vision of one old man, but his eyes were fixed stolidly upon the wall.

Now and then one of the mourners offered a long, loud sigh, vocalizing it "Oy!" The others would respond. They, too, shook their heads or nodded to emphasize their belief about the inevitability of this course which, ultimately, they would all have to run. Others just nodded into their hands and rocked gently back and forth.

There were subdued murmurings around the room as neighbors leaned over to whisper briefly to one another. I suspected the talk was about the deceased, what a fine woman she had been, what a devoted mother and wife. One or two, I noticed, suddenly became involved in a narrative, probably a reminiscence of an encounter with the deceased. I couldn't hear what they were saying because the voices were so subdued.

In one corner, an elderly woman sat on a box. Evidently she was related to the deceased. Her head was covered with an old kerchief, and she was bowed over, reading from a prayerbook. Her lips moved furiously, but I could not hear a sound. Nobody was concerned with her as she rocked back and forth over the open pages, moistening a finger swiftly to turn a page, pausing frequently to hold a handkerchief to her eyes and her nose.

Once or twice, someone in the room exclaimed, "Oy vay!" but it was not noticed by the others, who pursued their own course of meditation and mourning.

My mother had already advanced to the two principal mourners, and I followed her, curious about what she would say to them. Then I thought I would walk back to the kitchen to explore the legendary wealth of eatables.

My mother said, "What the earth covers, we must forget."

I thought, What an odd thing for my mother to say. The father barely raised his eyes and nodded slowly. He looked like a beaten man. Jennie smiled weakly into my mother's face, took her hand and kissed it. For a moment I was touched. Then, as I watched her, she raised her head and gazed into the gloom spread by the dim light of two mourners' candles. Suddenly her eyes dilated, and she sprang to her feet.

"That's him!" she screamed hysterically. "That's the felsher. He gave my mother an evil eye! *An evil eye!* He killed her, he killed her!"

Uncle Herschel had started into the room, but this sudden outcry stopped him. He stared at this girl, who a few days ago had welcomed him into her home. He smiled dimly and said, "Don't talk like a child. Nobody has an evil eye."

The spectators on all sides drew back. Some exclaimed, "*Oh! Oh! Oh!*"

"What you think is a large foolishness," Uncle said. "What is an evil eye? Who has an evil eye? The only evil eyes are in your own heads, in your own minds. I came in to look at this poor sick woman. So because I looked at her she died? Foolish! Foolish!"

"*You gave my mother an evil eye!*" the girl shrieked.

"No, my dear, don't say it. We tried to save her, but she was already half dead when Doctor Padilsky and I looked at her."

"You are an evil eye. My mother was only sleeping when you came, but when you looked at her twice, she died."

"Come," Uncle Herschel said to my mother and me. "What else can I say?"

"*Wait!*" the girl screamed after us. "I will yet go to the police. They will yet arrest you, you evil one!"

None of us spoke until we came into the street. Then my mother said, "What does she want from you?"

"I don't know," Uncle said. "She's upset and full of grief."

"But to say you've got an evil eye!"

"What's an evil eye?" I asked.

They were ahead of me on the stairs as we walked up to our flat, so I thought they had not heard me. When we came into the house I asked again, "What is an evil eye?"

I waited for Uncle to light a cigarette and bring his bottle and a glass to the table.

"People try to explain for themselves what they don't understand," he said, "or for which there is no explanation. Hundreds, thousands of years ago, people were terrified by thunder and lightning. They thought this must be the voice and the will of God. They worshipped the thunder and they worshipped lightning. They worshipped the sea and the stars and fire and water. Then, when a man came to the tribe, a stranger who did not look like the others—if he had a lame leg or if his head was bald—then, he was something to be afraid of. If he happened to be in the village when something disastrous happened, when someone was hurt or killed, the tribe would blame it on the stranger. They would say he had cast an evil eye on the victim, and they would kill him to get rid of the evil eye. That's what that girl wants to do to me."

My mother was shocked. "Oh, Herschel!" she exclaimed.

"So," Uncle said, "she wants to have me arrested."

"How can she do that?" I demanded.

I was upset, not only by the possibility of such an occurrence, but also by the affront to Uncle Herschel's dignity. After all, he was a felsher, and one did not reduce a felsher to the level of a common criminal. I would see. Tomorrow I would speak to Callahan, who would know how wrong it would be to arrest a felsher because a woman said he had an evil eye.

My father had gone to bed, but my mother brewed tea for us, which we drank with some of the delicious egg cookies she had baked the week before.

"You think he's got an evil eye?" I asked.

My mother stared at Uncle, who was swallowing tea so scalding we didn't even dare approach it. "Vay!" my mother said.

"I hate stupidity," Uncle said. "A roomful of people, most of them older than me, but not one to stand up and to say ' "an evil eye" comes from a stupid head!' Ach!"

"So why do you worry about it?" my mother asked.

"Worry about it, worry about it! We are only people. We are made of flesh and blood, and we have nerves, so we worry. You have nothing to worry about—your Schiya just became a citizen. You belong here. Me? I'm yet a stranger, and I told you what happens when a stranger comes into a tribe when a disaster takes place. I have an evil eye! I used this evil eye to kill this woman. No?"

"No!" my mother exclaimed.

Uncle got up. "Enough! For one night, I have heard all the stupidity I can stand."

"And if she goes to the police?" I asked, almost breathlessly.

"I will tell the police I don't have an evil eye. This, I have read about the courts in the United States. Here, I would not have to prove that I do not have an evil eye. The police and that girl would have to prove I have an evil eye and it was my evil eye that killed her."

I breathed in that simple logic. I did not know if he was right or if he did not understand the thought in American law, but what he said had such a true ring, believing it was quite irresistible.

I went back to my homework, Uncle to today's news in the daily *Forward*, and my mother to yesterday's paper, where she had marked off three or four articles she had not yet read. In this fashion we passed the evening until my mother looked at the big clock on our mantle and told me to prepare for bed.

Uncle went into the front room and closed the door, but I knew he did not go to sleep when the lights went out. I could hear him moving around the room restlessly, walking back and forth, back and forth, for the longest time. I could tell he was smoking as he walked, because I could see the sudden burst of light when he struck a match, and the light did not always originate in the same spot. My eyes would close and then snap open with the spark and the light, and I would wonder how he could go to sleep so late and yet be up and around so early each morning. At last, I could no longer resist sleep; I became oblivious to his restless tramping and his incessant smoking.

Eighteen

I did not see Uncle Herschel the next morning, because again he had dressed and he was gone before my mother woke me. I could only guess that he awoke as my father puttered quietly around in the kitchen. My mother knew that my father prepared his breakfast quietly and efficiently, so she was not concerned about him; but she did fret about Uncle until she counted two glasses in the black iron sink and she knew that Uncle had shared my father's breakfast.

School was a drag that day. I had wanted to talk about the evil eye to my friends but I didn't, because I knew that before very long their probing questions would drag the story out of me and they would regard me with horror as someone who lived intimately with an evil eye. Several times during the day I had looked speculatively at my teacher, as I wondered how much he knew about the evil eye and whether he could offer me any solace or consolation. I cannot explain how my thinking went, but I did not apply to my teacher; I sensed he did not have the resources to temper my disquiet.

I hurried home, buttered a roll and told my mother I would eat it on my way to the store. I found Uncle there, in a corner near the window, reading. He looked up when I came in, laid a marker in his book and closed it.

"What are you reading, Uncle?" I asked.

He looked down at the book. "Chekhov," he said. "He is a very good writer of short stories and plays."

"In Russian?"

He nodded.

"Would you teach me to read Russian some time?"

He smiled. "You're a good boy. I'll be happy to teach you Russian."

I walked around the room appearing to inspect the bottles but I wasn't really looking at them. There were so many questions I wanted to ask him. There was so much I didn't know about him. Would he be angry if I asked those questions? For so long I had been taught to be recessive, to be reticent about talking to adults.

"Uncle," I said, almost impulsively, "tell me something about your family."

He clasped his hands over the book. "What do you want to know?"

"Oh . . . how many children do you have?"

"Six."

"How many boys?"

"Three."

"And how old is the youngest?"

"It's a girl, and she is just seventeen."

"Are they like you, Uncle?"

That question he did not answer readily. He laid his fingers on his little goatee and, for about half a minute, stroked it gently as though he could not quite decide how to answer this question. Of course, I did not understand in my child's mind that I had asked a question that demanded not only thought, but selection. In what ways were they like him? In what ways were they not? He would evidently have to review the façade and bank of each child and hold it up against his own structure.

"I would first have to tell you what I am," he said.

"Oh," I said, sure of my own strength, "I know what you are."

He smiled. "Tell me," he challenged.

"What you are?"

"Yes."

I plunged in impulsively. "You are a very smart man. You know a lot about a lot of things, and you know how to make up your mind about something and stick to it."

When I stopped, he looked at me as though he were waiting for me to take a deep breath and continue.

"That's all?" he asked.

"Sure, isn't that enough?"

He shook his head. "No," he said almost gently, "that's not enough. That's what you see and what you hear. That doesn't tell you what a man is thinking, what makes him do what he does."

"But how could I know that, Uncle?"

"Ah, that's the important thing, and for that a man has to grow old and wise. I'll give you one example. Your father and your mother don't drink branfen. I drink branfen. For me, branfen is important. You see me drinking branfen, but have you ever asked, Why is he drinking so much branfen?"

I shook my head and I marveled at his wisdom. I thought, Why had it not occurred to me to ask that question. I had never questioned his drinking habit, although in my house it should have impressed me as an odd variant.

"Why do you drink branfen?" I asked.

"Well," he said, "I could tell you I drink branfen because I like the taste, and that would be true. But that would be only the reason that appears on the surface. A man doesn't drink only because he likes the taste. It could be because he's lonely, it could be because he wants to forget something, or it could be something in his body that presses him to drink."

When he stopped rather suddenly, I wanted to ask him which of these was motivating his drinking; but again I was inhibited by the teaching in my home.

He said, "Now, about my children. They are not like me. They are more like their mother. They want to get married and have children of their own, and they want most of all to come to America."

I listened, but I was not satisfied. I felt he had actually told me nothing about his children. He had simply said they were not like him. What *was* he like? I had not thought deeply enough about that question until he had laid out for me the facets of his character which were not exposed.

Nineteen

The regular daily visits of the letter carrier were events no kid in the house ever missed or overlooked. Because he was very punctual, and because ours was the third house on his route, all the kids raced down the long hall to be among those present as he came to the foot of the stairs.

His name was George, a nondescript name for a nondescript person. He was short and round, his face was always the color of a half-turned beet. Every kid on the block knew he had acquired that high color leaning against a rail in a dimly lighted saloon on the corner, where his letters gave out every day.

Everybody knew him by his name, but he was only aware of their names when he read them on envelopes. Somehow, he never bothered to associate names with faces, because he always shoved letters at an outstretched hand and he said only "here." The kids were around him like flies, buzzing over his shoulder (he was so short) to anticipate the reading. Normally, because he always started his day here, he was troubled on Saturday; on other days the kids who read faster than he were in school. Saturday he detested because on this day the children waited for him near the door to escort him down the hall and to fight over a choice position on the stairs behind him. The taller boys stood in back; the shorter ones clambered up the stairs in the hope they would be there to hand up the letters as the listening tenants responded to the names George called.

Often the pushing, jostling kids would irritate him so violently he would exclaim, "Get the hell off that bag before I break your ass!" The kids would pull back and look at him wide-eyed until he would resume his letter calling. Then they would crowd in on him almost relentlessly. Once the press became so unbearable he swung a strap from his mail pouch and clipped one of the children on the head. The others retreated frantically and, for that morning, stayed away from him until he could complete his rounds.

George had a well established routine. In this house we had no mailboxes into which he could drop the mail, so when he came to the foot of the stair, he would hold up a long whistle, toot long, once, twice before he would yell "mailman!" All the kids had evolved into a choral group. They reserved first solo for George but instantly gave out a long, fruity "*mailman*," drawing out the final sound so it reverberated up the deep stair well.

By this time every tenant in the house was leaning over the banisters, their heads cocked over the stairs. A hush always preceded the first long call of names. Then he commenced his uninspired name reading. Always after the third name, which George had begun to slur because he could not pronounce some of the foreign-sounding names, we heard the first "*whoooo?*"

Instantly a chorus of young boys and girls took up the chant. "*Whooooo?*" they sang, their voices rising to a falsetto. The din was almost unbearable, and George would stamp his foot in exasperation. "Shut up, goddamn it, before I break your asses." In two years of conscientious attendance at this scene, I had never heard him vary the pitch of his threat.

There was one tenant who lived on the fourth floor whom no one could put down. She was not deaf, but she wasn't always sure she heard the names George called from the bottom of the well, four flights down. When she shrilled "*who-o-o-o?*" her voice swelled to a piercing intensity. Her problem was that her surname, Gorinsky, sounded irritatingly like another neighbor's, Gorodinsky's, and very often George mistook one for the other.

In fact, this unhappy similarity had erupted into several violent scenes when Mr. Gorodinsky opened a letter intended for Mr. Gorinsky—a dunning letter from a customer peddler. Customer peddlers, vital operators in the Jewish community, moved from home to home, equipped only with cards and order blanks. They took orders for any kind of merchandise from clothing to jewelry to furniture. They wrote the order, they delivered what was ordered, and they visited the buyer's home regularly to collect the installment payment, fifty cents to a dollar a week at the most. They served a useful purpose in our area, where wages were low and needs moderate. Items purchased were almost never repossessed, because the people had a moral obligation to the customer peddler, who made his living in this fashion and who laid out the price of the merchandise himself before collecting from customers. If a customer could not pay, the peddler usually understood and said, "Don't worry about it. I'll be back next week." In rare cases, when he had been turned down many weeks, the customer peddler sent a letter. Mr. Gorinsky never forgave Mr. Gorodinsky for opening the dunning letter, but Gorodinsky shrugged him off.

"If it bothers you so much, Gorinsky, why don't you change your name?" Gorodinsky asked one very hot night on the street.

Mr. Gorinsky regarded him with distaste for a moment before retorting, "Why don't you change your face, you stupid thing."

"You say that again, you cockroach, and I'll change your face!" Mr. Gorodinsky threatened.

I was standing nearby and I thought both men were very funny. Mr. Gorinsky was a tailor who sat over his needle and thread for twelve or fourteen hours a day. His chest was a hollow, his shoulders a fine arc, and his arms two sticks, indifferently covered with skin. He could not have weighed more than a hundred pounds. Compared to him, Gorodinsky looked like an apple. He was about an inch taller and ten pounds heavier, and his cheeks were scooped out of his face because he had lost almost all of his molars.

There were three or four other kids around who had also heard the challenge thrown down.

"Fight, fight!" they yelled, and instantly twenty more swarmed around the men, who were eye to eye like two game cocks. Mrs. Gorinsky was seated near the curb about five feet to the right, but she had her back to the eruption. When the cry dinned around her head, she paused in the description of her daughter's new flat on Hewes Street because the other woman, facing the imminent fracas, was staring.

"What is?" Mrs. Gorinsky asked.

"Your husband?" the other woman said faintly.

Mrs. Gorinsky elevated her bulk, saw her husband's chin thrust out belligerently and let out a scream. "*Looey!*"

She scrambled over to the two men and wedged herself firmly between them. "You should drop dead," she told Mr. Gorodinsky.

"I should drop dead?" he said. "You should drop dead, and he should drop dead."

"You are a bum, a gambler, a rotten stinker, you should want to hit him. He's such a sick man."

"Who wants to hit him? Who? He wants to hit me. So let him try. I'll break every bone in his head!"

"Don't be such a knocker. I'm not afraid of you, and Looey ain't afraid of you either. He's a sick man."

"If he's such a sick man, let him keep his goddamn mouth. He wants to fight. I don't want to fight. Can I help it if the letter carrier gives me a letter that belongs to you. I didn't ask for it. He brung it to me. So? So pay your bills, and you wouldn't have nothing you should be ashamed."

There was no fight because Mrs. Gorinsky laced her fingers around her husband's spindle arms and led him away. The kids were disgusted and disappointed. Many non-Jewish kids in their school would report with considerable graphic exposition the fights that took place in their neighborhoods, particularly on Saturday night, which they called "drunk night." In our area, where only Jews lived, nobody fought.

This Saturday morning, some of us were playing soccer with our homemade stuffed stocking when George appeared. Today he was walking with a pronounced list to his right, since the bag was enormously overloaded. We pranced into the long hall to escort him to the foot of the stairs.

When he got there, George weighed off the great load in his big bag and set it down on the second step. As he took a new hitch in his belt, he looked around and said, "First kid crowds me, I'll kick his ass."

Having laid the ground rules, he leaned over the bag to pick up the bundle of letters he had corded for this house. We didn't crowd because we knew George was quite capable of implementing his threat. Each of us respected the rights of the others who were there, particularly the younger, shorter kids; if George didn't boot us for our overeagerness, they would.

We watched him unwind the cord. George never hurried. We observed this manuever with considerable impatience because we remembered the one episode when some big lunkhead behind George (who didn't even live in our house) had demanded, "Come on, hurry up, George." This had infuriated him so much that even before we could talk the kid down, George had seized a strap from his bag and flailed it wildly, sweeping us all out of the hall.

We held on quietly while he performed this ritual of unwinding the first batch of letters for Seventy-nine Manhattan Avenue. Then we watched him reach for the whistle attached to a braided leather strap, and we put our hands to our ears as he gave out two long blasts. As we took our hands away we could hear the doors being opened on all the floors, and a moment later I could look up into a swarm of heads and faces leaning expectantly into the well.

He began, as usual, to slur the names, except as he approached names easy to read—Goldstein, Goldberg, Cohen. These he always broke into two syllables—Gold-stein, Gold-berg, Co-hen. He got affirmative responses for the first five letters, passing them up to the cooperative young fingers, outstretched and eager to move the letters up to the descending tenants. Once or twice Mrs. Gorinsky leaned in and gave out an inquiring "*Who-o-o?*" which George ignored and which all the kids echoed gleefully.

As usual, my family had received no letters, and I had expected none. I came here regularly just to play out this charade with my friends. Now he held one letter in his hand, and he stared and stared at the name. I thought he would turn to the taller kids, as he sometimes did, to ask them to decipher what he could not read.

Today, however, he simply stared and muttered, "Ain't seen this name before." Then he said the name Kessler, and a dozen mouths repeated it. Suddenly I jumped.

"That's my uncle!" I exclaimed.

George looked doubtfully at me. "Why din't you know it when I first said it?" he demanded.

"I don't know. I didn't hear the name so often in my house," I said, and I knew how lame it sounded.

"I don't know," said George as he pulled back the letter.

"Yeah, his uncle lives with him," Muttel called. "I seen him. He's a greenie, and he's a felsher."

"A what?"

"A felsher."

"It's like a doctor," Muttel said, but at this point both his knowledge and his nerve gave out. "Wynchu tell him?" he called to me.

"It's my uncle," I said. "He lives with us. He just came from Russia about a month ago."

George continued to stare at me before he shrugged and gave me the letter. I seized it, swung around and dashed up the stairs to my flat. My mother was in the house.

"Look," I said, "a letter for Uncle Herschel." She came over to stare down at the typed name and address on the letter. Both of us were awed. We rarely had a letter, and never before one whose name and address had been typed.

"It's from the District Attorney," I said, and my voice shook a little. "What's a District Attorney?"

"I don't know, but it looks very important," said Mother.

"I'm going to take it over to Uncle right away," I said.

I flew to the door, shoved the letter into my pocket and raced for the street.

Muttel was waiting for me. Evidently he was as excited as I about this letter. As I started to go by him, he grabbed my arm.

"Where you goin'?"

I shook him off. "I gotta take the letter to my uncle. It's from the District Attorney."

"What's the District Attorney?"

"I don't know, but I'm going to find out."

"Kin I walk you?"

"Nah, I'm in a hurry. Besides, it's his letter."

I did not explain why he could not walk me if the letter was addressed to my uncle, and as I flashed by him I saw that the expression on his face was puzzled and hurt.

I cannot recall an errand I had executed more swiftly than this one. Many sights, familiar and unfamiliar, flashed by me as I alternately ran and walked to the store.

I was quite breathless as I burst into the store, where Uncle was talking to Sam. They turned as I clawed my way into the room.

"Uncle!" I exclaimed, and because I was quite breathless I held out the envelope for him.

Sam and I waited for him to tear open the flap. He gave me the envelope, and I said to Sam, "It's from the District Attorney."

His eyes widened, and his lips expanded as he repeated, "District Attorney!"

After he opened the letter, my uncle glanced at it and held it out to me. I read: "You are instructed to appear in this office at nine A.M. on April 22. Failure to appear may subject you to arrest."

When I looked up from my reading, Uncle asked, "Who wrote this, and what does the letter say?"

I told him, but he did not understand. "Who is this, and why do I have to go there?"

I said I did not know, but Sam intervened. "The District Attorney is a lawyer for the government. When someone commits a crime and he's arrested, the District Attorney brings them into court and he has the cases against them."

Uncle Herschel stared at Sam, and I could see from Sam's face that he was equally perplexed.

"Do you think it's because I threw that chemical in that boy's face?" my uncle asked.

Sam shook his head. "That can't be," he said. "That kind of man doesn't run to the police."

"Then," Uncle thought aloud, "was it because you threw that man through the window?"

Again Sam shook his head. "In such a case they would have sent the letter to me," he said.

For a moment everybody was silent; as I looked at Uncle Herschel I could see that a very deep thought was surfacing in his mind.

"I have a thought," he said finally, "which I don't like but can't help thinking. This is the second instance I have found in this country where one Jew wants to hurt another Jew, and I cannot understand it." He turned to me. "That daughter of the woman who died–she said she would try to do me a harm because she thinks I have an evil eye and it was my evil eye that killed her mother. Do you think she went to this District Attorney?"

I didn't know, and Sam shook his head. My uncle stared down at the letter. When he looked up he said to me, "Will you go with me to the District Attorney?"

My pulse leaped a little that my uncle, the felsher, should consider my presence, indeed, my help, important enough to ask for it.

"Sure," I said, and my face grew warm as I stirred around. Sam smiled down at me from his great height.

"He's a good boy," Sam said.

My uncle smiled only thinly, as he always did when he did not wish to be too expansive over something that pleased him. When he had returned the letter to the envelope and thrust it into his pocket, I said, "I'll go home and ask Mama if I can go with you next week."

"Good," he said.

I think I ran all the way home. As I burst into my flat my mother looked up from the herring slices she was laying out to bake on sheets of manila paper.

"You know what?" I exclaimed. "The District Attorney wants Uncle to come to his office next week, and the letter said if he doesn't come he'll be arrested."

"Oy vay!" my mother said. "What do they want from him?"

"The letter doesn't say, but Uncle says he thinks Jennie went to the police, and that's why they're calling him, and you know what the District Attorney is? They are lawyers, and when somebody does something wrong he's arrested, and he has to go to court, and the District Attorney is the lawyer who asks him questions in the court."

"No, it can't be. She's such a good girl."

"But she said Uncle has an evil eye. You heard her. And she said she would do something to Uncle. Maybe she went to the District Attorney. And Mama, Uncle asked me to go with him to the District Attorney."

My mother turned to look at me, and instantly I knew what was in her mind. "You will be absent from school," she said.

"Yes."

"What will you tell the teacher?"

"I'll tell him I had to go to the District Attorney with my uncle who's a greenie."

"But won't he send you to the principal?"

The thought of being accosted and interviewed by those big, bulging, ice-cold, blue eyes was disturbing. In the Jewish tradition the school was associated with the synagogue and, therefore, with God, and one did not readily take liberties with God. A child was really sick when he did not go to school.

"I don't know if he'll send me to the principal," I said.

"Then, tell your teacher on Monday, and he'll say if you can go."

I needed a lot of courage and probably waited until my flow of adrenalin was strong enough before I approached my teacher on Monday. I left my seat while the class was chained to a problem in percentages. The other kids looked up as I tiptoed to the front of the room; such a deviation was very unusual. They watched me bend over the teacher's desk and whisper, "Can I talk to you?"

My teacher raised his head. He, too, was surprised. Normally only an impending disaster would motivate a kid to leave his seat while the class was working on an exercise.

He said, "Yes?"

"My uncle is a greenie. On Saturday he got a letter to come to the office of the District Attorney, and he can't speak English."

"So he wants you to go with him?"

"Yes, sir."

"Why can't your mother go—or your father?"

"My father would lose his job, and my mother doesn't speak enough English."

"All right," he said, "but if you're through before three o'clock, come to school."

I promised and returned to my seat. Almost forty pairs of eyes watched me, hoping to see despair or rejection in my eyes, and Muttel's were the widest of all. I hardly looked at him, knowing I would have to put him off because one just did not discuss, even with a friend, his family's involvement with the District Attorney.

Twenty

On Thursday I was up early and I got into my Sabbath suit, shoes and shirt. My mother supervised my dressing and even helped me achieve a good part in my hair. I watched Uncle Herschel drink his tea and munch on a small piece of buttered roll, marveling that he was so calm; my own stomach churned busily before I ate and after. He just sat there, his stick emplaced between his legs, smoking cigarette after cigarette while I ate.

When I looked at our mantle clock, he took out his pocket watch, sprang the lid open and compared his time to the time on the clock.

"We should go," he said.

"Go, go," my mother said, and I ran for my jacket.

When we got to the street I said, "You know that policeman who came to our house?"

"Yes."

"If I could find him, he would tell us how to go to the District Attorney and why we should go there."

My uncle smiled at me. "But already we know why we're going. We're going because I received a letter telling me to come."

"But that isn't enough. Maybe he can tell what you did that was wrong."

Uncle nodded. I had probably struck a logical nerve.

"Then find him," he said.

I looked up and down Manhattan Avenue, but I could not see the pot hat and the long blue coat of the policeman. "I'll run up this way," I said, pointing toward Boerum Street. I began a medium-paced trot in that direction. If I could not find him there I would retreat and hunt the other way as far as Broadway.

I found him just beyond Johnson Avenue, staring into the window of a liquor store, his hands clasped serenely behind him. I ranged myself on his right side, wondering how I should approach him. When he saw my face in the window he turned to stare at me.

"Didn't know you kids was innerested in liquor. Why ain't you in school?"

I had to hurry to enter a disclaimer on one count and to explain why I was loitering here by his side instead of in school.

"Oh," I said, "I don't like liquor, and I'm not going to school this morning because I have to go to the District Attorney's office with my uncle. You know my uncle—he has that medicine store on Cook Street."

He took a little while to assimilate everything I had said, staring at me all the time as though he wanted to separate the truth from some odd piece of fiction.

"Now," he said, "what would the District Attorney want with your uncle?"

"We don't know. He hasn't done anything wrong."

"Maybe it's on account of them drugs he's sellin', but I give the captain a good story about them. If the District Attorney wants you, it's because you committed a felony."

"What's that?"

"It's an important crime like stealin' or murderin'."

"My uncle didn't steal, and he didn't murder," I bristled.

"No, I don't think he did. So it must be somethin' else."

What else?"

"I don't know. Maybe if I talked to your uncle I could find out."

"He's waiting in front of my house."

Officer Callahan swung off toward Boerum Street in that leisurely, unhurried stride we kids had learned to recognize so well. I think he would not have quickened his pace even if some disaster had struck Manhattan Avenue. His sense of dignity was splendid, but I wished he would forsake that attitude of aloofness just this once and yield to my need for urgency.

At last we got to Uncle Herschel. He had watched us come down the block and must have wondered why I was bringing the fountainhead to him. As we approached him, Uncle nodded, waiting for me or for Callahan to open the dialogue.

I said, "Officer Callahan is going to tell us why we were called and how to get there."

The cop listened for me to dispose of these preliminaries. Then he said, "You musta done somethin' pretty bad, Uncle."

When I translated for him, Uncle Herschel shrugged. "Tell him I'm in this country only a short time, and I didn't hurt anybody, and, so far as I know, I haven't broken any laws. Besides, I haven't had time enough."

"Ah, they all say that," the policeman said; but he was smiling, and I knew that he, too, did not believe my uncle had broken any laws.

"Maybe you been foolin' around with somebody's wife?" he suggested, and I looked askance at him, not being sure how I should translate this accusation and if my uncle would be upset. However, when I managed to put together a full offering of what the policeman had said, I was rather surprised to see Uncle Herschel lay his head back and cackle. I looked at Officer Callahan and I saw that he was grinning. I knew these two men had laid out something very funny between them.

"They musta made a mistake," Callahan said. "I can't see you committin' a felony, but you gotta go there. Now, you take this train that goes to East New York, you get out at Myrtle Avenue

—that's one stop—and you take the Myrtle Avenue train that goes to Park Row. But you get out at Boro Hall."

My uncle listened carefully to the names that dropped off the policeman's tongue, watched my face and, when he thought I had not assimilated all the information, he brought out his pen and a little book and said "write."

I sat on the curb, rested the book on the pavement, and wrote what I recalled from Callahan's exposition. When I read it back to him he smiled and said, "Smart boy."

The ride to the office of the District Attorney was not eventful except for one near miss. While we were standing on one of the platforms of the Myrtle Avenue train, I saw Uncle Herschel reach into his pocket for his cigarette case. Before I could get to him he took out a cigarette. The guard watched him put the cigarette in his mouth, and I could see a line of anger settle the guard's mouth.

"Uncle," I said, "it is forbidden to smoke on the train."

He remembered and returned the cigarette to the case while I took a long deep breath of relief. The guard turned away, and his look, too, relaxed.

We had no difficulty finding the tall building that housed the District Attorney's offices. As we walked into the lobby, we were surrounded by many hurrying men who carried leather bags or brown paper folders. When I spotted a man in a uniform, I asked him where we could find the District Attorney. He gave me an odd look, as if I had done something unpleasant or said something profane.

"Sixth floor," he said shortly.

Wow! I thought, that will be quite a climb for Uncle and even for me. If ever I had to find my way to the fourth floor in my house, I had to pause first on the third for a long deep breath. However, if the man said sixth floor—and it was apparently his business to know—then we would simply go to the sixth floor, and I would see to it that Uncle rested well on every second floor or even after every floor. I looked around.

"Where are the stairs?" I asked.

The uniformed man stared at me. I must have said something really stupid this time, because his stare was even a little hostile.

"What do you want with the stairs? What's the matter with the elevator?"

Now it was my turn to stare. I said, "What?"

He raised his voice. "Elevator, elevator. Dinchu ever ride in a elevator?"

He said that loudly enough to attract listeners, and I was embarrassed because many had paused, even in their haste, to hear how this controversy would come out.

I said, "I don't know what an elevator is."

"What does he want?" Uncle asked, and I felt he was uneasy about the prying, curious eyes around him.

The attendant was happy with the audience his loud, incredulous yawp had attracted. He hoisted up his pants, prepared to take me and my uncle apart.

I said to Uncle, "I don't know what he wants. He says we shouldn't walk up to the District Attorney. He wants us to go up in something he calls an elevator."

"I know what that is," Uncle said. "I rode in it when I went to New York for those collars. They showed me. It's good. Come, we'll go."

He took my hand just as the attendant had taken off his hat to begin an exposition on the virtues of the elevator as opposed to stair climbing. As we walked past him he stared at us, dismayed that we had pushed him from the center of the stage.

Uncle Herschel led me forward to stand opposite a wall that was built of iron like a fence. I stared at it because he had not yet explained to me what an elevator was.

"It will come down soon," he promised, and I waited patiently. I heard a great whirring noise and a rattling of heavy chains. As my eyes opened wider and wider, a metal box which measured about six feet square descended as through a ceiling and settled itself on something level with the floor. Then I heard and saw a gate being flushed open and a heavy iron door being thrust from one side to the other. The big box stood revealed. About four or five people stepped out and walked away as though they had just disembarked from the car of a balloon. I was beside myself with ecstasy and excitement.

"This is the elevator," Uncle said, and I think he was delighted that he, the greenie, could reveal this miracle to me, the American.

The elevator man stood by the door, holding it with one gloved hand. "Going up," he said.

I said, "Can we go this way to the District Attorney?"

"Sixth floor," he said without any interest.

I looked at Uncle Herschel. "Do you want to go in?" I asked.

"Of course," he said. He stepped forward boldly, and I took his hand. We moved into a far corner from which I could stare out to a grimy hall through the grillwork enclosing this iron box. Two or three other men came into the elevator, but they stood near the door. They were either braver than we, or they wanted to be ready to run as soon as the elevator door should open. I watched in some fascination as the operator used a cable to start the elevator and stop it level with each floor as he called out its number.

I heard him say "sixth floor," but I was so bemused by what I was watching that I didn't stir. Then he turned to us with a patient, tolerant look in his eyes.

"You want the District Attorney, dontcha?" he asked.

This caused me to start, and I nudged my uncle's hand, which I was still holding. As we left the elevator, we were confronted by a large sign: DISTRICT ATTORNEY. COMPLAINT. INFORMATION. Under each department an arrow pointed the way.

I read the sign to Uncle and explained each department in rather faltering terms. For a few seconds he stared at the two titles, while men crossed in front of us, busily moving down the corridors to the right and left. Then he raised his cane and pointed to "Complaint."

"Let's go there. I have a complaint," he said.

We swung off to the left, and two doors down we saw the

same word on a glass-paneled door. We entered a rather large room. Four or five feet from the door, a young man sat behind a desk. All other areas in the room were inhospitably fenced off. The man appeared to be stacking sheaves of papers. While we stood by the door for ten or fifteen seconds, he inspected us, moving his eyes inquisitively from me to Uncle Herschel, where they remained for almost a half minute, evidently attracted by Uncle's impeccable dress and walking stick.

At last he said, "Yes?"

I said, "We want to see the District Attorney."

"Tell him we have a letter from the District Attorney," Uncle said. But before I could offer this reference, this hateful character laid his head back and racked up a nasty laugh. I waited for him to subside. When he did, Uncle asked, "Why is he laughing?"

I told Uncle I didn't know—I had simply told him we wanted to see the District Attorney. Then Uncle took the letter from his pocket and laid it on the young man's desk. The clerk read it, took up a pencil and wrote "606" on the letter.

"Go to this room," he said.

I retrieved the letter, showed the number to Uncle and told him we had to go to that room. Again we moved into the corridor to look for Room 606. Uncle noted the numbers on the doors we passed and pointed down the corridor, as he surmised that the numbers were descending in that direction.

This floor appeared to be extraordinarily busy. Men hurried in front of us and behind us as they went about their business. I noticed that those who faced us stared—at me for a moment, but much longer at my uncle's suit, his shoes, and his walking stick.

As we entered Room 606, we were at once impressed by its unusual poverty and by its dusty, dirty appearance. We saw three or four straight-backed wooden chairs propped on the walls as if they were ashamed to be seen in the middle of the room. A huge desk stood in the middle of the room. The desk was almost bare except for a few manila folders stacked in one corner. In a far corner of the room another, smaller desk was tucked into a wall. The walls were bare except for three or four calendars whose sharp, striking colors contrasted vividly with the dismal, dirty gray of the walls.

Two men sat at the desks. We could not see the face of the man occupying the chair in front of the large desk in the middle of the room. We could see only his hands, which held a newspaper spread open.

We stood near the door for a moment as I wondered how to get the attention of this man. Uncle Herschel, however, was not so patient. He rapped sharply on the concrete floor with his stick. The man at the far desk turned to look at us but he said nothing. The man behind the newspaper did not stir.

My uncle said, "This room is filthy like for pigs," and banged his stick again as if he were using a gavel. Now the newspaper was moved to one side so this reader could see around it. We could see only half his face; one eye regarded us without blinking. He measured us from our shoes to the hats we still wore.

Then he said, "Well?"

"Tell him we want to see the District Attorney," my uncle said. I could not detect even a hint of patience in Uncle Herschel, who was always so everlastingly calm.

When I repeated Uncle's request, the man lowered his newspaper. Now we could see him full face, and his full face was bland and unharried. He was an overblown man who ate too much, and if I had known more I would have judged from his florid face that he also drank too much. His lips, however, were sharply carved into his round face, and his eyes were cold and uninviting.

"Hear that, Tom?" he said between tight lips he just barely activated when he talked. "He wants to see the District Attorney. When was the last time you saw the District Attorney?"

"About a month ago."

"And when do you expect to see him again, Tom?"

"Who knows? Maybe in a month, maybe two months."

Uncle Herschel watched and listened to this dialogue, but only I was aghast because only I understood. They stared at us as Uncle asked me what they had said to each other. When I told him, he took the letter from his pocket, advanced upon the desk and laid it on the bare surface.

"If the District Attorney is not here, ask them who writes his letters and who signs his name?"

I asked the question of this fat-faced one as he reached across his desk for Uncle's letter. "Oh, he's got boys who do his jobs—good boys like Tom and me. Now let's see what we have here," he said.

He read the letter and looked over it at me. "No speak English?" he asked.

I shook my head.

"And who are you—his kid?"

"His nephew."

"Ah, that's a good boy. Jewish?"

When I nodded, my uncle asked, "He's an anti-Semite?"

"I don't know," I said.

"Tom," the man said, "get me this file."

He held out the letter, which the younger man picked off with the same gesture I had seen used by carousel riders at Coney Island as they plucked rings from the post beside the revolving disc.

The man with the newspaper raised it again as Tom sauntered out of this room in search of the file. Now Uncle and I had a longer time to review more closely what had dismayed us at first glance. From both Sam and Officer Callahan I had heard the District Attorney was a rather important authority in the city government. This ill-kept hole, however, did not impress my young mind.

"For pigs," my uncle said, looking around for a clean chair to sit on.

I didn't know many public places, but those I had seen, all maintained by women, were immaculate and pretty. The local branch of the public library was dust-free and adorned at regular intervals with potted ferns. My classrooms were always so clean; the teachers appointed monitors to wash the blackboards and the chalk troughs every morning, water the many potted plants that graced the window sills, and dust the desks. During the long holidays, Christmas, Easter and summer, the boys begged for an opportunity to take the plants home to care for them. Even my present teacher, who was a man, involved us in these same routines.

As a little boy, I was introduced to the washing ritual that always happened a few minutes before three o'clock dismissal. The woman teacher would look at the watch hanging from a pin on her chest and signal one of the boys. As he went for the basin, the teacher would instruct us to get our books together.

When the boy returned, cautiously bearing half a basin of water, she would take out a cake of soap and a small towel. All of us little boys would watch in considerable fascination as she washed her hands carefully and delicately, rinsed them and dried them on the towel.

I knew why we watched with so much interest: we never saw such fastidious behavior at home. We learned from observing our teachers, even if none of them ever talked about what she was doing.

"Ask him if we can sit down," my uncle said, stirring me out of my reverie. When I had translated this request, the man creased his paper and said, "Sure, sure, sit down."

Two chairs stood on the wall facing the desk. We moved to them, and I waited while Uncle ran his hand over the seats and backs. The seats were clean, but the back of one was dusty.

"People can live like pigs," he said, taking a handkerchief from his pocket and slapping the dust off the chair. There was a rustle of folding paper behind us as the man stirred to watch this operation. He went back to his newspaper, but I heard him murmur, "Damned greaseballs."

When Tom returned, he carried a white folder, and we watched him lay the folder on that man's desk. Then, for the first time, we saw him elevate his head and eyes in a positive display of interest. He actually folded his newspaper and moved it to a far corner of his desk.

We knew, of course, that the manila folder held the information about Uncle Herschel that would reveal the reasons if not the source of the summons to this office. We waited for the man to open it. I saw that Uncle was leaning forward on his stick, both fists closed around it, knuckles white and drawn.

Apparently the man at the desk needed only a swift glance to refresh his memory. He raised his head and bent his index finger at us. Uncle got up, and I got up with him. We approached the desk.

"Ask him," he said to me, "if he's a doctor."

I said, "No, he's not a doctor."

He sucked in his lips as though he had just tasted something detestable. "Ask him," he repeated with a quiet hateful kind of tolerance.

When I turned to Uncle, he asked, "What does he want?"

"He wants me to ask you if you're a doctor."

"You know the answer to that."

"Yes, I know the answer, but he wants to hear your answer."

Uncle looked into the man's eyes and said, "No, no doctor."

The man nodded. "A woman came in last week to complain you had treated her mother and her mother had died. She came in with a lawyer, and they said you had an evil eye, whatever that is. What do you say to that?"

When he paused I turned to Uncle, who was waiting for me to translate. I could see anger mounting in his eyes as the charge unfolded.

"No," he said, banging his stick on the desk, "tell this idiot I am not a doctor, I don't tell anybody I'm a doctor, I did not treat that girl's mother, and I do not have an evil eye. Tell him, and tell him I want to see the District Attorney."

I took a deep breath before I would tackle this formidable assignment. I knew I would have to be selective about what to tell this man and what to omit. I certainly couldn't call him an idiot, and I would try to reduce the anger in what Uncle had said. I plunged into the translation and, almost out of breath, said that my uncle wanted to see the District Attorney.

"Tough guy, your uncle," the man commented. "Tell him I'm the District Attorney. I'm the Assistant District Attorney, and I take the place of the District Attorney. Now, does he deny the statement of that woman?"

"What?" He evidently forgot I was a little boy.

"Does he say the statements made by that woman are not true?"

"Yes," I said, "he says they are not true."

"What does he want?" Uncle asked.

I explained to him that I had denied (a new word for me) the statements made by the Teitelbaum woman.

"Tell him," Uncle said, "she should be immediately arrested and thrown in prison. In Russia such a woman would be sent to prison for five years."

"You want me to say that?" I asked. I had sneaked a look into that man's watchful eyes, and I suspected he would flip over Uncle's anger.

"Yes, of course, tell him. I'm not afraid of him. I'm in America, not Russia."

I looked at him, marveling that he was so inconsistent in his words about Russia. I turned to the man and delivered Uncle's estimate of what should happen to his accuser. He listened and nodded, then he slowly closed the folder.

"Tell your uncle American law protects a person's right to make an accusation and protects the right of the accused to fight back and he'll have plenty of fighting because I think they want to sue him for using an evil eye."

And as he wound up that assessment, he reopened his yap, laid his head back and bellowed his laughter to the ceiling.

After I had relayed to Uncle Herschel the sum of that man's message, Uncle stared at him and said to me, "Ask him why he's laughing?"

I asked.

The man dried his eyes with a handkerchief as we waited. I

looked at my uncle and saw on his face the same fury that possessed me.

"Tell your uncle," the man said, "that when he comes here the next time he'll have plenty to worry about. Tell him if he wants to, he can come with a lawyer."

"Why do we have to come here again?" my uncle asked after I had translated for him.

"Because," the man replied, "I want to give you an opportunity to face your accuser and to see how the two stories hold."

"Tell him," Uncle said, "I wasn't the doctor there. She had a doctor every time I came into that house."

When I conveyed this fact to the man, he paused and ruminated over it. "Who is that doctor?"

I told him and I gave him an approximate address.

"We'll have him here," he said. "Now you come back on the twenty-ninth of April."

He wrote the date on a sheet of paper he had torn off a pad and handed it to me. We understood that we could leave.

We did not speak on the way home, and when we walked into the house Mother looked inquiringly at us, but I waited for Uncle to tell her what had happened. He took his cane and coat into the front room, and I waited at the table for the lunch my mother would presently serve us.

"Heaven, earth and swindle," Uncle said as he sat down.

My mother looked at him, her eyes large with concern. "What does she want?" Mother asked.

"Money. I couldn't help her mother, and Padilsky couldn't help her mother, but she can't accuse Padilsky because he's a doctor with a license, so she is going to accuse me of what I don't know."

"But you didn't do anything for the mother."

"No, but I was there, and I talked to the girl."

"But Padilsky was there, too, and he told her what to do."

"Yes."

"So what does she want from you?"

"I don't know. We'll have to wait until I can hear what she

says. Then I'll know what to do. Where can I get a lawyer?"

My mother stared at him. Lawyers were fearsome characters in my home; they always involved trouble and court, and the receipt of a "lawyer letter" in any home in this Jewish enclave forecast impending disaster.

I said, "Maybe the Fried boys know."

My mother responded happily to that. "Oh yes, they work in New York. They will know. Let me go in tonight while they're eating dinner."

Later I went with her and waited with her as she knocked on the door. Mrs. Fried opened it and stared out into the dark hall until she recognized my mother.

"Good evening," my mother said.

"Come in, come in," Mrs. Fried said. "How are you? Sometimes I don't see you for days. How is your family?"

"Good evening," Mother said to the family, who were eating their soup course at the moment. "Good appetite."

They greeted her, and Sam, one of the boys, went to the front room for a chair.

"Don't bother," my mother said. "I don't want to disturb your dinner. I came in to ask you a question. My brother, a greenie, lives with us. He needs a lawyer. Do you know a lawyer?"

The two boys and Mrs. Fried deliberated over this question. Lawyers were not as common as, say, doctors. Then Mr. Fried said, "Lawyers cost money."

"Yes," my mother said, "lawyers cost money."

"And does your brother have money to pay for a lawyer?"

"No."

"Then let him go to the Legal Aid Society."

"What is that?"

"Those are lawyers. They take cases for poor people who can't pay."

"That, I never heard of."

"So you're hearing it now."

"But he speaks only Yiddish and Russian."

"Many of them are Jews."

"This is a gift from God."

"I have a friend who went to the Legal Aid Society once about a year ago. I'll see him in the shop tomorrow, and I'll bring home the address."

"Oh!" my mother exclaimed, "you are such good people. Thanks, thanks."

"For what?" Mrs. Fried asked.

Back in our home Mother said, "You don't have to worry," and she outlined for Uncle Herschel what Mr. Fried had said. My uncle shook his head as if he could not believe what he had heard.

"Wonderful! wonderful! Jews don't desert each other."

"No," my father said. He was near the sink slicing my mother's chalah on our breadboard. "This is a golden country. Someday our children will know."

"I'm learning already," my uncle said.

Twenty-one

We went through the routine of dinner: marinated herring, soup and thick egg noodles, boiled chicken, boiled carrots, mashed potatoes, a compote of prunes and other dried fruits, many glasses of tea and apple cake. We devoured everything. Only Uncle did not eat the chicken. However, he sat over his four glasses of tea for the longest time, smoking interminably without talking.

We had experienced his periods of silence before, so we talked around him, and I was happy that he didn't seem disturbed that we did not remark on his abstraction. His eyes seemed drawn to something, some phenomenon beyond the walls of this little flat.

When he had snuffed out his fourth or fifth cigarette and did not reach for another from his silver case, I suspected he was getting ready to leave the table. He turned his glass mouth end down on his saucer, a signal to my mother not to pour him another glassful, and ran his fingers over his little mustache. Then he got up.

"I must go to see that Padilsky," he said.

He did not ask for a discussion on the matter. This was his determination: he was going to see Dr. Padilsky, and we didn't know why. But, of course, we did know. Padilsky and this woman who had complained to the District Attorney were bound up in his mind, and he had to resolve one, apparently, before he could make up his mind about the other.

"Can I go?" I asked.

My mother said "oh" as if I had suddenly become an intruder, but Uncle Herschel simply looked over at me and said "come."

I jumped to my feet and ran for my outer garments.

As we walked down Manhattan Avenue, I had to reflect on the extent of Dr. Padilsky's expanse of awe in the neighborhood. Many had told of his shrill bad manners in their homes as they entertained him for a sick child or a sick husband. Somehow, women always managed to make it to his office, thus reducing their fee to fifty cents. Muttel had told me this story over and over. His father had developed a violent cough, and after days and days of home treatment with milk, eggs and honey whipped into a delicious drink, he had finally been persuaded to go to Dr. Padilsky. As soon as Muttel's father had walked into the consultation room, Dr. Padilsky had said, "Look at you, you fat slob. Whatever is wrong with you, it starts with your belly. And throw away that filthy cigarette. How long do you expect to live smoking those things? Shut up, don't say anything. You can't convince me about anything."

The legend around the doctor had grown to enormous heights. Everyone knew about his acidy approach to his patients. "You want to eat chicken, you'll be as strong as a chicken." They had heard rumors—or had circulated them—that he taught a class in Bellevue Medical College, so he was talked about as a professor. In local circles, where medicine was concerned, "professor" was regarded as the highest level of attainment; it rendered the doctor who had achieved it most knowledgeable.

This rumor grew as Dr. Padilsky unveiled his new carriage, which was drawn by a magnificent animal. Now and then Dr. Padilsky would pull up on our block and drop the weight that was attached to the horse's head by a long lead. The kids would run to stare at this beautiful chestnut animal. We knew nothing about horses but we could compare him to the dray horses we saw normally—heavy-legged, low-browed animals that sometimes dropped dead on our street.

The legs of this horse were so slim, and his head was so long and narrow; and he held it so high and tossed it so imperiously that he must have known whose carriage he was pulling. He would raise and lower his legs and turn his head from side to side so he could see us in spite of the blinders on both sides of his head. We kids would stand around and rehearse his virtues, arguing about the speed his legs could carry him on a straightaway.

We always backed off in a hurry when he spread his legs, because his urine bouncing off the cobbles could spray for a good distance. We admired the force and the heat of the expulsion and even speculated on the amount in terms of gallons.

When we came to Padilsky's house, Uncle Herschel stepped forward boldly and pushed the button. On previous occasions I had performed this rite; now he had learned. He even kept his finger on the button long after the sound had bounded and rebounded off the walls.

I got behind Uncle, suspecting that whoever would come to the door to answer this summons would be blazing. I was right. Already someone was yelling, "All right, all right, get off that bell."

Then the door was swept open, and we beheld Padilsky in his home undress—his feet in carpet slippers, his suspenders hanging and his pants trailing.

"Without mercy! Without mercy!" he cried.

"I have to talk to you," Uncle said.

"So you have to talk to me. Does that mean you have to break my door down?"

"I wanted to be sure you heard me."

Dr. Padilsky glared at Uncle Herschel, but my uncle did not seem intimidated. Padilsky didn't ask us to come in. He just turned away from us but he did not close the door. We followed him into his consultation room, where he struck a switch on the desk lamp and flung himself into the swivel chair. It responded to him, yielding to his weight, and the back of the chair dropped off. He did not ask us to sit down.

"So?" he demanded. "What do you want?"

"You remember that woman on Manhattan Avenue who died a few days ago? She had a form of sleeping sickness and never came out of a coma?"

Dr. Padilsky looked at Uncle Herschel as he probably tried to recall which of his patients died.

"So?" he asked.

"That woman's daughter says I killed her with my evil eye. She went to the District Attorney."

For a long, horrible moment Dr. Padilsky stared at my uncle, and I wondered if this story was so incredible he was stunned or if he were mustering the words to answer what he had just heard. Instead, he laid his head back and let out a long hateful yawp. He laughed and laughed, while Uncle and I stared back at him, waiting for him to stop. His face still looked strangely blemished and, in spots, almost raw.

When he had brought his chair back to a normal position and stopped howling, Uncle Herschel said, "Why are you laughing?"

"Why am I laughing? I'm laughing because you wanted to play doctor, and if you want to play doctor, you sometimes get kicked in the face."

"What are you talking about?" my uncle demanded. "Who was playing doctor?"

"Then why were you there every time I came?"

"Because I'm a human being, because I heard the girl screaming for help."

"It would have been better if you had stayed in your own house."

"You don't mean that."

"I do mean that."

"And let a woman die without even trying to help her?"

"If you had helped her you would have been playing doctor."

"That's child's talk! If a building is burning and I run in to save a woman, do I have to worry that I'm not a fireman?"

"A fireman is not licensed by the state to practice his trade."

"So I should have remained in my house and not gone in to make the kind of suggestion any intelligent person would have made?"

"What suggestion?"

" 'Call a doctor.' "

"That girl would have decided that for herself."

"But what else did I do that I shouldn't have done?"

"You diagnosed the case before I could look at her."

"That's not permitted?"

"It's not permitted if you say you're a doctor and you're not."

"How could I say I'm a doctor when I told the girl to send for a doctor?"

"Maybe you thought it was too much for you."

"You're only flattering yourself, Doctor Padilsky. I don't have a license to practice medicine, but what you know about medicine is only a small part of what I know."

"All right, so you're a professor. So what do you want from me?"

"You should tell the truth to the District Attorney."

"Oh! And what is the truth?"

"That I wasn't treating this woman—that you were."

"That's all?"

"That's all."

"No!"

"Why not?"

"Because you're a charlatan, because you pretend to be what you are not and now you want me to swear to a lie."

"What lie are you talking about? The only lie I've heard so far is that I'm a charlatan. Who are you to make such a judgment on me?"

"I'm the doctor you want to go in and lie for you."

"Pig! I'm not asking you to lie. I'm asking you to tell the truth

—that I did not treat this woman, that I told the girl to send for a doctor, that this boy ran to you to get you."

"No!"

"Then I will make you tell the truth."

"So! How will you do that?"

"You will find out when the time comes."

Dr. Padilsky got up slowly, almost regally.

"Do yourself a favor. Tell the District Attorney you made a mistake, that you will never do it again, and go sell your patent medicines."

"And how do I explain her complaint that she died because of my evil eye? Is that the mistake you're talking about?"

He stared at my uncle for a long speechless moment. Then, again, he laid his head back and roared his laughter to the ceiling.

"In medicine, my friend, there is no evil eye," he finally said.

"You know it, and I know it, but that stupid girl doesn't know it."

"If you had stayed in your house—"

"But I didn't stay in my house. I'm a human being, and I hear a call for help when I see suffering," Uncle said.

"So now *you're* suffering."

"So now I'm suffering, but why should that be when you can change all that?"

"I?" he asked in a kind of hateful tone of mock bewilderment.

"Yes, you."

"And how can I change all that?"

"By telling the District Attorney that she's a foolish, stupid girl, and that you, not I, treated her mother."

"Oh no, I don't get involved in anything like this. I didn't call you in for a consultation."

"That's right. You didn't. I called you."

"I don't stick my neck out. You went looking for trouble. Now get yourself out of the trouble. After all, you're a felsher."

"Whether you like it or not, you're in it, Doctor Padilsky."

The doctor smiled, and I detested the pity on his lips.

"The District Attorney is going to call you," Uncle said.

"You gave him my name?"

"I did."

"So you tell him what he wants to know."

"He won't ask me. He'll ask you."

"Then I'll tell him what he wants to know."

"That's all I'm asking."

"But not anything about you. I know nothing about you, and I won't answer any questions about you."

"You're a very stubborn man, Doctor Padilsky."

"Sometimes being stubborn can be a virtue. It keeps you out of trouble."

"But it won't keep me out of trouble."

"That's your problem."

"No, it's your problem, too. It's humanity's problem."

"Hah! I have to worry about all humanity!"

"If you're a wise man, you'll worry."

"So let's say I'm not a wise man."

"If anybody has the evil eye, I'd say it's you."

"You see all my good points."

"You'll see when we face the District Attorney. He's not a stupid man."

"He can't make me say what I don't want to say."

"He won't be the only one there."

"Ho! Felsher, I'm not afraid of you."

For a short interval the two men looked balefully at each other. Then Uncle Herschel licked his lips, and I expected a sharp thrust from him.

"Doctor, your face is badly broken out. You're a doctor. Why haven't you cured yourself?"

"Who asked you to come here and ask impertinent questions?"

"Doctor, I don't sell a preparation for it, but I can cure that misery on your face."

"I was sleeping so peacefully—"

"Let's say I'm a witch doctor, but why should you be afraid of what I can do for you? I won't complain to the police that I can do for you what you can't do for yourself."

"You're even a worse charlatan than I thought before. Don't you know there is no cure for what is bothering me?"

When Uncle smiled down at the other man's rage, I knew that he had worn down the doctor's assurance.

"I know that," Uncle said, "but you don't. For the rest of your life you'll wonder what I know that you don't, and you'll probably be too proud to ask. So you'll continue to suffer with that nasty mess, but you won't come to me because you're convinced I'm a charlatan."

"You even talk like a charlatan. You're using the same kind of salesmanship to draw me out and make me want to come to your cheap store."

The smile did not leave my uncle's face. "But you won't come, so you'll never have the satisfaction I could give a man who doesn't have your anger and prejudice."

"You can't convince me by laughing at what you call my anger and prejudice. Of course I'm angry. I've spent at least three years studying medicine. How many years did you study medicine? What right do you have comparing yourself to me?"

"Every right. My brother is a doctor in Odessa. I worked and studied with him in his office for at least ten years. Whatever you have done for every kind of patient, I have done. In addition, for at least fifteen years I've studied in pharmacology. I've experimented with the preparations my brother and I used. It may not be easy for you to understand, Doctor, that I know more about drugs and chemicals than all your doctors in Brooklyn rolled into one. And if I have to, and if you push me to it, I'll prove to you and everybody that I'm not a charlatan. So . . . I feel better now, Doctor. I know about American courts, too. I may ask a lawyer to make you prove that I'm a charlatan. You may regret such a test."

Dr. Padilsky glared at us as Uncle turned and stalked toward the door, and I was undecided whether or not to turn and give this hateful man a proper rejoinder for that word—"charlatan." However, we were on the street before I could decide that this was my uncle's quarrel and I had no place in it.

On the way home we held our heads higher, and I could tell from the emphatic rhythm with which Uncle's cane punctuated our walk that he was pleased with his part in the dialogue.

"Do you really have a medicine that could cure the doctor's face?"

He turned to smile at me.

"Doctor Padilsky would give a year of his life to find out."

"Do you?" I persisted.

I did not understand this kind of chess. In my home nobody ever lied to me. We had no need for subtlety. I had to know if my Uncle Herschel was answering Padilsky's charge by daring him to ask about the cure.

"You would be disappointed if I didn't have a cure for that?" Uncle asked, and I marveled that he would know how I felt.

"Yes."

"Why?"

"Because! Because he said things about you that aren't true."

"How do you know they are not true?"

"Because you said so—you told him how long you studied with your brother and that you had studied by yourself from all those books."

"I have a cure. I've tried the cure on many people in Russia, and the skin trouble went away."

I rejoiced. "Sure," I said.

"He'll come," Uncle said.

"The doctor? Why? He called you so many names."

"Because man is an animal with a great deal of curiosity, and because an intelligent man is even more curious, and because a sick man will be even more curious about a possible cure, even if he is a doctor who doesn't believe."

I tried to memorize the sequence of what he had just pronounced for me, but it was not easy. I wanted to remember because I could not assuredly keep to myself the triumph I had just witnessed; and when I would tell the sequence to Muttel tomorrow, I intended to fashion every facet so it would enhance the color of my story.

When we got home, before I took off my coat, I told my mother, "We went to Doctor Padilsky a couple of minutes ago, and you should have heard Uncle holler at him."

My mother stared, dumbfounded, from me to her brother, because nobody went to Dr. Padilsky unless he was sick and absolutely *nobody* hollered at Dr. Padilsky.

"This is how it's going to be," Uncle Herschel explained, "if I try to be what I am, if I try to do what I can. Nobody has anointed me yet, and for that reason I am not yet among God's chosen people, like Doctor Padilsky. The difference between me and him is that if he makes a mistake or even if he doesn't make a mistake and he doesn't know what to do for a patient, and the patient dies, that's the end of it. He's a doctor, he has been anointed by the state and he can do no harm. If I see a patient and everything goes well, then I'm a good felsher–not a good doctor, a good felsher. I'm not anointed, but I'm not shunned. But if my patient should continue to be sick and if my medicine cannot help him or if he should die, then not only am I a bad felsher, but I also have an evil eye. An evil eye! This kind of stupidity I thought I would never meet in America, but I guess they haven't given up their old world superstitions. So what becomes of me? All those years I studied with my brother and with other doctors, I must now throw away. Maybe I should hang out a sign like Doctor Padilsky's–'Evil Eye Administered Here.' A good idea. I wouldn't need a license because the state doesn't know about evil eyes, and I could practice my medicine that way. What have I done with my life? What can I show for myself in addition to a lot of children? A crazy world! A man should plan better. Maybe I could have been a very creative, a very efficient tailor or a bookkeeper. Then I would have worked in a large store or a large establishment, and I wouldn't have the heartache of rejection or going to the District Attorney to explain why I used an evil eye to kill a woman who was almost dead when I first saw her.

"What would I have said to me if I were Padilsky? Would I have laughed? Would I have taunted the poor felsher? Why did he do this? What pleasure did he derive from seeing me in a ditch? And what do I do if the District Attorney doesn't believe me? How can I explain to my wife and children that even in America, even in this golden land, I am a failure, an out and out failure, even in what I feel I do best? This will be the hardest for me to do. I must tell them about my evil eye and that my evil eye will keep them in Russia for only God knows how long. There must be an answer for this failure."

I carried my buttered roll to the store the next day. Uncle Herschel was sitting in a chair near the window. I liked the way he placed himself there. With his goatee and his starched shirt, he was good display for his business. I noticed as I approached the store that people stopped to look.

When I came in, he raised his eyes from the book he was reading and nodded. I took my roll into the back room, and when I returned to the store, I asked, "What can I do, Uncle?"

He leveled his eyes at my face and unclipped his glasses from his nose.

"There is nothing to do, my child," he said. "We will now wait for people to come in."

I nodded, and, as he went back to his book, I moved in front of the bottles, lining them up like good staunch soldiers, row on row.

Then I heard a faint scraping at the door and I turned. At last, a customer.

My mouth dropped, and I swung around to face Uncle. He was peering over his glasses toward the door.

"Come in, Doctor Padilsky," he said.

Dr. Padilsky rammed his fists into his pockets and sauntered over to the shelves that the monstrous Ferd had overlooked. He touched some of the bottles, shook one or two to enrich the sallow liquid that had risen, and studied the full color. He held up one bottle, shook it and pulled out the cork.

"May I?" he asked.

"Taste it, taste it."

The doctor dipped his small finger into the mixture and brought the finger to his lips. "*M-m-m*," he said.

He repeated his probing three or four times, each time repeating the murmur. I was eager for him to spell out for me what that humming sound meant. Did he like what he tasted or was this only a noncommittal courtesy to a host?

"I smell a lot of chemicals in these bottles, Felsher," he said.

I was proud that the doctor had called my uncle by his title.

"You'll smell more if you open more bottles, Doctor."

"I stole away from my office for a few minutes. Maybe some other time. Felsher, I had to come because of what you said about my skin condition. Understand, I don't believe you can do anything for it. I know you can't. However, I now have two cases even worse than mine. I want to hear what you have to suggest so I can try it on them."

"I understand," Uncle said, and he didn't smile.

Dr. Padilsky looked around at the bottles on the shelves. Apparently he expected Uncle Herschel to pluck a bottle from a shelf for instant salvation.

"You have your prescription paper?" Uncle asked.

"Yes."

"Then write yourself this prescription."

The doctor pulled his pad from his coat pocket.

"You don't have it prepared and on a shelf?" he asked.

"No, no, then I would really be a charlatan. You will see after you write the prescription I'm not allowed to write in America."

Then he dictated a few words and figures that I did not understand but that, evidently, the doctor caught and entered on his pad.

When Uncle had stopped dictating, Dr. Padilsky reread the prescription he had just written. I watched his face because I had no other way to measure the effect upon him.

He said, "I've never seen these drugs put together this way."

"This cost me many mistakes and many hours of worry and concern."

"You've tried this on people?"

"On many people."

"And your results were good?"

"The skin cleared up completely."

"Did you get any resistance when you told your patients to take this internally?"

"Perhaps you won't believe this and perhaps you will think I'm talking about what you said to me. Once, one called me a charlatan, and another one suggested I had gotten this prescription from my grandmother."

Dr. Padilsky looked up from the prescription pad, and for a moment I thought I saw a sheepish look on his face, as if Uncle had caught him deep in a honey pot.

"I'm sometimes such an ogre, I even scare myself," he said.

"I won't come to find out if you used it, but you can take the word of a very successful charlatan that it will clear up your skin."

"Sometimes even a charlatan can make a contribution to medicine."

Twenty-two

When we came home my mother looked from my uncle to me. She was seated by the kitchen window reading the day's installment of the novel in the *Forward.* My father was sleeping in the bedroom.

Uncle Herschel went directly to the front room after my mother had asked if he wanted a glass of tea. He shook his head and I watched him hang his coat on the back of a chair, kick off his shoes and lie down on the leather lounge. I went to the space behind the stove, where my mother kept the old newspapers, for yesterday's *Forward.* I, too, liked to read the installments of the novel as well as the many articles on health, literature, world events.

I sat at the kitchen table, where I could spread the paper comfortably, and I dug into yesterday's segment of the novel. After a few minutes I got up and looked in the icebox where my mother kept those large, luscious Spy or Cortland apples. Then I returned to my reading.

I wondered how long my mother would endure this silence and how long she would refrain from asking me what had happened two days ago in the confrontation with Padilsky. I could only guess she was waiting for Uncle to fall asleep. It was as I suspected.

When she rustled her paper extensively and turned slowly in her chair to face me, I knew she was getting ready to ask her questions.

"What happened in the doctor's office?" she whispered.

I raised my head from the newspaper and leaned toward her. "Doctor Padilsky," I said, "is a dirty dog." I paused so the full impact of this total assessment would sink in.

"What happened?" she repeated.

"Nothing happened. Uncle asked him to go to the District Attorney to tell him he was the doctor and he treated Mrs. Teitelbaum, but Doctor Padilsky laughed at Uncle."

"Aye, aye," she said.

"And he laughed at Uncle when he said the District Attorney would call him, too."

"Aye, aye."

"And Uncle got very angry when Doctor Padilsky laughed and told him he was no good."

"Good, good."

"And Uncle was very sad, and he talked a lot on the way home from the doctor's office."

"What did he say?"

"He said he didn't know what he was going to do if every time he sees a patient he'll have to worry about an evil eye. And he thinks he's a failure and he'll never be able to bring his family over from Russia. Is he a failure, Momma?"

"No, my son, your uncle is not a failure. He's a very wise man, but he's upset and discouraged by what happened. Maybe I can go in to talk to Jennie. Maybe she doesn't understand what she said or how it would hurt Uncle."

"Are you going to tell Uncle?"

"I don't know yet. I'm afraid if I tell him he'll say I shouldn't."

"When will you go—now?"

My mother got up and tiptoed to the front room. For about a minute she stood at the threshold, watching the smooth sleep-tempered motion of Uncle's chest. When she turned back to me she said "come."

I was at the door almost immediately, but I did not realize that the "come" was just preliminary to what she had planned. The command was actually meant for herself. She got out a large bowl and filled it with the almond bread and apple cake she had baked for the Sabbath, and I felt ashamed that I had forgotten how a Jewish mother should prepare for a visit to a bereaved neighbor.

When we came into the street I was happy that none of my friends was visible or waiting for me. We went quietly into the next house and up the two flights of stairs to the Teitelbaums' flat. I waited for my mother to do the neighborly thing at the door. She knocked briefly and immediately pushed the door open. We had not heard an invitation to enter, but that didn't matter; protocol and formality were loose in this enclave.

The house was quite dark, and we paused at the door because no one was in the kitchen. Then we saw Mr. Teitelbaum and Jennie in the front room. They were seated at the two windows, staring out into the yards at the rear of the house, where tall, skinny, shaved timber poles held one end of the clotheslines extending from each tenant's window.

Hanging the clothesline was always the first vital task after moving into a flat. Specialists at the job, peripatetic pole shinners, moved from yard to yard, rendering a call I have not heard in many years—"*L-l-l-i-i-i-ine up!*" The shinner was always trailed into the yard by a retinue of kids who waited for him to chant his first bid so they could join with him in the next chorus. He approved of this because it brought to the windows all the neighbors, interested to see if their youngsters had joined the chant.

We had many odd-ball vocal salesmen who made their pitches in our back yards. One around whom the kids rallied delightedly was a tinker whose cry they adored. "Fixen, fooxen, foxen, iceboxes, teplach, kreplach, vahness."

This line the kids howled over no matter how often they heard it, and they belted it out with a vigor and excitement that brought lucrative bids from the neighbors. Another vendor offered nostrums against "cockwooches, wahten, mize." The kids who imitated his liquid consonants with gleeful accuracy could only guess what he was selling, but they accepted his bellow so wholeheartedly they spurred his sales, too.

My mother said, "Good evening."

The girl did not turn at all, but her father rolled his eyes over toward us and nodded. "Good evening," he said.

My mother walked to the sideboard on the left, where she set down her dish. "I brought you some almond bread and some of my apple cake."

He nodded again. "Thank you, thank you."

"How are you?" she asked, and I marveled she was not discouraged by their totally negative reception.

"How should we be?" he asked. I noticed that our Jewish people very often answered a question by asking a question, as though to emphasize the futility of asking the first.

"She was a good woman," my mother said.

Not even this seemed to rouse him. He looked down to the carpet slippers he was wearing and sighed weakly. "She was a good, true wife."

"She was a good mother, too," Jennie suddenly exploded.

I looked at my mother. She never quarreled with her neighbors and only occasionally said something sharp to my father. She had come here to be kind and neighborly to these people.

"Oh, I know," she tried to soothe them, "I know. She was a very good mother and a very good wife."

"Then why did she have to die?" the girl demanded.

My mother spread her hands. "How can I answer that, my dear? All this is in the hands of God."

"No," the girl replied fiercely. "God wouldn't bother with little people like us. Your brother killed her with his evil eye."

"How can you say that? My brother is a felsher. He cures people. He loves people. He wouldn't hurt a fly."

"He wouldn't hurt a fly because he doesn't try to cure flies. And if he can't cure somebody he kills her with his evil eye. I know. I watched him."

"But Doctor Padilsky was here—"

"When Doctor Padilsky came, it was already too late."

"How can you say that? After all, Padilsky is a doctor. My brother is not a doctor. He told you to send for Padilsky."

"Your brother looked at my mother. That's all he had to do. When I first saw your brother, I knew something was wrong. He doesn't have a beard like all good pious Jews. He has that little thing on his chin like a devil."

"That's a style with European doctors."

"European devils."

"In a month you'll feel better, and you'll understand that my brother only wanted to help."

"And why does he carry that stick? Is he a cripple, or is that to keep the other devils away from him?"

"The stick? In Europe many doctors carry a stick. So what?"

"So he has an evil eye."

My mother turned to the girl's father. "You don't believe my brother cast an evil eye on your wife."

He shook his head; he seemed too bewildered to have an opinion. "I don't know what to believe. Why should somebody like your brother cast an evil eye on my wife? He never saw my wife."

"*He believes, he believes*," the girl shrieked.

"But you shouldn't have to go to the District Attorney, he should make trouble for my brother," my mother said.

"If the District Attorney makes for him trouble, then good. He should suffer the way my mother suffered and the way my father suffered and I suffered."

"It's not good," my mother persisted. "One Jew should not make trouble for another Jew. We Jews have enough trouble without we should make trouble for another Jew."

"By me he's not another Jew. He's a man with an evil eye," the girl said.

"You talk like an anti-Semite."

"If he's a Jew, then I'm an anti-Semite."

"So already you made up your mind that's how it's got to be."

"That's how it's got to be. I want to see him lie to the District Attorney. I want to hear him tell the District Attorney he don't have an evil eye. And when the District Attorney sends him to prison because he has an evil eye, then my lawyer says he's going to sue him because we know he has a business, and he'll pay and he'll pay and he'll pay." Her voice rose and rose until it reached an almost hysterical pitch on her last word.

My mother said, "You're a very wicked woman." She held out her hand to me, said "good night" to the girl's father and swung around to the door. As we came to the door, we heard Mr. Teitelbaum's pallid voice. "Good night," he said.

As we came into the hall I said, "Ma, she's crazy."

"Maybe she's crazy, maybe she's not crazy. Who knows what a lawyer can tell her."

What my mother had just said was a new concept that I did not understand at all. I did not ask what she meant until we came into the street. Then I said, "What did you mean when you said that about a lawyer?"

"Well," she said, "Mrs. Kornut's son is a lawyer. He's already married and he lives on Vernon Avenue. That's how he makes a lot of money. He hears about an accident or somebody died, and he goes there to find out how the accident happened or how the person died. Sometimes he hears a little something, and from that something he builds something big. Somebody must have come to a lawyer and told him that Jennie thinks her mother was killed by a felsher who has an evil eye. You hear? Two things: in America only a doctor can treat a patient, not a felsher; and in America if you do something wrong to somebody he can sue you for money."

"But Uncle doesn't have any money."

"He has a store and he has merchandise in the store."

"But if they take away his store, how will he bring over his wife and his children?"

"That's what's worrying your uncle."

"Oh, Ma, I wish I was a lawyer."

She smiled down at me. "And what would you do?"

"I'd go to the District Attorney and tell him he's making a terrible mistake. Then I'd go to that lawyer and I'd tell him he's lying about my uncle and I would send him to prison."

She touched my cheek. "You're a good boy," she said. "Uncle will be so glad to hear what you're saying."

When we entered the flat, we dipped along on our toes, but we woke my father and Uncle Herschel anyway. My father asked where we had been, and, because Uncle had sauntered into the kitchen, she made a noncommittal gesture and he understood that she did not want to talk now about her excursion but she would develop it at a later hour.

"I will make tea," Mother said, and my father and Uncle sat at their places to wait.

"It was not good," Uncle Herschel said.

"What was not good?" my mother asked, not because she did not know, but because she did not want him to feel we had been talking about him.

"We went to see Padilsky, but he's like a mule. He admits he was there, he admits he treated the woman, but he won't tell it to the District Attorney. He says if I want to play doctor, I have to accept all the responsibilities of being a doctor. Play! Didn't I know she was dead the minute I laid eyes on her?"

"The truth will come out," Mother said.

"And if it doesn't, what will I do? How will I bring my family to America?"

"God will find a way."

"Whose God? Mine? Yours? My God tells me He'll suggest a way in my mind, but I must find a way to do what is in my mind. So far, I've been failure. I must admit it even if I don't like it."

"How can you say you've been a failure when you haven't

really undertaken to do anything? You opened a store, but you haven't given it a chance to grow, for people to get to know you."

"Who knows? Maybe I'll have to close it."

"A person has to look to God and to himself, or he can't live."

"We will see, we will see."

After that he drank enormous quantities of tea, gulping vast draughts and looking moodily out the window. We matched his feeling. I said nothing, and my parents spoke of their relatives and of their plans to visit my father's brother on Saturday.

As before, anticipating the trip to the District Attorney with Uncle Herschel, I told my teacher where I would be on Wednesday. Again I was surveyed by a large battery of inquisitive eyes, but I did not yield to their frank questions.

Twenty-three

On Wednesday we did not go as we did last week, haltingly and unfamiliar with directions and our surroundings. We knew where we would find the District Attorney as we got into the elevator that had once confronted us as an automatic monster. I was even familiar with the way my stomach whooped into my mouth as the elevator stopped short at our floor. Today we did not flounder. We turned down the right corridor and came to the office we had explored on our last trip.

I waited for Uncle to open the door, an act he carried off with his old aplomb; I was delighted to see his shoulders squared and his walking stick at carry. What we had seen in this room on our first excursion was still very much in place with only two differences. The man at the corner desk was now facing us, and at the Assistant District Attorney's desk sat a new man whose face was even more bland and noncommittal than the last one's. On the other side of the room, perched on three chairs, were Jennie, her father, and a strange man who held a pad of yellow, ruled paper in his lap. I guessed that he was the lawyer the girl had flung into my mother's face.

The Assistant D.A. turned to the man at the rear desk and said, "Get Horowitz." Then he swung around and said to us, "Sit down–over there."

"Over there," where he had pointed, stood three chairs. We

sat in two of them as he opened the same file the man had brought out during our last visit. The stage was being set for the drama, this confrontation, and I wondered about this Horowitz. I stared over at Jennie, and I hoped her eyes would meet mine so I could stare her down and warn her that I, too, had seen what had happened in her house and I, too, could testify that my uncle had instructed her to send for a doctor. But she did not look at me, and I had no way of knowing whether it was because she was afraid of me or because I was really nothing in her life. Her father sat completely immobilized, staring down at his hands. I had to guess that he was either unhappy about the entire proceeding or he was wholly indifferent to it. Certainly he showed no enthusiasm for the impending trial.

When the door opened, everybody raised his head. A young man preceded the messenger. He raised his hand to the Assistant District Attorney like a gladiator greeting Caesar and came immediately to Uncle Herschel and me. He touched my shoulder. "Sit on the next chair," he said to me, and I moved over to leave a place for him next to my uncle.

"My name is Horowitz," he said to Uncle in Yiddish, "and I'm here to help you. I'm a lawyer from the Legal Aid Society, and I speak and understand Yiddish. Don't be afraid to say whatever is on your mind, because you won't be asked to swear that what you say is true. The Assistant District Attorney will probably ask the young woman to state her complaint. I will translate for you as she speaks. You understand?"

"I understand," Uncle said quietly, and he folded his hands over the head of his stick.

Horowitz raised his head and nodded to the Assistant District Attorney, who squared himself around toward Jennie.

"Do you understand your rights in this complaint? You don't have to answer any questions after you make your complaint unless you so wish."

The girl had transferred her blank gaze to the man who spoke to her and, when he stopped, to her lawyer, who nodded.

"Yes," she said.

"Very well," he said. "This is only a hearing where we will decide if there is enough substance in your complaint to take it before a grand jury. Now, you go ahead and state your complaint."

I was actually more attentive to Horowitz, who was whispering a swift, accurate translation of what the girl had said and what the Assistant District Attorney had just announced. Uncle listened impassively to the translation, his eyes fixed upon Jennie's face.

She stood up and pointed to Uncle Herschel. "That man killed my mother."

For a moment, everybody appeared immobilized by this sharp, spare denunciation. Then the Assistant District Attorney scratched a light out of a kitchen match and held it to a cigar. Immediately Uncle reached into his pocket for his cigarette box. This was his only response to Horowitz's translation. He held a light to his cigarette, exhaling smoke through his mouth and his nose, but he did not take his eyes from Jennie's face.

The Assistant District Attorney seemed to wait for the girl to enlarge on her thesis, but when she did not he said, "Are you charging this man with murder?"

"Yes," she declared boldly, and I watched my uncle's face as Horowitz translated this brief exchange for him.

"She's simply crazy," he murmured.

"Tell us how he murdered your mother," the Assistant D.A. said. He had turned to the papers in front of him for a moment, perhaps to look for the word "murder."

"He used his evil eye on her," she said. For a moment, for one flickering moment, she looked venomously at Uncle; but his eyes did not retreat.

Then Uncle Herschel turned to Horowitz and whispered, "Ask her to tell that man what an evil eye is."

Horowitz raised his eyes to Uncle and grinned.

The man standing at Jennie's side coughed and cleared his throat. "If I may. That statement by my client is perhaps unfortunate."

"All right," the Assistant D.A. agreed.

"I would like to make a substitution in our complaint. I would like to make it read that my client accuses this man of practicing medicine without a license."

Horowitz was on his feet. "If I remember correctly, 'evil eye' was in the complaint as submitted."

"Yes, it was," the Assistant D.A. agreed.

"My client respectfully requests that 'evil eye' be retained in the complaint."

The face of the Assistant D.A. grew large and red with pleasure. He enjoyed a good scrap between lawyers and sensed that Horowitz had involved the other man in more than semantics.

"That's silly," the girl's lawyer said. "Before I knew what I was doing, I permitted her to toss that in. That really isn't the issue—"

"If it isn't the issue, then why worry if it stays in?" Horowitz asked.

He leaned down to Uncle, who had suddenly tugged on his coat. "Ask the girl to explain what an evil eye is," Uncle said again.

Jennie's lawyer leveled off his hands in a deprecating gesture. "We're bickering about a really small matter. The vital issue is practicing medicine without a license."

"All right, let's dispose of one issue at a time," Horowitz said. "Suppose you permit your client to tell us how she knew my client had used his evil eye on her mother. In fact, you might ask her to describe an evil eye."

Jennie jumped up, her eyes blazing at Uncle Herschel and Horowitz.

"No," her lawyer yelled. He laid his hand on her arm.

"Yes," she hollered back. "I know what an evil eye is. I can see it right now."

"No," the lawyer repeated.

"Aw, come on, Counselor. We're not in court," the Assistant D.A. said, "and, besides, I'm curious to know what a Jewish evil eye is."

Jennie's lawyer looked askance at the Assistant D.A., but he sat down.

"All right," Horowitz said, "tell us about the evil eye that murdered your mother."

"You want to know what an evil eye is, so look at him. Only the devil has a thing on the chin," she said.

Everybody turned to look at Uncle as Horowitz translated for him what the girl had said. That seemed to amuse him. He said to Horowitz, "I thought she was talking about my eye. How does the beard fit in?"

When Horowitz put Uncle's words into English, everybody laughed except Jennie and her lawyer. He was on his feet again.

"I don't like this," he said.

Horowitz said, "I think my client has a right to this question."

"It makes a mockery of these proceedings," her lawyer persisted.

"I don't think so. Your client came in with a complaint about my client's evil eye. We have a right to explore the complaint revolving around his evil eye."

"I have asked that it be stricken."

"We have objected, and we will insist that it stay. Now," he turned to the Assistant D.A., who had followed this colloquy with interest and very evident amusement, "we'd like an answer to my client's question."

The Assistant D.A. nodded. "Counselor's right," he said. "Remember, this is only an inquiry, and nothing goes on the record. The question was: How does the beard fit in? Is that right, Counselor?"

Horowitz nodded, and everybody was attentive to Jennie. She had not sat down; she waited like a batter for the pitch to be thrown. "Yes," she exclaimed, "I'll tell you. It isn't the beard alone. He has a beard to scare everybody and make everybody look him in the face, and that's how he uses the evil eye."

"Ask her to describe how I used my evil eye on her mother," Uncle said to Horowitz. He translated again, and again Jennie's lawyer rose to his feet; but the Assistant D.A. waved him down.

"Keep your pants on," the Assistant D.A. said. "Go ahead, young lady."

"What's to go ahead? Everybody knows how a man makes with the evil eye."

"I don't," Horowitz said. "I'd like to hear your explanation."

"What's to explain? He looks on somebody and he says 'you're gonna die,' and it happens," she said.

"And you say my client did just that. He looked at your mother and said 'you're gonna die,' and she died?"

"Yes."

"And you heard him?"

"I didn't hear him. He had it in his mind."

"Ask her if I had it in my mind in Yiddish or in Russian," Uncle said.

Horowitz looked at Uncle's sober face and he ran his hand across his grinning mouth as he translated for Jennie.

"Now that's too much!" her lawyer exclaimed.

"I don't think so," Horowitz said. "After all, it was your client who indicated where my client recessed this power of the evil eye. We have a right to explore that."

"Answer the question," the Assistant D.A. said.

"How can I answer such a crazy question?" Jennie demanded.

The Assistant D.A. looked at Horowitz, who was listening to Uncle say, "Ask her to say why this is a crazy question. If she knows what's in my mind, she knows if I thought evil in Yiddish or Russian."

Horowitz nodded and rendered Uncle's declaration in English.

"*I know it, I know it. I just know it. How do I know I'm alive?*" Jennie screamed.

When Horowitz had translated this last outburst, Uncle said, "Ask her how she knows she's alive."

"How do I know? Because I'm breathing, because my heart is beating, because I'm talking!" she yelled.

"Ask her how she knows it's not my evil eye that's permitting her to do all these things?" Uncle asked.

Jennie stared fearfully at Uncle Herschel when Horowitz had translated that, and once again her lawyer was on his feet.

"Hasn't this joke gone far enough?" he demanded.

The Assistant D.A. waited for Horowitz to defend the course his inquiry had taken, and my uncle brooded over his walking stick.

"Ask her who introduced this joke?" Horowitz said.

"We didn't introduce this as a joke," the lawyer said indignantly. "This is a serious matter."

"Very good, we accept this as a serious matter," Horowitz said, "and we are inquiring in kind to your client's statement. If we are reducing the credibility of those statements, you should have thought about it before you presented it as part of your complaint. Now"—he turned to the Assistant D.A., who had banked the back of his head on his clasped hands—"may I have a few minutes to consult with my client?"

When the official nodded, Horowitz said to Uncle, "Is there anything else you want to ask this girl?"

"Yes," Uncle said, "I want her to tell us in detail just how my evil eye killed her mother."

Horowitz nodded and turned to Jennie. "We would now like to hear in some detail how this gentleman killed your mother—how his evil eye killed your mother."

Jennie's lawyer looked up at her disturbed face and then down to his hands. He knew it would be futile to protest, because the Assistant D.A. had already ruled on this question.

"What do you mean, how his evil eye killed my mother?" Jennie asked.

"Just that," Horowitz told her. "Just that. You can kill with a knife or a gun or poison. You say this gentleman killed with his evil eye. Tell us how. Show us how. We're interested. How does an evil eye kill?"

"I can't explain it. It just happens."

"Yes, that's what you said before. We want to know *how* it happens. What did this gentleman *do* to your mother?"

"I don't know." She clasped and unclasped her hands. "I

don't know. It's a secret in his mind, and I can't get into his mind."

"Well, if it's a secret in his mind, then how did you know what he was planning to do or what his mind told him to do?"

"I could see it on my mother. *She died!*" Her voice rose to a shriek.

"We know she died, but we want to know how you connected your mother's death with what was in this gentleman's mind?"

"I knew what was in my heart."

"What was in your heart?"

"I knew she was going to die from the evil eye as soon as I saw that little thing on his chin and that stick he carries."

"Tell us about the stick."

"Only the devil carries a stick. Who else carries a stick?"

Uncle tugged on Horowitz's coat. "Ask her if I waved my stick or if I just held it over her mother?"

Horowitz looked a little startled, but he asked the question. Jennie stared at him, sensing for the first time that the path down which she was being led had many odd, crooked turns.

"I don't know what you mean," she said.

Horowitz used his arm to illustrate the question. Jennie shook her head.

"He didn't wave his stick."

"Doesn't she know," Uncle demanded sternly, "that waving the stick is an important part of applying the evil eye?"

Horowitz did not change a crease in his face as he repeated Uncle's question.

Jennie looked even more confused. "You're trying to mix me up," she exclaimed.

Her lawyer jumped up yet again. "Now look—this farce has gone far enough. This is not the vital area of our complaint, and Counselor knows it. He's using this to cover up his inability to answer our charge that this man is guilty of practicing medicine without a license."

"Not guilty," the Assistant D.A. cautioned. "He is only being accused."

"I'll accept that, but this nonsense has reached the limit of our patience."

Horowitz poked his tongue into his cheek as the other lawyer spoke. When that man had finished, Horowitz said, "I'll agree with you when you characterize your client's charge of evil eye as nonsense, but you wouldn't deny me the privilege of reducing it to nonsense."

"We're willing to withdraw that charge," Jennie's lawyer said.

"Of course you are, but we insist on retaining the charge."

"Well," the Assistant D.A. said, "it's Counsel's privilege to withdraw it if he wishes."

As he completed that sentence, the door opened, and Padilsky walked in. Everybody turned to the door, grateful for any interruption; the tension had become almost unbearable.

Uncle Herschel did not raise his head. He just rolled his eyes up to the man who stood poised at the door, waiting for an invitation to come in.

"Trouble," Uncle murmured to Horowitz.

The lawyer sat down by Uncle's side and whispered, "Who is he?"

"He's the doctor who signed the death certificate. He thinks I'm a fraud and a charlatan."

"Is he coming to testify for them?"

"I don't know. All I can tell you is, I came to him to ask him to tell the District Attorney that he was the doctor for this woman, not I. He laughed in my face."

The Assistant D.A. had waited for Padilsky to declare himself, but before he could frame a proper inquiry Horowitz called out, "May I take a ten-minute recess with my client?"

When the D.A. looked surprised, Horowitz held out his hands. "Language difficulties. I just want to reconcile certain expressions."

The assistant glanced at Jennie's lawyer, who nodded briefly.

"We're going to stop for ten minutes," Horowitz said to Uncle Herschel. Instantly Uncle was on his feet. He strode over to Padilsky.

"What are you doing here?" he demanded.

Padilsky regarded my uncle with a hateful coolness. "You're sweating pretty hard aren't you, Felsher?"

"Sweating? Of course I'm sweating. Why shouldn't I sweat when a crazy girl is tearing the bread from my mouth and preventing me from bringing over my family? Sure I'm sweating, but with blood and not water. And now you've come here to help her to make sure I can never do what I can do best."

"Do I have to get permission from you to go where I want to go?"

"You might have had the decency to tell me when I came to you, 'No, I can't be a witness for you because I'm going to be a witness for the girl.' Instead, you let me talk my heart out and you said no to me without warning me you were coming here to testify against me."

"I've come here to tell the truth."

"The truth as an American doctor sees it."

"And what's wrong with the way an American doctor sees the truth?"

"What's wrong? Better you should ask me what's right. You're all like dogs in a farm yard. There's more than enough to eat for you and the other dogs, but should another animal want to come in to share with you what is so plentiful, you jump on him and try to destroy him. I can't forgive myself for having been so stupid that I thought you could forget for a minute you're a doctor and acknowledge that I, too, can do something in the medical profession."

"What can you do in the medical profession?"

"Maybe I could wash hospital floors scientifically."

Padilsky smiled, and I could have killed him for that.

"That I'll accept, and I'll even be a witness for you."

"Why did you come so late? Why didn't you come earlier so

you could hear that crazy girl explain about my evil eye and how my evil eye killed her mother? Maybe you're going to help her with the story so we'll have it told by a crazy girl and a crazy doctor."

Again that Padilsky smile, but this time Uncle returned it.

"Maybe," said Padilsky, "maybe I can help her story about your evil eye. What did she say? How did she discover you had killed her mother with your evil eye?"

"Ask her. You and she ought to get together. You could tell each other all about my evil eye."

"How did she say she recognized your evil eye?"

Uncle Herschel glared into Padilsky's altogether sober face. As my eyes sped from one face to the other, I could not tell whether my uncle was getting ready to talk further or to strike him. Uncle's fury seemed enormous.

"You, look at me," Uncle said. "Can't you see the evil in my eyes? Can't you see the evil eye in my goatee? Can't you see the evil eye in my walking stick? And if I take off my shoes and socks, you'll see my cloven hooves."

"Very interesting," Padilsky said, and he made an effort to stare into Uncle's face.

As my uncle glared back, Dr. Padilsky said, "I must talk about the evil eye in medicine at our next county meeting."

The Assistant District Attorney clapped his hands and announced in a loud voice, "I think we're ready to resume this inquiry."

"Go and sit with the other scientist over there," Uncle said.

Padilsky shook his head. "I want to stay near you. Maybe I can yet see how your evil eye works." He cackled briefly.

"That kind of laughter comes only from a fool or a charlatan," said Uncle Herschel.

"Let's get on with this now," said the Assistant D.A. "Sir"—he turned to Dr. Padilsky—"I don't know your name or what concern you have with this inquiry."

"You sent me a letter ordering me to appear. I am Doctor Padilsky."

"Oh, fine, you've come just in time. Now, gentlemen, I'm going to inquire into Doctor Padilsky's concern in this matter. Then I'll give you time to question him."

Horowitz and the other lawyer nodded. The Assistant District Attorney pointed to a chair that stood midway between our group and Jennie's.

"Won't you sit down, Doctor," the Assistant D.A. said. "Let me explain, first, why you are here. This is an inquiry to determine whether we have enough reason to institute a criminal action against this gentleman for practicing medicine without a license and for applying an evil eye to this lady's mother, causing her death. Now, sir, how did you become involved in this action?"

"They sent for me."

"Who?"

"That boy"—he pointed to me—"came for me."

Everybody's eyes turned on me, and I squirmed a little in my chair.

"Young fellow," the Assistant D.A. said, "who sent you?"

"My uncle"—I inclined my head to my right—"told me to run for Doctor Padilsky."

"And when you arrived at the Teitelbaum home, Doctor Padilsky, what was this gentleman doing?"

"He was smoking a cigarette."

"He was not ministering to the patient?"

"He was smoking a cigarette."

"And what else was he doing?"

"He was looking at the patient."

"As a doctor, would you say this gentleman was applying an evil eye as he was looking at the patient?"

"In medical school we did not study evil eyes."

I took a deep breath and turned to watch my uncle, who was staring at Dr. Padilsky.

"As a doctor, how would you characterize the evil eye?"

"Nonsense, stupid superstition."

"You signed the death certificate?"

"I did."

"And do you recall what you wrote on it? Could you tell us?"

"Yes. All her vital functions had ceased. She had become comatose and never survived that condition."

"And do you not think an evil eye could have induced that condition?"

"In medical school—" Padilsky began.

The Assistant D.A. raised his hand. "I know," he said. "Evil eye was not in the course of study. Now, let's get back to this gentleman. He is being accused of practicing medicine without a license. What did he do for the patient before you came and after you came?"

"Nothing."

"Nothing? Did he prescribe for her?"

"No."

"Did he take a fee from this young lady for anything he might have said to her?"

"I'm not sure, but I would say no."

"Why?"

"Because he sent for me."

"He did give her advice."

"Yes, the same advice I gave her, but that isn't practicing medicine. If a neighbor comes into a sick house and says to the mother put a hot compress on the sick child's throat, she isn't practicing medicine. Nobody calls her a doctor."

The Assistant D.A. grinned. "You're all right, Doctor. Maybe you'd like to join my staff."

"I have enough trouble with patients, doctors and felshers," Padilsky said, turning to chuckle into Uncle's disbelieving eyes.

"Felshers?" The Assistant D.A. was puzzled.

"Oh yes, felshers. They're the most troublesome. You see, a felsher is an educated registered nurse. We don't have them in our country, but they do in Russia, where they don't have enough doctors and a felsher is permitted to treat patients. This gentleman is a felsher, but he knows he can't practice in this state without a license. Now before I stop, I want to say this:

I don't like this man because he behaves like I was a beginning doctor and he was a professor of medicine in a large university. But he knows the human body, and he knows a lot more about chemistry than I do and, for that matter, than most doctors. And if he would stop looking down his nose at me, maybe I could get him a good job as a clinical assistant in a good hospital."

This time Dr. Padilsky did not turn to grin at Uncle Herschel, but my uncle continued to gape at the man, who had just made a most unlikely declaration.

For a full minute nobody spoke; everyone appeared immobilized by what Dr. Padilsky had just said. Then the Assistant D.A. cleared his throat, turned to Jennie's lawyer and said, "He's all yours, Counselor."

The lawyer shook his head sadly. "No questions," he said.

The Assistant D.A. swung his head to Horowitz and waited for him to complete a translation of everything Dr. Padilsky had said. When Horowitz had finished, my uncle said, "I don't believe what you told me."

Horowitz grinned, shrugged broadly and said, "Ask him yourself."

"Mr. Horowitz," the Assistant D.A. asked, "do you have any questions for this witness?"

Horowitz shook his head. "No," he said, and he held that word a long time, "no questions."

"Then," the assistant said, "I see no cause for action. I have nothing to take before a grand jury. What you choose to do in a civil action is your concern. This hearing is over."

Horowitz touched my uncle's arm. "You can go home," he said. "You have nothing more to worry about."

Uncle Herschel turned to him briefly. "What do I say to a man I've just called a liar and a charlatan when he turns out to be an angel?"

Horowitz grinned. "You'll think of something. You weren't without ideas when we were questioning that girl."

Uncle's fingers flittered across his mustache, as Dr. Padilsky began to move toward the door. "Doctor Padilsky," he called, "wait a minute."

Dr. Padilsky turned slowly, as though he were rotating on a rusty swivel.

"What now?" he demanded a little crustily.

"It is human I should say I'm sorry for what I said to you," Uncle said.

"So–so you're human. Should that excite me?"

"No, but if I'm human enough to say I'm sorry for what I said, you should be human enough to accept what I said."

"I see you're at it again–teaching me, telling me what to say, Herr Professor."

"Yes! Yes, you are *verdommed,* and it's about time somebody told you how to behave like a human being." My uncle's voice was loud and furious.

"*Shah! Shah!* Don't holler, don't holler. Remember, I'm the one who has the license."

"Yes, and you can take your license–" my uncle raged.

"*Sh! Sh!* What would Hippocrates say to such talk? Don't try to change me, and I won't try to change you. Good? Will you take that job if I can find it for you?"

"Now you're bribing me not to tell the truth about you."

"Everybody knows the truth about me. I hate people, I hate doctors and if I knew more felshers, I'd hate them, too."

"All right. Knowing one felsher should be enough for you."

"Ach, do me a favor. I meant what I said about a job. Let me get it for you. I know how much you know. Look, I'll even confess to you that the compound you gave me for my face is beginning to work."

Uncle stared at him, not thoroughly convinced.

"The truth?" he asked.

"The truth."

"Then what do I do with my store?"

"Cut it out like an appendix. In the hospital you'll be something to the doctors and the nurses. You'll work in the laboratories. You won't make a fortune, but you'll be earning, and soon you'll be able to bring your family over. Why do you want to be a storekeeper? A man like you ought to be ashamed to even think about it."

When Padilsky's voice rose, Uncle Herschel took a deep breath.

"*Shah!*" he said. "Don't holler. You sound like a doctor all over again."

Jennie and Mr. Teitelbaum walked by. As she turned to stare at Uncle and Dr. Padilsky, they did not continue their conversation.

"No matter what they say," she hissed, "you are still a murderer. You still have an evil eye, and you, Doctor Padilsky, are just helping him out. You probably have an evil eye, too. All doctors have an evil eye, and you're all murderers!"

I saw my uncle lay his hand on Dr. Padilsky's arm, cautioning him to restraint. My eyes bulged as Dr. Padilsky patted Uncle's hand. For the first time, I felt they understood and appreciated each other. They watched Jennie and her father leave the room. Then Padilsky said, "Come to me at four o'clock tomorrow afternoon. I'll have news for you."

Twenty-four

The way home was jubilant. Uncle had smoked two cigarettes before we boarded the Myrtle Avenue train so he would not again be tempted to smoke on it. We rode in blissful silence, watching the sweep of homes that lined both sides of the tracks. We could even peek into some kitchens, where women were beginning to prepare the evening meal. In a few minutes we were back on Manhattan Avenue, walking from Broadway to my home.

"I never thought he could be so nice," I said.

Uncle nodded, bringing his stick forward in rhythm with our step, and he smiled his slow, enigmatic smile.

"Even a crazy person has his moments of clear thinking," he said.

"But he was so nice, and he said such nice things about you."

"These nice things I should translate into something worthwhile for my family. Then they will really be worthwhile."

"Yes, but he said you know as much as he knows about medicine."

For a long moment he stared out, out, far and beyond. I thought perhaps he hadn't heard what I had said until I recalled that every now and then he responded this way, as though I had stimulated a sensitive line of thought.

"And you'll be able to work in a laboratory almost like a doctor," I cheered on.

This seemed to rouse him. "A golden land," he said, "a golden land."

He permitted me to tell the whole exciting story to my mother, while he sat by without interfering or offering to help once, even when I could not recall the true stress of some of the questions he had suggested to Horowitz. I enlarged upon Jennie's reference to Uncle's beard and to his walking stick, trying hard to paraphrase the hopeless answers she had given to his intimidating questions.

My mother walked around the kitchen, her mouth open, trying to assimilate the whole disturbing picture as she brewed tea for us. She paused only when I began to talk about Dr. Padilsky and his surprising testimony that Uncle did not have an evil eye, that Uncle knew as much about medicine as he, and that he, Padilsky, had attended Mrs. Teitelbaum and had signed the death certificate.

When I told her about Dr. Padilsky's offer, she began to cry.

This seemed to rouse Uncle Herschel. He stared his surprise at my mother and said, "Foolish woman, why are you crying?"

"Why shouldn't I cry when you have had so much trouble and now the trouble is all over and you can do what you want to do?"

Uncle reached into his pocket for his cigarette case, took out a cigarette, held a light to it and drew on it fervently.

"What's a man's life?" he said with a smile. "What's a man's life?"

I smiled, too, and my mother kept crying.